Dearly Departed

Dearly Departed

A Love Me Dead Romance

Heather Novak

Dearly Departed

Tule Publishing First Printing, September 2022

The Tule Publishing, Inc.

First Publication by Tule Publishing 2022

Cover design by Erin Dameron-Hill

ISBN: 978-1-958686-30-0

Dedication

To Eliza: This book exists because of our friendship. Love you.

For those who carry grief in their heart, I see you and sit with you.

Shout out to all my fellow allergy/digestive condition/restricted diet friends—don't let anyone make you feel like a burden! You're a badass.

Jen Luerssen—"Tit's up!" Thanks for your constant support.

And to my mom, who left a letter for me to find when I needed it most.

Prologue

Eliza

Twenty-eight months ago

WHEN MY FIFTH-GRADE teacher had asked me what I wanted to do for the school's talent show, I'd said, "I could write a letter to your dead mom." This resulted in my first detention for lying, despite the fact my teacher's mother had passed away the summer before, and I never lied. I may not have been old enough to drive or vote, but I had the power to alter someone's last words to a dearly departed loved one. It forced me to grow up *fast*. Especially because the transaction came with a hefty price tag for the sender—one year of their life.

What I hadn't known was that I paid a price, too.

That price felt exceptionally cruel today as I watched my fiancé's ashes being lowered into the ground from a safe distance. My white knuckles locked around iron posts that separated me from Applechester Cemetery, the flaking paint stabbing my palms. I couldn't look away from his black headstone. I'd paid extra to have it erected before the burial.

He was forever immortalized as "Benjamin Dylan Somerset" instead of "Ben" or "my love," which he preferred.

Thirty years of heartbeats, laughter, and I love yous were shoved into one little dash between the date of his birth and death. That tiny line could never tell a passerby about the amazing new thing his daughter had done, or about the time he was accidentally an extra in an action film, or how much he loved basketball.

My body trembled with silent tears, and it took several paralyzing moments to realize the earth wasn't shattering around me. Huge flowerpots with red, white, and blue petals to celebrate the Fourth of July lined the sidewalk, their cloying scent suffocating. How dare they rejoice under the hot summer sun when my entire body was ice cold.

My hold on the bars was the only thing keeping me upright as my stepbrother Jake helped my daughter Daisy throw a shovelful of dirt onto her dad's ashes. I wished I'd gotten to see Ben's body before they cremated him, to kiss his cheek, to smooth his hair off his forehead one last time, but morgues aren't much kinder to me than cemeteries. I was thankful Ben never wanted a visitation or memorial service, especially since funeral homes weren't any easier to bear. I just had to get through the last ten minutes of this burial.

Usually, the din of the dead was just a buzz in my head, something I was able to keep in the background of my thoughts until I needed to communicate. This close to a cemetery—or any place with a high concentration of the dead—it was deafening. I was like a magnet; each spirit had a story about why they needed to get in contact with a loved one, and they were determined to tell me. Someone tugged on my hair hard, making my head snap back.

"No," I whispered firmly. "Do not touch me."

My left arm prickled, as if stung by several bees. Scratches, red and angry, raised up on my fair skin. A retort.

I shook my head. "No," I repeated. While I could see ghosts, the spirits here *wanted* to stay invisible to pick on easy targets. Either their deaths had made them so resentful they couldn't cross over, or they were bullies in their former lives.

Sometimes I hated being a medium, hated that I not only had to worry about creatures in this world—the kind that everyone thought were fictional, like vampires and demons—but also those in the afterlife. I wished I could throw dirt on my Ben's grave, tell him I loved him one last time. It wasn't worth the risk. If the spirits were this restless and violent outside the cemetery, it would be so much worse the moment I stepped onto consecrated ground. I was a single mother now, and my six-year-old needed a parent who wasn't possessed by a handful of ghosts.

Jake kissed Daisy's cheek before throwing his own shovelful of dirt. He passed the shovel first to Ben's parents, who were clinging to each other as if existence itself depended on it, and then ours. My brother asked for the shovel one more time, and he scooped one last pile of dirt. He lifted his gaze to mine, and I knew this one was for me. He poured the rocks and dirt into the hole.

My knees disappeared and I sank to the sidewalk, my chest aching. *I was alone now.* How was I supposed to do this? How was I going to get up off this cement and put one foot in front of the other? How was the earth still turning?

"Mommy!"

I looked up and saw Daisy releasing Jake's hand and run ahead of him. She was the reason I *had* to get off the ground and figure it out. *Get up, Eliza. Don't let her see you break down.*

"Help me or go away," I told the ghost who had tugged my hair again. Something poked me under my ribs hard, and I scrambled to my feet to get away. "Thanks," I grumbled.

Daisy rounded the gate and pushed her red face against my leg. *Shit, how was I not going to completely ruin her childhood? Was it possible to live without ever really breathing again?*

My daughter mumbled something through her sobs. I bent down and scooped her up, holding her close. "What, munchkin?"

"Why did Daddy leave us?" she wailed.

Oh god, I didn't think there was anything else that could destroy my heart, but those five words sucked all the oxygen out of the atmosphere. I struggled to fill my lungs once, then twice.

"It wasn't by choice," I promised her. "He'd never leave you on purpose. He loves you so, so much, even now."

She buried her head in my shoulder, and my chest cracked open. *Could I have stopped this? Should I have seen it coming? Had Ben suspected?*

The flowerpot next to us on the sidewalk exploded. With a shout, I pulled Daisy closer, a chunk of shattered terracotta catching my arm and leaving a bloody gash. Jake propelled us across the street.

"Was that a ghost?" he asked.

"Probably," I said, straightening. "Go check on Ben's

parents."

I looked down at Daisy, whose gaze was glued to the small trail of blood on my arm. "I'm sorry, Mommy."

"Shh, shh." I ran my hand over her head. "This wasn't your fault, baby girl."

She tilted her head up, sky blue eyes filled with tears. "I did it."

"Why do you think that?"

She buried her head against the crook of my shoulder. "I wanted to explode something."

I rubbed her back and looked over at the pile of dirt and clay. It had just been the ghosts, right?

Chapter One

Eliza

Present day, eleven days before Thanksgiving

ROBINSON FAMILY DINNER had been a source of stability in a life full of devastating losses. I thought I was safe with my family, safe *from* them. When I could barely get out of bed, when it took everything I had just to feed Daisy and send her to school, someone in my family would come by and provide us with a home-cooked meal. On one memorable occasion after a particularly bad week, Mom had shoved me fully clothed into the shower. They were the only people I trusted would never betray me.

Until today.

Until my mother destroyed our family before dessert was served.

I didn't know how many times I could break and still be mended, but I must be close to totaled. So far, no amount of compartmentalizing or therapy quotes put me back together again.

"I don't want to leave!" Daisy complained as I pulled her through the front door of my parents' house, then handed her the coat I'd grabbed on the way out.

"Put this on," I ordered, ducking my head against the ice-cold rain that pelted my face.

She grabbed the coat and shoved her arms through the opposite way, wearing it backward. I wanted to argue with her, but I didn't have the energy.

The front door opened and my mom walked out, bathed in the porch light. "Eliza! Don't leave until we've discussed this like adults!" she called.

"Twelve years, Mom. You lied to me for *twelve years*!"

"Stop fighting!" Daisy tried.

"You have a daughter. Are you telling me you wouldn't do everything you can to protect her?"

I put my hands on my hips. "How was lying to Jake and me protecting us? You could've given us closure!"

Mom mirrored my position. "You would've lost all hope! And then she wouldn't be back now." My mother may look like me, light blue eyes and red hair with streaks of gray, but I didn't recognize her anymore.

I shook my head in disbelief. "You've got to be kidding me."

"Don't use that tone with me, young woman!"

"You know I don't tolerate lying."

"And you think you're a better mother because of it?"

"Yeah, I think I've got a leg up!"

The decorative gourds on Mom's porch exploded, sending chunks of skin and seeds everywhere.

"STOP IT!" Daisy screeched.

We both looked at Daisy who had her hands over her ears and her eyes shut tight. A shimmering light dissipated around her.

I bent down so my face was level with hers and brushed her hands away. "Are you okay, baby girl?"

"Stop fighting," she whispered.

"We've stopped. I promise. Let's go." I looked over my shoulder at my mom, who stood wide-eyed, glancing between the vegetable carnage and Daisy. "She's okay, just overtired," I explained. "She'll call you later."

Mom nodded. "And you?"

I shook my head and hurried Daisy to the car. I reached for the back door handle and swore when it didn't budge. I made sure it was unlocked and tried again, but still nothing. I sucked in a sharp breath, making a mental note to get the car to the shop. *Stupid latch.*

Daisy brushed me out of the way. A scattering of blue sparks emitted from her hand, and then the door opened with ease. "I got it, Mom."

"Thanks, baby," I sighed, my voice stretched tight to cover the rest of my emotions. The magic fix wouldn't last, but it would hold for a few days. "You can have tablet time."

She nodded and grabbed the tablet from the back seat pouch as I closed the door and rounded the back of the car. My knees were shaking, and I held on to the trunk as I tried to put one foot in front of the other, without looking behind me. Mom had gone inside, but no doubt she'd be back to clean up the porch. I needed to go before she tried to stick another Band-Aid over the knife she'd plunged into my chest.

"Eliza!"

My spine stiffened as I turned to face the one person I never wanted to see again, Paris Evans. My new partner at

Supernatural Human Accountability Partnership, known as SHAP. The woman we were celebrating tonight for saving Jake's and his soul mate Poppy's lives. The same woman who had destroyed mine.

I tried to tell her to go away, only to have a sob escape. The key ring around my finger hit my lip hard as I clamped my hand over my mouth. I closed my eyes and focused on relaxing the tightness in my throat.

"You can't drive," she stated.

I opened my eyes to find Paris standing too close, studying me as if I were three-week-old trash. I welcomed the heat of anger over the coldness of sadness. "Been doing it since I was fifteen. No tickets, no accidents," I spat back.

"You're shaking." She pressed her lips together.

"I'm—" I held out my hand to prove her wrong, but it betrayed me. The voices of the dead poked at my mental defenses, always ready to pounce whenever I let my guard down. Their white noise stampeded into a loud static, blocking out the howl of the wind.

"Just let me drive you and Daisy home." She reached out and grabbed my keys, her fingers brushing my knuckles.

My stomach dipped, and the voices immediately quieted like they always did when she was around. I dropped my hand and glared. "Don't touch me."

Paris gestured toward the passenger side.

"I know how cars work," I barked, swiping at my eyes, then stepping away from her. I climbed in and slammed the door like a petulant child.

"If I did that, you'd ground me for two days," my daughter, Daisy, said. At eight years old, she was full of sass and stubbornness, a combination of me and her late father.

"Damn straight," I agreed.

"Then why do you get to do it?"

"Because I'm an adult."

"I think that's an excuse adults make to get away with things they know are wrong."

She was right in this case. "One of the perks of getting older."

Paris climbed into the driver's side, filling the car with her soft sunshine and gardenia scent. It burned through me and robbed me of breath, as if I'd inhaled fire. I yanked at my seatbelt, but it twisted and fought back.

"Need help?" Paris asked.

"No," I growled, tugging one last time. The belt finally released, and I nearly sighed in relief. "How are you going to get home? Your car is here."

"I'll figure it out," she promised. She put on her own seatbelt with one smooth motion, then checked Daisy was buckled before starting the car and backing out of the driveway. Her long, thin fingers wrapped around the steering wheel, her grandma's emerald ring sliding off center on her right middle finger. I turned away, resisting the unexpected impulse to take her likely cold hand in mine to warm it.

The rattle of the glovebox and the squeak of the windshield wipers filled the silence, and I focused on two raindrops racing down the passenger window. Another tear escaped and I tugged my sweater sleeve over my coat cuff to wipe it away. I could feel Paris's eyes burning a hole in the side of my head, but I refused to acknowledge her.

My heart beat hard, trying to fight against the pressure

building under my ribcage. The urge to scream, to cry, to break something swirled faster and faster until a tornado was trapped in my chest. *Four more miles.* I closed my eyes when we passed the cemetery, avoiding the temptation to stare at the sidewalk under the streetlamp.

"If you want to talk..." she began.

I clenched my jaw.

"Your parents—"

"No." My parents had known we'd lose Poppy one day, that she was a grim reaper, and they never warned us, never confessed what happened when she disappeared. She had been my best friend and Jake's first love, yet they'd refused to give us the closure we so badly needed. They'd let us search for her for years and only admitted their deception after a miraculous series of events had given Poppy her human life back.

"I know." Paris navigated the left turn onto my street. "I'm sorry."

Her apology weighed between us, as if it were not just a platitude about tonight, but an attempt to revisit our past. I shoved it away. Nearly everyone I loved had either ended up dead or betrayed me. I would do anything and everything to protect Daisy, to give her a life full of joy and smiles so she never had to feel her chest caving in. My inner circle could no longer be infiltrated, not even by my parents. It now only consisted of my daughter, Jake, Poppy, our friend Mina, and her partner Carma.

There was no more room for Paris in that life.

We pulled into the driveway and Paris shut off the car. The sudden silence was deafening. I focused on unbuckling my seatbelt as if it were open heart surgery. My body was a rung-out dishrag and it was still hours before Daisy's bedtime. All I wanted was to pull the blankets over my head and sleep for days.

"Why is your bedroom light on?" Paris asked.

I ignored the pang in my chest at her remembering such a simple detail and narrowed my eyes at the small brick ranch. In an effort to keep the energy bills reasonable, I had a self-adjusting thermostat and never left lights on, except the porch light. So why was my bedroom light on?

We had been running behind after Daisy spilled juice on her first outfit. I'd rushed out of my bedroom to help her clean up. Could I have left it on?

"I'll check it out," she said, unbuckling and climbing out of the car.

"That's not necessa—"

She closed the car door, then pulled her gun from a hidden holster and located my front door key on my chain.

I opened my car door. "The alarm's on!" I warned, then growled. "Daisy, stay here."

Daisy gave me a thumbs-up from the back seat, too engrossed in her game to care. I wished I could relax at that level. I shook my head and hurried after Paris while fumbling to grab the stun gun out of my purse.

I jumped up the porch step and barreled through the door and directly into Paris. She spun and grabbed my forearms to steady me. I sucked in a breath at the contact before rushing out, "Sorry! Didn't expect you to be standing in the entrance."

"I thought you said the alarm was on?" She let go of my

arms and gestured to the panel.

"It is." I looked at the panel which read disarmed. "How is that possible?" I grabbed my phone and opened the alarm app. Armed at 4:37pm via keypad. Disarmed at 5:15pm via app. It was now 5:45. I held up my phone to show Paris. I didn't trust her farther than I could throw her, but she was still an active agent.

"Did you hit it by accident? Who else has your code?"

"Only the people at dinner," I explained. "And I don't remember turning it off, but maybe?" This whole day was super fuzzy. I usually only used my alarm via keypad, but after the time I forgot to turn it on a few weeks ago—although, I swear I had armed it—I downloaded the app. While the keypad couldn't tell me how and when the alarm was activated, the app could.

"Wait here." She side-stepped down the hall, peering into the living room, then the kitchen. I looked through the storm door to check on Daisy, who was still safely inside the car.

"Living room, kitchen, and Daisy's room are clear," Paris called.

I inched deeper into the house, looking around for anything out of place. I paused at the picture frame on the entertainment stand of Daisy and me at her last birthday party. My arms were around her shoulders as she blew out a candle on top of a pile of waffles with whipped cream and rainbow sprinkles, both of us wearing tiaras at her insistence. Paris had taken the picture.

The photo had been moved.

I hadn't had time to dust recently with Daisy's schedule,

Jake nearly being killed, and Poppy returning. I ran my finger over the rectangular patch of dust free wood where the photo used to sit, as if it could give me answers. I turned around when I heard Paris's footsteps.

"All the windows are closed, locked, and untampered with. The front door was locked," she offered.

"Who would have a key and the alarm code and just sneak in to do nothing? Why would they leave the light on in my bedroom and not reset the alarm code? It doesn't make sense."

"You came home early."

A chill ran down my spine. She was right. We usually went to my parents' every Sunday night for dinner until eight. What if I hadn't come home early? Would they have reset the code and turned off the light? I glanced back at the photo.

"This was moved." I gestured to the dust-free patch.

Paris studied the photo then searched my face. "I'll run it for fingerprints. I've got a kit in my—" she made a face. "I don't have my truck." All active field agents had a SHAP-issued SUV, black with bulletproof glass, strengthened body, and top-of-the-line safety features.

I gestured toward the front door. "Let me get Daisy inside and I can bag the photo for you, as long as you promise to bring it back."

"I will."

When I got to the front door, Daisy was already walking up the porch stairs. "Finished the level," she said by way of explanation. "Didn't even use magic this time." She'd yawned most of the sentence.

"Proud of you." Having a daughter with swiftly developing magical powers who hated to lose was a lesson in patience, for both of us.

She handed me the tablet as she walked into the house, then shrugged her jacket off and let it fall to the floor.

I cleared my throat.

"So tired," she complained, but bent down and scooped it up, then shoved it onto her coat hook.

I studied her, noticing she looked paler than she did a half an hour ago. I cradled the side of her face in my hands for a full three seconds before she shoved me away. She didn't have a fever, but she looked like she hadn't slept for days. I'd been warned that the strength of her magic at such a young age would be hard on her. If we knew what kind of witch she was, there might be ways to mitigate her magic fatigue.

That information, however, died with Ben. My attempts to contact his parents or dig further back through his family tree had proved unsuccessful.

"Do you have the energy to shower?" I asked.

She lifted her shoulders. "I guess."

"Shower and I'll make you a snack. We can watch that ghost show you like."

She nodded and moved to her bedroom with no enthusiasm. She paused in front of Paris. "I miss you."

Paris looked as if Daisy had punched her in the stomach. "Me too," she whispered back.

This was not a good idea. I cleared my throat. "Daisy…"

She huffed a dramatic sigh, then turned and went into her room.

I set the tablet on the counter, then grabbed a clear storage bag and carefully maneuvered the frame inside without touching the glass. I handed it to Paris.

She took it from me and studied it, smiling. "She looks so happy here."

I smiled back. "It was a great birthday."

"You're a great mom."

I blinked. That wasn't what I expected her to say. "I—thank you."

She nodded, her eyes unfocused, her thoughts clearly somewhere else. "I'll work on this." Her gaze sharpened and she looked up at me. "Unless you want me to stay?"

Her offer weighed heavy between us. If it had been *before*, if it had been someone else with identical beautiful brown eyes the color of dark chocolate, silky dark hair that I wanted to run my fingers through, and creamy skin with a small scar on her chin I'd kissed a hundred times, I would've said yes. I didn't want to be alone tonight, knowing I wouldn't sleep. Waking up at every sound, even after I changed the alarm code.

I shook my head. "How are you getting home?"

"I called a car." She lifted her phone. "I'm sorry about tonight."

"Wasn't your fault." This was one thing that wasn't Paris's fault. No, that blame rested solely on my parents' shoulders. "Thanks for driving us home."

"Anytime," she rushed out. "Eliza…" She took a step forward as her phone buzzed. She looked down, hesitated, then nodded. "Car's here. I'll text." She hurried out of the room as if it were on fire.

I followed her to the door and locked it, then changed the alarm code and armed the system. I stood in the middle of the hall, inhaling the remnants of Paris's perfume. I needed to change, make something for dinner since we hadn't finished eating, and find a way to shove all these inconvenient emotions into a neat little box I could put in the corner of my mind.

Daisy padded across the hall to the second bathroom and turned on the shower.

This jolted me from my spiraling. "Call me when you're ready to comb!" I loved that she got my thick, curly hair, but it was a learning curve for a kid who still forgot in what order to use shampoo and conditioner. I'd installed a dispenser and told her to start on the left, which seemed to help.

I unbuttoned my shirt as I walked to my bedroom, yanking it off and unhooking my bra. I sighed at the release. I slipped into my sweats and hung up my dinner outfit.

The closet door was halfway closed before I gave into the urge. I shoved the door and clothes aside, revealing a false back. Fitting my fingers into small holes at the top and bottom, I slid it to the side revealing my evidence board.

I reached up and touched the photo of Ben. He was wearing a navy-blue suit for a friend's wedding, hands in pockets, and smiling. Then I moved my finger to the list of people in the case file investigating his death.

~~Jim Summers~~

~~John Franklin~~

~~Adrien Ramsay~~

~~Justin Waterstone~~

~~Celine Joyner~~

Paris Evans

I grabbed a pen from the shelf and circled Paris's name for the fifth time. *Why did it have to be her? Why was I always destined to lose what made me happy?*

Loving Ben had been like jumping into a sports car with no seat belt and driving toward a concrete wall at a hundred miles an hour: fun, thrilling, terrifying, and knowing we were trapped on a one-way street, about to crash. We'd made it work because we wanted to raise our daughter together.

Loving Paris was like the beginning of spring, when everything came back to life, when the sun shone down from an endlessly blue sky, and there was this overriding feeling of *hope*. After too many years of pain and grief, Paris had been my own personal springtime. Until she turned into a brutal winter.

I stepped back and looked over the board, blue glitter yarn from one of Daisy's forgotten craft projects connecting the dots between the hours before his death. The police report was only one page long, ruling Ben's death an accident, that the motorcycle flipped over the Folk River Bridge and he drowned.

Ben taught courses on pursuit driving and was a licensed deep-sea diver. He didn't drink, didn't do drugs. I checked the printout of the weather report for the eight-hundredth time. Dry and fifty-five degrees. Wind speed topped at twelve miles an hour. Sunset had been only ten minutes before. Traffic was clear.

So what had really happened that night?

My phone buzzed and I yanked it from my pocket.

Jake: *You make it home safe?*

Me: *We're fine. You okay? Poppy?*

Jake: *Yeah*

Jake: *All things considered. Wanna talk?*

Me: *Not tonight.*

Jake: **thumbs-up emoji* See you tomorrow.*

Jake: *Want me to grab a pizza?*

Me: *I'll want to cook*

Jake: *k. Love you*

Me: *night *sleeping emoji**

Me: *Ps. Changed the alarm code to 9022*

Jake: *Why*

Jake: *What happened???*

Me: *Everything's fine*

"Mom! I'm ready," Daisy shouted.

I jumped at the interruption, then secured the closet's false back. "Be right there!" I promised.

I moved the clothes back into place and then closed the closet doors. As I hurried out of the bedroom, a whiff of evergreen made me freeze in my tracks. I breathed sharply through my nose, then again. It was gone.

Had I imagined it? Did I want to talk to Ben so badly that I was phantom-smelling his cologne? I shook my head. It was probably just exhaustion from all the betrayal.

Chapter Two

Paris

I HELD MY breath as I dusted the picture frame for prints, hoping, wishing, praying that this was the answer. That whatever I found would be the key to finishing this vixen case and Eliza and I could go our separate ways. Being apart from her was heartbreaking but working with her was torture.

My former partner Jake and I had discovered vixen—an oral powder vampire venom street drug—while investigating an oral liquid venom source. Vixen promised to cure any ailment…with the side effect of turning the human into a vampire-human hybrid. It may have worked if the distributer hadn't laced it with fentanyl for her own scheme, which also revealed a leak at SHAP. We'd secured all remaining liquid venom and vixen after the lab was destroyed, and since then things had been eerily quiet. Now, Eliza and I were forced to work together until we closed the case, since our boss refused to trust anyone outside our group.

The irony that we were the only two he could trust when Eliza would never trust me again was not lost on me.

I refocused on my task, trying to keep my eyes on the

glass and not the photo beneath. I'd taken that picture the morning of Daisy's birthday back in May. I sucked in a sharp breath, the memory still so strong, for a moment I believed I could fall into the photo. I'd thought I was one of the lucky ones who'd found everything she wanted, and I would get to love and cherish them for the rest of my life. Then, four days later, the dream imploded. Guess it was a good thing she'd kept me a secret.

Focus. Stop looking at the photo. An impossible task. Eliza's cheeks pink, her smile relaxed. Her eyes were practically hearts as she looked up at me, her arms around Daisy, who looked just as happy.

Logically, I knew that pictures never told the whole story. Daisy had broken a glass that morning with her magic when Eliza wouldn't let her have orange soda for breakfast. Eliza had cut herself with a knife, and I'd burned my hand on the stove. Despite the rough start, the morning had been full of joy and celebration.

I knew that having kids, especially ones with magical powers, was difficult, but I'd never seen my own mother as happy as Eliza was in this moment. Especially not around my birthday. I'd been the surprise.

I got it. I couldn't imagine being in my early twenties and suddenly having a surprise daughter. I'd escaped detection until six minutes after my brother was born. For a young couple who'd scrimped and saved and prepared for a boy, to have not only a second baby, but a girl, was a shock I don't think they ever recovered from.

I shook my head. *Stop feeling sorry for yourself.* I was thirty-three years old. Sure, my parents weren't the most emotionally available people on the planet, but I always had enough food and a roof over my head. When I finally got a family of my own, I could make amazing memories with my kid. I just needed to find someone I cared for as much as Eliza and Daisy, because it was clear we were never going to be the happy family we almost were.

My stomach twisted and I swallowed hard. Eliza was not an easy woman to get over and being forced to close this case together was torture.

Tell me what happened that night, she'd demanded, her blue eyes glacial.

It was my fault, I'd whispered.

We're done.

I rubbed my eyes and let out a long breath. I needed to get out of my head. I grabbed the remote for my stereo and turned on my streaming channel. I picked a throwback pop playlist and turned it up as loud as I dared with Doris Manalin, Countryside Village Apartment's nosiest neighbor, across the hall. The music pushed out all errant thoughts as I concentrated on a partial print on the edge of the frame. It was a larger diameter than the other two prints, which were likely Daisy's and Eliza's.

I turned on my handheld scanner then held it over the print I'd dusted, isolating it on the screen and taking a high-resolution scan. While this technology was still new, it was one of my favorite projects from when I worked in research and development. It would save so much time if we could run prints at a crime scene, instead of lugging samples back to the lab. The scanner should connect to the SHAP database and display results within twenty-four hours.

It was still recommended to run the prints through the lab for accuracy, but since we hadn't pinpointed the leak yet, I wasn't going to take my chances. This print could too easily go missing or be misfiled. After typing in a code name for my investigation, I plugged in the device to my SHAP laptop.

My stomach growled, reminding me that I hadn't finished dinner. I picked up my phone to text Eliza and see how she was doing but opened a message to Jake instead. The fact that he still spoke to me likely meant Eliza had never told him about my role in Ben's death. Guilt pressed down on my chest as I typed.

Me: *Checking on you and Poppy*

Jake: **thumbs-up emoji* Made very alcoholic hot chocolate and watching a romcom*

Jake: *sorry dinner went wild*

Me: *No apologies needed! Been to a few dramatic dinners myself*

Me: *I'm here if you need to talk*

Jake: *Thanks *smiling emoji**

I set my phone down and moved to the kitchen, shuffling in time to the music. I put a slice of gluten-free bread in the toaster and grabbed peanut butter from the cupboard. With a banana microphone in hand, I slid across the kitchen in my socks, throwing up my arm for the chorus of "The Best" by Tina Turner.

When the toast popped, I slathered it in peanut butter then cut up the banana to put on top. I had a mouthful when I two-stepped back into the living room and past my phone. It lit up with six missed calls.

I tossed the plate onto the coffee table and nabbed the phone as it began to ring again. UNKNOWN NUMBER. I swallowed and winced at the half-chewed mouthful, muted my speakers, and then answered.

"It's me," my twin brother, Dallas, said. "Secure line. Why didn't you pick up?"

"Didn't hear my phone."

"Why are you running prints on a Sunday night?"

I paused, gaze flashing to the device on my desk. "What are you talking about?"

"You assigned the model numbers to the devices, P. Of course you picked our birthday. Also, I monitor all our equipment, just in case."

"Just in case of what?"

"Just in case…you need help running a print on a Sunday night."

I sighed at his deflection. "Someone may have broken into a friend's house. We're not sure."

I heard typing in the background. "Most people would call the police."

"We are not most people."

"Good thing you know me. I can run this faster for you. Also, you going to Thanksgiving?"

"Do I have a choice?"

He sighed and I heard more keystrokes. "I know you're morally against Thanksgiving, and that's fair, but you know I can't come this year and Mom and Dad—"

"Want *you* there."

"Need *you* there. And since *you're going*, you need to talk to Mom about food."

I shrugged. "Why bother? She's just going to make the recipes the way she always does, I won't be able to eat anything, she'll get offended and cry in the bathroom, I'll do the dishes, then come home and drink a bottle of wine by myself."

"Liar. You don't drink."

"Why don't you have any food intolerances or allergies? This is bullshit." I wasn't someone who could "cheat" on their diet and only get a stomachache. Eating something on my "don't consume" list could cause anything from hives to vomiting, an altered mental state, or even a trip to the hospital. It took years of elimination diets to feel normal, and I didn't want to—and frankly couldn't—risk the reactions getting worse.

"It is bullshit you got all the allergies," he replied. "I'm not jealous though. Keep that shit to yourself or I'll return your Christmas present."

"You wouldn't go through the hassle. What is it?"

He chuckled. "It's good."

"You say that every year."

"Am I ever wrong? I know my baby sis."

"Six minutes, Dal. I'm only six minutes younger."

He sucked in a breath. His chair squeaked as he shifted. "Paris," he whispered, all teasing gone. My grip on the phone tightened. He never used my full name unless it was something serious. "Holy shit. Where'd you get this print?"

"I told you, a friend's house. Why?"

"Which friend?"

I didn't respond. I trusted Dallas, but I didn't always

trust secure phone lines.

"You can't run this again, okay? I can cover it up from here. If someone else had—*shit*—wipe the frame. Reset your handheld, okay? Forget this existed."

"I can't if she's in danger! Who is it?"

"She—Eliza?"

I was silent.

"What the hell, P? I thought you were going to stay away."

"We're working a case together. And you know I will always protect her."

"You need to stay away from her in case whoever was after Ben comes after her. You'd be at risk if whoever killed Ben connects him back—"

"I KNOW!" I shouted. I never raised my voice, and Dallas's sharp inhale proved I'd shocked him. "That's why I'm keeping an eye on her, okay? Now, whose print?"

He didn't respond for a beat, then two. "I'll handle it. Won't happen again."

"Dallas—"

"It's a ghost. It's from a ghost."

"A dead person left this print?" I frowned. "Impossible."

"For certain ghosts, it's possible. I don't know why they were in her house, but they won't be back. Okay?"

I threw my hand in the air. "What am I supposed to tell Eliza?"

"Tell her you couldn't find a print."

"I don't want to lie."

He sighed. "P, this print is from *my* active case. It was just a ghost passing through. I'll handle it. They won't touch you or Eliza."

That took the wind out of my sails. "You better be safe. You're my only twin."

"Promise. Just make it disappear on your end, okay?"

"Okay."

"Love you."

"Ditto."

I hung up and tossed my phone next to my cold toast. I'd lost my appetite anyway. I unplugged the handheld as if it were a bomb, all soft touches and shallow breathing. I reset the device and turned it off. Then, I cleaned the frame until it was spotless.

My chest was hot with worry and indignation. Whose print was on the frame? How was Dallas connected? What was my brother into? What mess had found its way to Eliza? If someone had gotten to her, it meant I was failing at keeping her safe.

When everything was put away, I stared at the photo for one more moment before flipping it over on the desk.

Me: *Sorry, no unfamiliar prints on frame*

Eliza: *Thanks for checking*

My thumbs hovered over the keyboard, debating asking her how the rest of her night went. *We're done.* I locked the screen and set my phone upside down next to the photo. I needed to get out of this apartment.

I slipped my feet into sneakers and grabbed a hoodie, then walked to the building's foyer. My favorite ghosts sat around a group of tables pretending to play board games, but in reality, they were just gossiping.

"Ah, there she is!" Clint called, waving me over. Clint, a former rock star with dark hair and colorful tattoos covering his fair skin, was locked in a chess match with his boyfriend, Reggie. "Amber just made cookies."

"You look like you could use one," Amber said, pushing a plate of cookies toward me. "Dark chocolate caramel." Amber wasn't a ghost, rather an elderly neighbor who adopted everyone who needed someone to love them, including a demon named Belphegor and all of the building's dead. She resettled her glasses perched on her tiny nose, her earpiece chain tinkling. Her tight gray curls were pulled back in a claw clip so tight, I had a headache looking at her.

"Thanks, but I can't." I was allergic to dairy and intolerant to gluten, which meant the cookies were off-limits.

Amber clucked her tongue. "That's right dear, I forgot. I'll make you a special batch soon."

I waved her off. "I don't need cookies, just company."

Belphegor, a graphite-colored demon with a nose as long as his horns, giant caterpillar eyebrows, and a thin tail, grunted. He was hard to look at, as if he were just a little out of focus. "Shit day?"

I plopped into a chair opposite him as he carefully shifted his hands, which were wrapped in yarn that Amber was using to make a sweater. "Yeah. A lot of family drama."

Belphegor made a face. "I have eighty-four siblings. Been fucking there."

I cringed. I had enough trouble with one sibling. I squeezed his arm, then turned to Clint. "Hey, do ghosts have fingerprints?"

Clint lifted his hand to inspect it. He leaned forward,

huffed a breath on the table, then pressed his fingers down. Him and Reggie surveyed at the dark wood from every angle. Clint studied his hand again. "Maybe if I were having a more solid day? It looks kinda smooth to me."

"Hmm." Interesting.

"What?"

I lifted a shoulder. "Work stuff." I turned back to Belphegor. "You hear about any venom on the streets?"

Amber pursed her lips and shot me a look over her reading glasses. "What'd we say about shop talk during off hours?"

I lifted my hands. "Sorry, sorry. I'm just not really off ever, at least until we close this case."

She looked at me over her glasses. "Well then, let's hope you finish it quickly."

I blew out a long breath and rested my head on the back of my chair. "Yeah."

Amber looked at Belphegor then back at me. "There was a lot of emotion in that one word."

I waved away her observation. "It's just..."

Belphegor leaned forward, his tail twitching in curiosity. "Just?"

"It's just that I'm partnered with someone whom I care...a lot about. And this will likely be the last chance I get to be an active part of her life. So while I want to rush it, I also don't."

"Was this the girl you were in love with?" Clint asked.

All eyes—human and supernatural alike—paused then turned to face me. My cheeks burned and I bet I glowed red. "Why do you know that?"

He lifted his eyebrows. "Because I may have seen you holding hands with someone, and I may have been curious."

"You followed us."

Reggie put his hand over Clint's mouth. "Callate, mi amor. You're incriminating yourself." Reggie was a Guatemalan-American man in his thirties with dark hair and light brown skin with no tattoos. He was wearing light colored dress pants and a polo shirt, the opposite style of Clint's torn jeans and ratty band shirt.

"What happened?" Belphegor asked, leaning toward me, listening intently.

I pressed my lips together and looked down at my worn shoes. "She discovered something in my past that she—rightfully—couldn't get past."

I shoved my fingers through my hair and blew out a breath. "She went out of her way to avoid me for five months and now—" I laughed without humor and picked at my thumbnail. "We are trapped together in a tiny office. It hurts so bad, but at least I get to be around her. Which, I know, is not healthy."

Cold radiated across my left arm and I looked over to find Sebastian in his full Victorian-evening-wear glory. He removed his top hat. "Remember that you deserve as much love as you give to other people. If another person can't see your worth, that's on them. Not you."

The entire room turned to look at him.

"Seb," Reggie prompted, "Is it time for another one of your 'do as I say not as I do' stories?" He leaned his chin on his hand and smiled. Sebastian and Reggie had become best friends after Reggie forgot to change the batteries in his carbon monoxide detector nearly a year and a half ago. Sebastian was known for his deeply annoying, yet often right advice.

I held Sebastian's gaze. "Did that happen to you?"

He flashed a quick, self-deprecating smile, then stared down at the brim of his hat. "No. I did that to someone else."

Reggie gasped and Clint reached out and grabbed his free hand.

"Who?" I asked.

He was silent for a long moment, staring out the window, even though it was dark as ink. He ran a hand along the front of his throat. I didn't know much about his death, but I knew he had broken his neck in an accident. Sebastian, while being a fountain of wisdom, was always closed off.

He looked back over at me. "Her name was Evie."

I took a breath, tempering my reaction so I didn't chase him away. "That's a beautiful name."

"And she was even more so." The corner of his lip lifted. "She was my best friend's younger sister and he doted on her. We'd let her tag along, getting her into trouble by teaching her how to play cards or going swimming when we she was supposed to be with her governess."

"You cared for her?"

He nodded once. "Not as more than a sibling at first. Hell, I barely noticed that she was out of braids and short dresses. Then at her coming out ball...she was..." he looked down and laughed once, touching the brim of his hat, "incandescent."

No one moved. The only sound was the patter of rain

outside and an analog clock over the building's main entrance. I held my breath, not daring to speak.

"It was as if her dress was made of starlight. She was draped in sparkling jewels, even in her hair," he waved a hand over his own head. "I was unable take my eyes off of her." He was looking at me, but I could tell he wasn't seeing me. He was back in that ballroom, staring at Evie. "I stopped speaking midsentence and practically jogged over to ask her for a dance."

"And?" Belphegor prompted.

"I was an unconscionable villain. I was mocked by the people I'd mistakenly called friends. We'd always proclaimed we'd never get married. Balls were for assignations in the garden with bored widows. Maybe if her brother had heard, he would have said something."

"Oh no," I breathed, unable to stop myself.

"When the dance began, I could hear them laughing at me. So, I enticed her out of the ballroom, took a few liberties—enough to ruin her—and left her in the middle of the garden crying. She'd told me she loved me and I…I ran, despite feeling the same way. I knew her brother would challenge me to a duel the moment he learned the truth, so instead I challenged him to a race to distract him. And I paid the ultimate price."

He looked over at me. "I should have danced, should have protected her, should have shoved my so-called friends into a bush. Instead, I ruined her, hurt my best friend, and destroyed my family. I would do anything to take back that night."

He set his hat back on his head. "Do not leave your heart

in the care of someone who is unable or unwilling to treat it with care."

I nodded.

He disappeared.

Belphegor leaned back on the couch. "Well, goddamn."

Clint studied me. "What are you going to do?"

"I don't know," I admitted. "Hopefully, figure out how to get through it while keeping my heart safe."

Chapter Three

Eliza

I GLANCED AT my watch for the fourth time in five minutes. Paris shot me a look, but I ignored her. If our boss, Jim, wanted to call a lunch meeting and make me late to Daisy's doctor appointment, I expected not to be kept waiting while he took a call. Thankfully, Jake was able to take Daisy, but I needed to be there. She'd been struggling to get out of bed the last two weeks, even after going to sleep early.

I cleared my throat, crossed my arms, and straightened my shoulders. My boss could force me to sit here, he could make me work with Paris, but I didn't have to pretend to be happy about it.

Jim hung up and glanced at me. "Am I keeping you from something, Eliza?"

"Yes, an appointment which I scheduled for my lunch break." I didn't need to look at Paris to know she just full-body cringed. She was never one for confrontation. I missed my former partner back in the Dead Letter Office, who'd never heard the word meek in her life.

"My apologies," he offered, without sounding sorry in

the least. "My friend at the DEA wanted an update." He eyed both of us. "It's imperative the vixen case is closed by the end of the month."

"That's only sixteen days away," Paris gasped. "Sir, even if Eliza and I were both seasoned agents, that's unlikely to happen. We haven't finished interviewing SHAP registered vampires and hybrids, we haven't gotten the approval for Eliza to write the letters to the vixen victims, and we're spending most of the day digitizing old case files. If we had help with the case files, maybe we'd have a chance."

Jim folded his hands on his desk and glared at Paris. "Let me be clear: The case will be closed by November 30th at end of day. This agent is former SHAP and is up for a promotion. The connection is *crucial.* Make a good faith effort to confirm vixen is off the streets permanently. Write up your report. Send me the case file." He turned to me, "Then you get to go back to your offices and lives."

"And the leak?" Paris asked.

"There's been no vixen activity since Fletcher blew up the warehouse and then died shortly after," he explained. "Looks like the leak problem solved itself."

I forced myself to unclench my jaw. "Let me get this straight. You force me to work with someone who had a hand in my late fiancé's murder—"

Paris stiffened.

"She was cleared of all charges," Jim interrupted.

"Yeah, I'm sure there was a *very thorough* investigation," I shot back. "And now you won't even let us do our job because you want a connection higher up the DEA food chain?"

He waved away my concern. "This is how the game is played. If you don't like it, you're welcome to find a new job. Of course, then you'll have to pay for Daisy's SHAP lessons, mentor, and clinic visits out of your own pocket."

He knew I couldn't pay for the lessons and for Jake to be her mentor. My brother would do it for free, but he'd need a new day job and then I'd have to pay for childcare. I wasn't even going to think about the cost of having access to a medical facility that knew how to handle an eight-year-old with powers most humans didn't know about.

On top of everything, I got paid more at SHAP than I would at comparable human jobs. I was effectively trapped, and he knew it. Rage filled my chest.

Paris grabbed my wrist and squeezed before I could open my mouth. Her hand was so warm, so soft. Sparks of awareness shot up my arm and I yanked myself free. I hadn't been touched by a non-related person in so long I nearly forgot how much I despised her.

I leaned forward. "Grant me approval to write to the vixen victims, and we'll close your case by the week's end."

"You'll finish the case with or without the approval. I'll review the request after I see your weekly report." He removed his glasses and folded them on his desk. "You're dismissed."

I stood and opened the door carefully, resisting the urge to slam it against the wall, and walked out of the office. Sienna, Jim's assistant, studied me with her yellow werewolf eyes as I walked past her desk. "I know that look all too well."

"He's infuriating," I mumbled.

She nodded. Paris brushed by me with her head down, dark hair hiding her face.

"She is, too," I added.

Sienna looked between us. "I'll see if I can find any files that might actually be useful."

Me: *On my way*

Jake: *With doc now*

I took the stairs two at a time to make it up four floors to Daisy's pediatrician's office. SHAP took care of all her medical needs for as long as I worked for them, deducting an annual fee from my paycheck pre-tax. I was breathing heavy with sweat beading at my temples as I leaned on the reception desk.

"Eliza Robinson. Dr. Marback." I swallowed, trying to moisten my tongue. "Sorry I'm late. Meeting with Jim."

The assistant made an understanding face. "I'll let her know you're here."

Before I had the chance to sit down, Jake and Daisy walked out of the patient area and into the waiting room. I crouched and gave Daisy a hug and kiss, much to her dismay, then straightened.

"We need to talk later," Jake ordered, his face betraying the seriousness his light tone tried to cover. He pulled his dark hair back into a low bun, revealing the deep lines of his frown.

I nodded. "I'll call." I looked at Daisy. "How are you

feeling?"

"Fine."

"How'd the spelling quiz go?'

She tugged on a curl that had come loose from her ponytail. "Got a B."

I held out my hand for a high five. "That's my girl."

Her tiny hand slapped mine without much force. I frowned.

"Robinson?" a nurse called from the doorway.

"Here!" I called, then nodded to Jake. "Call you in a few." I smoothed back Daisy's hair. "Love you. Have a good rest of your day in school."

I brushed my own tumbling curls out of my face and hurried to follow the nurse. They led me to Dr. Marback's office and announced me, before closing the door behind them.

Dr. Marback was a petite woman in her fifties, with gray eyes and slightly pointed ears. While she'd never confirmed her heritage aloud, it was easy to spot she was only partially human.

She nodded and gestured to the seat across from her desk. "I know you're on a time crunch, so let's jump right in."

"Perfect." I sat on the edge of the chair and leaned forward.

"Your brother is doing a great job with teaching Daisy how to control her magic, as best he can. I'm glad to hear she hasn't popped all the basketballs in gym class again."

"But?"

"The magic is still taking a toll on her body. She's so

young and it's developing at an alarming rate." She slid her tablet across the desk. "Her iron is low, her B12 is low. I don't like how her vitamin D, magnesium, potassium, and calcium levels keep decreasing. Her blood oxygen level is concerning. Her cortisol is really high, her inflammation markers have increased, and if her alkaline phosphatase level gets any higher, I'm going to schedule additional tests. She's lost four pounds since last month. Is she in any pain?"

I blinked down at the screen, then back up at her. "Not that she's complained about."

"That's good." She took the tablet back. "I'll have the pharmacy make up a liquid multivitamin for her. Mix it into some juice daily. We'll retest her blood in a few weeks." She leaned back in her chair. "But you know this is only a temporary fix to a long-term problem."

The ever-present pit in my stomach widened. After the exploding flower pot the day of Ben's funeral, Daisy went back to being a regular girl. Well, as regular as a kid who just lost her father can be. It took nearly a year before it returned, in small ways at first, floating pens and flickering lights. I told no one until it became impossible to cover up.

"The more information we can find out about her bloodlines, the better we can help her," Dr. Marback continued. "If we can identify what specific bloodline of witch she is, we can anchor her magic, ease her burden."

"Is it normal to not be able to classify the powers of an eight-year-old?"

She sighed. "No, which is why this is so concerning."

A child could only be a witch if there were supernatural genes on both sides. Magic didn't just appear out of thin air.

It was cultivated through long lines of supernatural pairings. So what genes had Ben and I given her that were wreaking havoc?

With Ben dead, my bio dad MIA, no magic on my mom's side, and no matches on any of the ancestry sites, we had no way to trace Daisy's supernatural lineage. They didn't make supernatural power DNA tracing tests yet, unfortunately.

"And we can't just try different rituals to see what works?" I asked. "We know I'm a medium, surely that narrows down the options. Not all witches have medium-compatibility."

She bobbed her head. "It does help, but not enough. Some witches can be identified by their spells, but Daisy doesn't seem to *do* spells, just intentions. If we tried a ritual, and it was the wrong fit, it'd be like forcing her into a shoe that's too small. Overtime, it would cause permanent damage."

I sat back in my chair, breathing out sharply in frustration. "Ben used to say one of his family members died during the Salem Witch Trials, but even if any actual witches had died, I couldn't trace his family back that far. Even with Daisy's DNA test, Ben and his parents were the only matches. Ben says they were both closed adoption, but how has no one from either side of the family ever done a test?"

"That is a mystery." She tugged on the front of her white coat and folded her hands. "There's another option on the table. It's a last resort, one we should only employ if we have exhausted everything else."

I frowned. "Okay?"

"There are ways to remove magic from witches."

"But?"

"Magic is sticky. It digs in and clings to a person. Some witches have given up their magic and only suffered emotional trauma, while others have had major physical trauma. It goes best when a witch gives it up willingly, but there's no way to predict what will happen. And at eight…"

Daisy loved her magic. And she was small and fragile. I scrubbed my hand down my face. "Looks like it's time to hire a PI or something."

The doctor checked her watch. "I'm sorry to rush you, but I have another patient." We both stood and she held out her hand for me to shake. "Try the vitamins. My assistant will call you to set up the lab work appointment. Keep me posted on what you find out."

I nodded. "Thanks." I hesitated. "How long do we have? Before the magic is too much?"

She paused to think, tapping her fingertips on her desk. "Truthfully? I don't know. I suspect it's a few months before we need to be truly concerned, but one bad day could change that."

I hurried out of the office and took the stairs to the lobby, then stepped out onto the sidewalk. The sun was peering out from thick clouds, the day struggling to stay above forty degrees. It was the time of year when sunny days were rare, but the weather could go from T-shirt to blizzard in a matter of hours.

Wrapping my sweater a little tighter around myself, I dialed Jake. Having my brother as part of my Daisy-team was something I tried never to take for granted.

He picked up on the second ring. "You freaking out?"

"Yep."

"Get that."

"She's sending a prescription to the pharmacy. I'll grab it on my way home."

He grunted. "Loren's wife, Raine, used to be a gray witch before she gave up her powers. I think you should talk to her."

"Whoa, a gray witch?" They were one of the most powerful witch lines. I let out a low whistle. "And I'm sure the story is fascinating, but I'm not taking away Daisy's powers."

"Not saying you should, but talking it over with someone who went through it will help. I've already talked to Raine. I'll forward her number. We need to know and understand all the options before we are forced into choosing."

I blew out a breath and tilted my head up to the sun. "Yeah, okay. What am I going to do about finding my sperm donor?" My true dad had always been my stepdad, Jake's biological father. "I can't afford a private investigator."

"If your bio dad is supernatural—which seems to be the only possibility—then you have to use SHAP resources to locate him. You're partnered with one hell of a detective."

"I can't trust her."

He grunted again. "We need to talk about this. Why?"

Did I tell him the truth? That she had a hand in Ben's death? Did I tarnish his relationship with his former partner after all that he went through?

What if he didn't believe me? What if my confession meant the end of our sibling relationship? His mentoring

Daisy?

I cleared my throat. "We'll talk later. I've got to get back."

"If you won't ask Paris, ask Loren. You're calling his wife anyway. You can kill two birds with one stone."

I sighed, hating to involve anyone else but knowing asking Loren was my best alternative to asking Paris. "I will, thanks."

He went quiet in a way I knew he wanted to say something but didn't know how.

"Jake?"

"Dr. Marback had said that this is the sixth time in two years that Daisy's made something explode."

"Yeah." I stepped on a dry leaf, enjoying the crunch it made under my shoe.

"She's only had her powers for like six months though, right?"

Oh shit. "I—It may have been…a little longer. She just wasn't showing them frequently and I didn't catch it."

"Bullshit."

"It's the truth! After the first incident, she didn't have any visible powers for a year. I didn't realize what it was until just before you found out."

"When was the first incident?"

I was silent.

He sucked in a breath. "You told me multiple times the flower pot at the funeral was caused by ghosts!"

I swallowed hard but didn't answer.

"I'm trying not to take this personally."

"I'm—"

"No," he interrupted. "I'll see you after work."

The call ended and my eyes stung. How did I explain why I never told him? That at first I didn't know what was happening, but then I kept silent because it was too much? It was one more thing to deal with in a cascade of never-ending things after Ben died and I just couldn't.

Daisy had just been floating pens and then cheating on her video games. It wasn't anything to worry about, until, one day, it was. The last two years felt like someone was holding me underwater and every time I broke the surface, I was pulled back under.

Was life supposed to be this hard all the time? My phone buzzed.

Paris: *Your 2 pm is here*

Me: *Be right there*

Chapter Four

Eliza

WRITING LETTERS TO the dead was like having very far away pen pals with a slight chance of death. After the incident in fifth grade, my parents discovered SHAP and found me a medium mentor. I learned how to set boundaries, when and where to let ghosts communicate, and met other children like me, who could talk to the dead. I could talk to ghosts on earth easily enough, but once they crossed over, I could only understand them through the letter writing process.

Most of my clients were SHAP attorneys looking for evidence from a victim who had passed, or family trying to find or contest a will. Today's client was neither, and definitely the highlight of my day. Edward Gardner's nurse pushed him across the foyer and to my office. I rounded my desk and met him at the door, leaning down to kiss his cheek above his oxygen tube.

"Beautiful Eliza," he crooned, his voice rough with age and pain.

"I've saved my best spot for you," I promised. I replaced the nurse and pushed him to my desk.

Paris stood and grabbed her purse and coat. "I'm going to lunch. Need anything?"

My stomach growled, reminding me I hadn't eaten lunch. "I'm okay."

She hesitated. "I'll bring you back a sandwich in case."

"You don't need to." I was sure I'd find some quarters in my purse for the vending machine. I had meant to grab lunch between Daisy's doctor appointment and meeting Edward, but it fell through the cracks.

"If I don't, you'll eat a candy bar."

I didn't respond, instead shifting my laptop and stack of manila folders out of the way to make room for the ritual, pointedly ignoring the way my stomach dropped. Why did she have to keep trying to take care of me?

Paris pulled on her coat and walked out. I watched her leave, forgetting to breathe until she closed the office door behind her. Sucking in a breath, my shoulders unwired themselves just a little.

Edward stared at the door then turned back to me, eyebrows raised.

"I don't want to talk about it," I warned.

"I didn't say anything."

"After three years, I know you better than you think."

"My Rosie took my breath away, too."

I shook my head. "She hurt me in an unforgiveable way."

"I see."

"It's not happening again."

"Again?"

I held up my finger. "Uh-uh. Today's about you. I heard you were causing trouble down at the city hall meeting."

He gave me an innocent look. "You say trouble, I say fun."

"Faking a demonic possession in the middle of the mayor's speech qualifies as fun? I'm doing this life thing wrong."

He chuckled and coughed, his thin chest rattling. "He's a putz."

"Rumor has it you were speaking in tongues."

"I'm learning Finnish on the Duolingo app."

"And calling for a priest to exorcise the town?"

He winked at me. "Okay, maybe I was causing a little bit of trouble."

We both laughed and I reached out and took his soft, frail hand. Pale blue veins stood out against paper thin skin. "How'd your last checkup go?"

He let out a shaky breath and shook his head. "Not so good."

I bit my lip. "Prognosis?"

"Long and painful."

I nodded. "Well then, I'm happy you're spending time with me."

"Me too, beautiful Eliza. Me too." He flinched and shifted, then smiled back up at me. "Did I ever tell you about the time I streaked across the school gym in the middle of an assembly?"

"No! Spill."

"It was the final round of speeches before we voted for class president. See, I'd been in love with Rosie since I first saw her two years before, but she was with that jerk Colin Odell. Still, when I found her crying by her locker because she left her speech at home, I had to do something."

"Oh my goodness, you really ran through the assembly naked?"

He let out a low chuckle. "That I did. I caused enough ruckus that she got home and back to school before the speeches even began. You bet your bottom nickel she won that election! And I won her."

He smiled and dabbed at his watery eyes with a crumpled handkerchief. "She was my everything. I can't wait to see her again."

I blinked fast, not wanting to show my tears. "Okay then, what are we going to write to Rosie this time? We did a poem last appointment and the words to her favorite song the one before."

His smile was bigger than I had ever seen it. "I'm going to recite the vows I read to her fifty-two years ago today."

I cradled his hand in both of mine. "That sounds perfect. And happy anniversary to you both."

He tried to gather his wallet out of his wheelchair pocket, and I swallowed hard. "You don't owe me a thing, Edward." I couldn't stomach taking what little money he got from Social Security when he was already giving up so much to talk to Rosie. "I don't charge on anniversaries."

"You've got a daughter to support."

"I'm salaried. I'm getting paid either way. Plus, my late fiancé left me some life insurance."

He sighed. "You remind me so much of Rosie. She was stubborn, too."

"I'll take that as a compliment." I removed a wooden box from my desk. "I need to go over the contract with you, like

I do every time."

He nodded.

"You will dictate the letter and I will write a draft. Once we confirm this is what you want to say, I will transfer it to parchment. I will use a sterilized lancet to draw a small amount of blood from your finger, which will be your postage..."

I held his hand as I explained the procedure to him, even though he'd heard it nearly a dozen times before. The lore went that many centuries ago, a medium who could communicate—albeit chaotically—with the dead became the first official postmaster when she passed. Over time, she took on additional dead supernatural creatures who could translate letters from living mediums.

It was almost like a mirror to what we did in the human realm. Instead of contacting a specific dead person directly, I'd send the message to the Dead Letter Office in the afterlife and they'd act as a hub. This was a safer and more reliable way. They would transcribe the message, locate the dead person, deliver the letter, take a reply, and send it back.

Time didn't really exist in the afterlife, not in any way I could understand at least. Sometimes replies took mere moments, other times days or weeks. Or in Ben's case, two years and counting.

"The cost for sending a letter—whether or not it is answered—is 365 days of your life. This is a permanent, non-refundable service," I finished.

A non-negotiable price paid to afford the letter runner the ability to cross between the realms of the dead without getting trapped. Poppy once told me that as a grim reaper, she'd drop souls off to be sorted into different realms but was never allowed to visit any herself.

While it would be free for me to contact a spirit by letter directly, it was like an unsecured dial-up internet connection versus a high-speed fiber optic one with strong security. A message could get through, but it could be interrupted, or a virus easily downloaded—although in this case a virus was a malevolent spirit or demon. I'd tried it once to contact Ben and ended up with a poltergeist that give me one hell of a scar on my thigh.

Edward nodded and sighed. "The fact that I'm still here means I would've been without my Rosie for ten years." He shook his head. "It's a life not worth living."

I took his hand again. "Is your will up to date?"

"Yes. I hope this is the last letter I have to write."

"Me too." I stood and walked around the table, and then wrapped my arm around his shoulders, kissing his nearly bald head. "But I will miss you and our visits."

He patted my arm. "I told you, you've got to start looking for a man your own age," he teased.

I laughed and squeezed his shoulder then returned to my seat. "You ready?"

"More than I've ever been."

"Let's begin," I directed, scooping up my red feather quill and homemade parchment paper, both ceremonial rather than required. I could write a letter with ketchup and a grocery store receipt. It was the postage that mattered most.

In careful cursive, I wrote DEARLY DEPARTED ROSIE GARDNER, followed by her birth and death dates. With smiles and laughter, Edward retold the story of his wedding and the impromptu vows that took everyone by surprise. I could feel the love, even after all these years. When we finished the letter, I read it back to him.

"It's perfect," he confirmed.

"Then it's time."

I removed an alcohol swab, a lancet, and a bandage from the wooden box. With a rub of the alcohol pad and a poke, I coaxed a drop of blood from Edward's finger and helped him press it to a small square of paper, about twice the size of a postage stamp. "Are you ready? You cannot undo the time you lose, even if she doesn't respond."

He held my gaze. "Yes, my dear. I am ready. I've been ready for the last two years and thirteen days."

I bandaged his finger, then started the communication process.

My preferred method of delivering a message was fire scrying, which could be dangerous. If I pulled too far away from my body, it was harder to get back. However, I'd been writing letters for so long, it was nearly second nature. I lit the thick purple candle, then stared into the flame, allowing myself to fall into the light.

I waited until I felt a transcriber's presence then began visualizing the words as written, pushing each one through as if guiding a croquet ball through a hoop. Then, I lifted the blood payment to the candle and set it on fire. It disappeared without leaving any smoke or ash behind.

I pulled back from the connection, leaving it open but shallow. If I needed to close off before a reply came, the transcriber would save the reply until another agent could receive it. There was always someone in the SHAP Dead

Letter Office taking correspondence. I really missed being there, with other mediums. Sometimes, if I went too long without taking a letter, the voices would become unbearable.

A tug at my connection alerted me that a response was forthcoming. I grabbed another piece of paper and made notes as I was bombarded with symbols of *joy* and *love.* I worked hard on suppressing my own emotions so they wouldn't interfere.

Spirits couldn't speak the way humans did, and often replies were illegible to the untrained transcriber. Luckily, I was extremely fluent. Someone poked at my thoughts, the mood of love and joy turning sour. Another soul was trying to cut in.

Both the other transcriber and I broke the connection, keeping the stray soul from accessing our line of communication. I threw up my mental shield and blew out the candle. My ears rang as a cold sweat beaded along the back of my neck, and I gasped in a few breaths to combat the nausea. The body didn't like touching death, and sometimes it had a fight or flight reaction.

After one last deep breath, I glanced up at Edward. His face was a little paler, his hair a little thinner, his eyes unfocused. His breathing had become more labored, a wheezing sound accompanying each inhale.

When I was confident my legs would hold me, I folded the response and walked around the table, scooping his hand into mine and pressing the letter in. "Rosie says she loves you and that she'll be waiting."

A smile ghosted over his lips. "Beautiful Eliza, I'll miss you."

I sat with my head in my hands for a several minutes after saying goodbye to Edward. He was not the first client I'd lose, nor would he be the last. It didn't make it any easier.

If I didn't have Daisy, would I have wanted to give up the rest of my life to be with Ben? In Edward's shoes, would I have written ten letters to hurry the years along? *No*, I thought. *I wouldn't.*

The office door opened, and I quickly dropped my hands and looked up. Paris walked in, cheeks pink from the wind.

I would've given up everything for her. I nearly gasped at the thought, busying myself with filing Edward's letters into a binder, which was kept for legal reasons.

Paris set a Café Eleonora bag and a cardboard coffee cup on my desk and then moved to her own.

I swallowed hard, the constant war of betrayal and longing churning my stomach. "How much do I owe you?"

She waved me off. "I don't have a kid to support."

I shook my head. It felt too much like a gift, too much like a date. *She hurt you*, I reminded myself. *Ben is dead because of her.* "I need to pay you for it."

She stilled for a moment, as if my words hit her like a fist, then glanced down at her phone. She sent me an electronic invoice for the total through the SHAP banking app, and I immediately paid. She'd been right; those nine dollars were likely more precious to me than to her, but I couldn't be indebted to her. Not any more than I already was for her saving Jake's and Poppy's lives.

"Thank you," I said, so low I didn't know if she could hear me.

She nodded, but kept her eyes locked on her laptop, sipping what I knew was a cup of peppermint tea.

I bit into the sandwich, pretending I didn't want her to look up at me and tell me it'd all be okay and that we'd figure it out.

Chapter Five

Paris

MY PRECOGNITIVE DREAMS weren't always nightmares, but when they crossed that line, they were horrific. Last night I'd woken up with a nosebleed, shaking, and covered in a cold sweat. I'd ran to the bathroom and thrown up. Not even a long shower before dawn helped.

Whenever I closed my eyes, I could see the dream werewolf-vampire hybrids, the ones we had fought in Hayvenwood during the vixen investigation. They'd been wandering through a mass of bodies collapsed in red-tinged snow, some I recognized, some I didn't. Loren, Raine, Mina, Jake, the owner of the deli on Main, my favorite grocery store cashier. The wolves paused at every human, sniffing them, and leaning close to check for a heartbeat.

When they came across someone alive, they'd howl, and a human-vampire hybrid would run over and shove a capsule in the person's mouth. A few moments later, the nearly dead person would heal and rise from the ground and join the vampire-hybrid army.

The most sickening moment was when Daisy slid off a hybrid wolf's back and picked her way to Eliza's body. She tucked a pill into her mom's mouth, but Eliza didn't wake. It had been too late.

I'd woken up screaming. I sucked in a sharp breath and shook my head, bringing myself back to reality. *It hasn't happened. Everyone is safe. Eliza is safe.*

The dream had left me unfocused. Even now, as I stared at my computer screen while sipping peppermint tea, the dream played out in front of my eyes. While I could sometimes see future scenarios play out while awake, they weren't usually this vivid, this violent. Eliza sitting a mere twelve feet away from me didn't help. I wanted to warn her, to share my nightmare so I didn't have to carry it alone, but I couldn't. Not anymore.

I'd failed her, failed Ben, and that was my burden to carry. I'd sworn to protect her and Daisy with my life, even after our breakup. It was harder now that she'd completely shut me out. At least I got to be near her until the end of the month.

I scrolled through the Excel sheet of interviewees I still hadn't heard back from. Two hundred and thirty-six emails ignored, one hundred and eighty more not reached by phone. How were Eliza and I supposed to investigate this case following protocol with so few resources?

"What?" Eliza asked.

I looked over at her, ignoring the way my stomach dropped when I saw her staring at me. "What do you mean?"

"You've sighed twice in the last five minutes."

I had? "Oh. Sorry." I turned back to face my laptop.

"Just tell me or you won't stop doing it."

I bit the insides of my cheeks. Did she really want to

know? Or was my sighing that disruptive?

"Sigh number three."

Okay, probably the latter. "When Jake and I were investigating, we had ghosts, witches, forensics, R&D. We were working weekends, existing on cups of coffee with no sleep. Why are you and I confined to this room doing paperwork during normal business hours?"

She eyed her coffee cup as if it had the answers. "Because I'm not an active field agent?"

"But I am. And for that matter, why aren't you allowed to write to the vixen victims? That's literally the job you were hired for."

"What are you saying?"

What was I saying? Did I think Jim was trying to sweep this under the rug, which was why he was using—what he suspected were—two under-qualified agents? Absolutely. *But why?* Was it only to help Jim's friend at the DEA? Or was it something else?

I unfocused my eyes and looked over Eliza's shoulder, trying to find any snippets of what might happen after we turn in the file. I wasn't fully clairvoyant, but I could see probabilities in certain circumstances. The vision of Eliza, dead on the snow, pushed its way through again. I scrambled out of my chair, returning to the present and pressing my hand to my chest to try and keep my thrashing heart inside.

Eliza stood too, looking out the window then back at me. "What? Are you okay?"

I nodded, despite still breathing like I'd just run five miles. "Sorry," I mumbled, slumping down in my chair, and then grabbing my tea. My hands were shaking as I lifted it to my mouth, and I hoped she couldn't tell.

She looked behind her again then turned back to face me. "What was that about?"

"Thought I saw something. I was mistaken." The crease between her brows deepened and I knew she wanted to pry, but she wouldn't. Because if she forced me to open up, she knew she'd have to return the favor.

I nearly laughed at the thought. When we were together, every personal story from her had been tempered to contain as little about her life and feelings as possible. She relied on her storytelling capabilities and humor to smooth over any gaps. I hadn't noticed at first, then I hadn't cared because I just wanted my hands on her body and my mouth sealed to hers.

"Okay…what's going on?" Eliza prompted. "You're acting strange."

"Nothing's going on."

She glared. "I've already had a really shit day and I have to go home and deal with a sick kid. I don't have time to babysit you, too. Just tell me."

"What's wrong with Daisy?"

"Nothing serious." She tucked a stray lock of hair behind her left ear, her tell.

I crossed my arms. "For someone who doesn't abide lying, you are exceptionally good at it."

She raised an eyebrow. "Protecting my daughter from the woman who killed her father is the most important thing."

Her words were like a punch to my gut. "I didn't kill him." My words were barely more than a whisper. I hadn't pulled the trigger, but it was my fault he was dead and we both knew it.

"If you weren't there, he'd still be here—"

"I get it!" I shouted, standing again. "I get that you never want to see my face again, that I've destroyed your life, that I lied to you. I'm sorry we are trapped in this damn office for the next month while we work on a case that doesn't seem to matter to anyone else. But I'm *trying* to make this work and you're hiding behind your 'trust no one' and 'my secrets will always be more important than yours' façade and I'm so tired."

She stared at me, eyes wide and mouth open.

I closed my laptop and grabbed my tea. "I'm going on a walk to cool down." I rarely raised my voice, and never at Eliza. Usually, any yelling was reserved for sports teams or suspenseful movies. Today, though, I'd reached my limit.

"The case matters to me," Eliza admitted, voice quiet, as if her soothing tone could undo the damage mine caused.

"Good," I managed.

She fiddled with a pen cap, keeping her eyes on her hands. "What do you think we should do?"

I gripped the edge of my desk. Had *she* just asked *me* for my opinion? It would mean she'd have to listen and consider what I suggested. It would mean she'd have to trust me again. I chewed on my lower lip, debating whether I should tell her my plan. I was considering doing it alone, but it'd be easier with two people.

She set the pen on her desk and looked up at me, waiting expectantly.

God, I could fall into her eyes forever. I cleared my throat and looked away to maintain my composure. "I think we should forget the paper trail and do some real investigating. Be ready tomorrow."

"PARIS, DID NO one teach you how to color?" Clint whispered.

I startled and glanced up at Clint then down at my paper. My mind had been wandering and my red pencil was coloring the table. I winced and rubbed at it with my thumb. "Just distracted."

"No shit. What about?"

"Work stuff." I waved him off, not wanting to share.

Sitting with the ghosts, Amber, and Belphegor after dinner had become my nightly ritual over the last few weeks. Tonight, I'd brought out a coloring book and a pencil case full of colored pencils and sat at an empty section of table, but it wasn't really helping me decompress.

Reggie was talking about his visit with his niece, who was staying with his brother down the hall. "And she sat next to me for the whole movie! Didn't get scared once. Mi sobrina was too scared to talk to me for almost a year but didn't even flinch at zombie movies." He shook his head. "I'm less creepy than a zombie."

Clint laughed and kissed him. "You are. But have you thought that maybe she's used to you now and feels safe with you?"

Reggie smiled. "That's true, mi amor. I am the best uncle. I can haunt all the people who are mean to her."

I pointed a pencil at Reggie. "That's going to come in

handy."

He laughed. "Did you hear about the time Sebastian chased one of Mina's suitors out of the shower because he talked crap about her? I laughed so hard, I would've cried if I had tears."

Dani, the ghost mom of the group, clapped her hands. "I was there. I'll reenact!" She pretended to slip out of a tub, then run out the front door as if she were naked.

I was laughing so hard, I snorted. A door down the hall opened and Doris Manalin, Applechester, Michigan's nosiest neighbor, peered around the corner. She was in her sixties and just over five feet with a yellow-blonde bob, but she could strike fear into the heart of humans and ghosts alike.

"Ms. Evans, I'd like to remind you this isn't a coffee shop." She shot me one more dirty look, then returned to her apartment.

I covered my mouth with my hand and sank down in my chair, silently laughing.

"Now *she's* scarier than a zombie," Reggie mumbled.

I buried my face in my sweatshirt, trying to keep my laughter quiet.

"I'm pretty good at scaring people," Belphegor added. "It's the baritone of my voice, I think. But that woman scares the shit out of me."

My hand hit the table as I tried to suck in a calming breath. It took me three attempts to get my giggles under control. "N-no one finds me scary," another breath, "until they see me fight."

"You fight?" Belphegor asked. "You're the size of a green bean."

Amber tsked him. "Don't shame people's bodies."

"I wasn't!"

"Even if you weren't, that wasn't nice." Amber paused her crocheting and looked over at me. "Tell us about your fighting, dear. Is it like those cage matches on television?"

"You watch cage matches?" Dani asked.

Amber nodded. "Just in the background while I'm baking."

"Is that the secret to a perfect cookie?" I asked. "That's what I'm doing wrong."

"Now you know. Keep it between us."

"This place gets weirder every day," Clint chimed in.

"The fighting?" Belphegor prompted.

I lifted one shoulder. "I was really sick as a kid, *really* sick, before we figured out food was causing the problem. Somedays I had to go to school in a wheelchair, others I would hurry out of class and not always make the bathroom…"

Amber reached out and patted my knee. The memory became bearable with her compassion.

"My twin got into a lot of fights with my bullies to the point of suspension, so my parents enrolled him in martial arts classes to focus his anger. I wasn't well enough to join him, but on good days he'd take me out to the backyard and show me things. In college, he joined an amateur fighting league. Thought he'd fight professionally, but he found a position at SHAP he liked better. He still trains for fun, and he's still practicing with me."

"If he's half as pretty as you, Reggie's going to fall in love," Clint teased.

Reggie shoved his arm. "Silencio." He turned to me. "What's he look like?"

"You have a boyfriend," Dani chastised.

"I'm not dead. Well, I am, but I can still look." He leaned over and bussed Clint's cheek. "Clint knows my entire heart belongs to him."

Clint smiled and gave him a quick kiss. "Yes, I do. Look all you want, babe."

"Gross," Belphegor grumbled.

"He looks like me, just with shorter hair and a nose that's been broken several times. He snores like the devil."

"Fun fact," Belphegor added, "the devil doesn't sleep and therefore can't snore."

Reggie *pfft* him. "Continue, Paris."

"Do you have that twin thing?" Dani asked.

"Sometimes," I admitted. "Like, last week I was listening to a new band and texted Dal about it, and he already had them on repeat. Or last Christmas we bought each other the same concert tickets in the same row."

"Does he live close?" she prompted.

"His apartment is just outside of town, but he travels so much for work I hardly see him." I scribbled a doodle in the margin of my coloring book. "I miss being around someone who *gets* me."

I hadn't had friends, close friends, in a long time. Sure, I had Jake and my brother, but when I left R&D to become a field agent, a lot of people who I assumed were friends stopped returning calls and texts. Eliza had been a bright spot until she became a black hole. For the first time since the breakup—even though most of this group was dead, and one was a demon—I felt like people wanted me around...if I used the term "people" loosely.

"I'll teach you how to crochet or knit, if you'd like!" Amber offered. "I'm bistitchual."

I laughed, my loneliness lifting. "I'd like that. Thanks."

Sebastian poofed in next to me with a tip of his hat. "It's a pleasure to see you smiling. Did I miss anything good?"

"Paris was telling us about her hot brother and how she can fight like a badass!" Reggie explained. "And Doris made an appearance."

"I just had the most terrifying thought," Sebastian offered. "What if Doris died and became a Countryside ghost?"

We all shuddered.

"Why you gotta bring us down like that, mano?" Reggie complained. "Well, Paris, now you'll have to show us pics of this hot brother." He made a gimme motion with his hand. "Let's go."

Rolling my eyes, I opened my phone's photo album and navigated to my favorites. "I only have two, for security reasons, and I shouldn't even have these." I held up a photo of us.

"You're my favorite human," he told me. "Don't tell Mina. No, wait, tell Mina. It's fine."

Clint let out a low whistle, "Good genes run in your family."

"Yeah, except for my food allergies."

Belphegor scoffed. "Shit like allergies isn't what matters. The right people know it and want you around no matter what."

Amber smiled, as if she were a proud mother. “Damn straight.”

The demon stared at her. “Language.”

I covered my mouth with my hand. When I finally composed myself, I turned to Amber. “Okay. What do I need from the craft store if I’m going to start crocheting?”

I jotted down the list Amber gave and for the first time in a while, I felt like I was in the right place at the right time. Maybe things would be more tolerable if I just kept trudging through the hard days. Especially if I could stop seeing Eliza’s broken body behind my closed eyes.

Chapter Six

Eliza

DAISY'S EYES WERE closed as she shoveled in the last bite of her dinner. I glanced at Jake, who was watching her, too, his fingers tapping soundlessly on the table. A few weeks ago, it was like she had slammed two energy drinks in a row. I forced my jaw to unclench. Adding dental bills to my worries wouldn't help.

"Mom, can I go to bed?" she whined.

"Finish your juice first," I commanded, "and then pack your backpack and pick out your clothes for tomorrow. Give your tummy some time to settle. Then you can go to bed."

She let out a groan but picked up her glass. "It tastes weird."

"It will make you feel better. Just drink it really fast, okay?"

She leaned her head back on the chair and looked up at the ceiling. "Do I haaaaave to?"

"Do you want to feel better?"

"Fiiiiine." She sat up straight, grabbed the glass, and finished it in two gulps and made a face. She slammed her water next.

I smiled at her. "Great job. Now you are excused from the table. I'll clean up."

Jake held up his hand for a high-five. "Way to go, munchkin."

Daisy slapped his hand, slipped off her seat, and headed for her bedroom. My brother dropped his hand and turned to face me. "I'm still really pissed at you."

I swallowed down the pain of his words. "I know. You have every right to be."

"You're such a hypocrite. You refuse to talk to our parents for the exact thing you did to me." He pressed his finger into the table. "I'm trying as hard as you to keep her safe."

"I know."

"What else haven't you told me about her?"

"Nothing!" I promised, grabbing his arm. "It wasn't a big thing at first. Outside of the funeral, it had just been changing channels and floating books. I knew I had to deal with it, but I..." I squeezed his arm, trying to figure out how to say the words without hurting.

The words came out slowly, as if I were extracting them. "I was overwhelmed with things and I didn't want to deal with it. So I didn't until I was forced to."

He rested his hand on top of mine and squeezed. "I get it. I checked out after Poppy died. And I didn't have a kid." He leaned back in his chair and shifted his permanently injured leg. I was happy to see he wasn't wincing anymore. "So, what are we going to do?"

I picked up my phone and turned it end over end. "I'm going to put Daisy to bed then call Raine and Loren."

He nodded. "Glad you're listening to me. I'm usually

right."

I rolled my eyes. "Sure, like that time when Joe Buell told you no one would suspect that your water bottle—"

"Yeah, yeah, I said usually, not always."

"To be fair, if you hadn't flipped over the front of the bleachers and ripped your pants, you may have gotten away with it."

"Hadn't really thought about *being* drunk, just getting drunk." He stood and balanced himself with his cane. "Let me know how the call goes?"

"Of course."

He headed to Daisy's room as I cleared the table, trying not to think about calling two people I didn't know. Sure, Jake and Paris knew them, but opening up to strangers was terrifying. Daisy's laugh bubbled into the kitchen and I paused, realizing I hadn't heard the sound in several days. I would do anything for my daughter, including making a call.

Jake walked through the kitchen on his way out the door. "Poppy wants you over this weekend for a movie night."

"Okay."

He hit my ankle lightly with his cane. "We're good. Just don't lie to me again."

I nodded and followed him to the door, then locked it behind him and armed the alarm. By the time I circled back to Daisy's room, she was fast asleep. I turned off her light and closed her door.

Deep breath. Time to adult. I opened a new text message.

Me: *Hi Raine, it's Jake Robinson's sister, Eliza. Do you have time to chat?*

I cringed. *Chat? Who says chat anymore? Why didn't I just say talk?* I pinched the bridge of my nose. I was overthinking this.

> ***Raine:*** *Definitely. Loren is with me if you'd like to do a video call. Jake mentioned you may need to speak with both of us*

I nearly groaned. Video calls made me so anxious. I straightened my shoulders and grabbed my laptop. Anything for my daughter.

I LEANED BACK against my headboard, processing Raine's story about giving up her powers to save not only Loren, but all of Hayvenwood. She was a beautiful woman, with white skin and long ice blonde hair that faded into a deep blue at the end. Loren, twice her size with skin tanned from years in the desert and a buzzed head, was protective of her, even over video. He was constantly touching her, soothing her, as she leaned into his shoulder.

Paris used to constantly touch me, something I hadn't noticed until she was no longer around. It had made the voices in my head so quiet, and I'd felt treasured, precious to her. Now that I had to sit across from her every day, the throbbing emptiness inside my chest only grew worse.

"Losing my power was like losing a piece of myself," Raine admitted, then laughed a little. "I mean, I guess that's what it is. An internal amputation." She pressed a hand to her chest. "For a long time, I felt hollow."

"Do you regret it?" I asked.

She smiled sadly but shook her head no. "How can I regret something that saved so many lives? And now I can touch Lucian freely without my magic interfering," she explained, using Loren's birthname. "I miss it, every day. But I don't regret it."

She looked down at her hand entwined with her husband's. "I think if someone had taken my power, it would've been much worse. It was hard making peace with who I am without it, even though I would make the same choice a hundred times over."

I slowly released a breath, trying to steady my emotions. "What if your power was hurting you?"

"I would've wanted to go down with the ship. I almost did. Removing magic is not always a successful endeavor, even if by choice."

I pressed my fingers to my forehead as I tried not to think about losing Daisy. Emotions which felt too big for my body swirled inside my chest before settling. "Looks like that leaves only one option," I managed. "Loren, can you help me track down Ben's family and my biological father? I need to find out what kind of witch Daisy is."

Loren nodded. "Tell me everything you know."

Chapter Seven

Paris

RETURNING TO R&D with its white tiled floors and blue doors was like visiting high school after graduation. A sense of nostalgia mixed with the need to see if anyone remembered me. I somehow still wanted to stake my claim on this place, despite no longer being part of it.

It had been an incredible job, one with great memories. When my old manager retired and my team was reassigned to work with a micromanaging bully, I knew it was time to get out. As if by magic, an active agent position opened, and Dallas put my name in before I'd even made up my mind to apply. Since he was an active agent, his recommendation landed me an interview. He helped me train every day for two weeks, and I passed the introductory test with flying colors. They hired me the same day.

I'd never once doubted I made the right move until I was assigned to Eliza. I glanced at her out of the corner of my eye, still surprised she'd agreed to come with me. We'd decided yesterday to start properly investigating this case against Jim's orders, and she hadn't changed her mind. Not that she often did.

She studied the hallway with interest, peering into any windows that we passed. The space between us was heavy with unspoken words. I missed when our conversation flowed freely instead of through a minefield. My pinky twitched, desperate to reach out and wrap around hers. I closed my hands into fists to prevent me from doing something embarrassing.

With a deep breath, I knocked on the door of my old dragon of a manager's office. Miriam, a grumpy woman in her forties with a white lab coat and hair pulled back in a tight bun, opened the door with an even tighter smile. "Ms. Evans. What brings you back here?" She glanced at Eliza. "And this is?"

"Ms. Monroe, this is Eliza Robinson, my partner. We're here on official case business."

Miriam's expression didn't change, but she turned back to Eliza. "Any relationship to Jake Robinson?"

"He's my brother," Eliza confirmed.

My old boss nodded once. "One of the best. Shame he retired."

Eliza opened her mouth to retort, but I placed a hand on her arm. Touching between us had virtually been nonexistent unless absolutely required since our split, and this felt like breaking a dozen rules. She tensed and I squeezed her arm once before letting go, a plea for her to keep her mouth closed. Arguing with this woman would mean not getting what we needed. She made Eliza's grudges look like kid's play.

"May we come in?" I asked, pulling out my more congenial voice. I fisted my hand, trying to hold on to the warmth of Eliza's skin.

Miriam eyed me wearily, then nodded. "You have five minutes. If you need longer, you can call and schedule—"

"Five minutes is more than enough time," I assured her, following her into her office. It was little more than a desk stacked with organizational containers and three chairs. While the top was cluttered with multiple inboxes and outboxes, along with a metal framed filing system, it was spotless. No doubt she could locate something in precisely fifteen seconds. Even micromanaging had its perks.

She took a seat, then stared at us until we sat. Realizing she wasn't going to offer even the briefest of small talk, I began. "We're on a confidential case that requires tracking sensitive materials. I think it would be an excellent opportunity to test RD131-T."

Miriam folded her hands in front of her on the desk, and I knew this was going to turn out exactly as I expected. She'd ask probing questions starting with "tell me about your case." I'd explain I'm unable to answer, she'd say something about having a higher security level than me and therefore she needed to know the details of the case first, I'd stand my ground, she'd pull the "they're only a prototype, and therefore unreliable," card and I'd leave the office empty-handed.

I knew the RD131-T were accurate. I'd been the one who built them.

"So, Ms. Evans. Tell me about your case."

My stomach dropped and my shoulders drooped. There it was.

"As much as I love small talk," Eliza said—I nearly laughed because she hated small talk more than she hated me—then reached into her suit coat pocket and pulled out a folded sheet of paper. "This is from Jim."

My mouth fell open. She'd managed to get Jim to sign a release form?

Eliza glanced at me out of the corner of her eye, and I knew. This was a forgery. Miriam looked nearly as shocked as me. She ran her finger down the page, combing through every detail. She looked up, then back at the form. I could practically see the questions bottlenecking in her throat as she rolled her tongue around her mouth, then swallowed hard.

Without a word, she stood and walked over to her closet along the side of the office. It was built flush with the wall, the only noticeable feature being a keycard reader. She swiped her card and a panel popped forward and slid open. She located a closed box and swiped her card again.

She reached in and removed a hard case, about the size of a thousand-piece puzzle, cradling it as if it were her first born child. Miriam always wanted the upper hand, which is why most conversations with her were like a tennis game. "Will these be returned?" she volleyed.

"The plan is recovery," I lobbed.

"What if they're destroyed?" she backhanded.

"I left detailed schematics, three different prototypes, and a how-to video as demanded by you before I changed positions." *It's not my fault if you don't have decent lab techs.* While my thoughts remained unspoken, they were as loud as a shout.

She tilted her head left and then right, the top of her ears turning red. "I expect a renewal form or a return in two weeks, as stated on the initial release."

I nodded once, then extended my hands. She hesitated then handed me the box, her fingers curling around the edge for a moment before releasing.

Match. "Thanks for all your help," I chirped.

Eliza bit down hard on her lip, presumably to keep from smiling, and widened her eyes. I tilted my head to the door and then walked out. She followed close behind.

We were dead silent until we got into the elevator. As soon as the doors slid shut, Eliza barked out a laugh. The sound was so unfamiliar, my entire body went weightless, or maybe that was just the elevator jerking to life. I turned to face her.

"No wonder you left. Was she always so charming?"

"Even more, sometimes. I think she might be half-troll or something. They are hoarders by nature, and she hides all her treasure behind locked cabinets." I shifted on my feet and stared at our hazy reflection in the door. Her shoulder was only a few inches away from mine. In another world, I could lean into her, rest my head on her shoulder, tilt my chin up until she pressed a soft kiss to my lips.

I averted my eyes and smiled. "I can't believe you forged a form so accurately it fooled her."

"I do write letters for a living." She gestured to the case. "What's our loot?"

"I'll show you in our office."

She hesitated then said, "You stood up to her."

"People often mistake my quiet for weakness. I just pick my battles." That was a lie. I let most of my battles pick me. Part of the reason being an agent was so appealing was my desire to be more confident.

When Eliza didn't respond, I glanced over at her. She stared at the elevator buttons as if they would give her an explanation to an unasked question.

The elevator dinged and the doors slid open. Four people walked in as we tried to step out, creating chaos as the doors tried to close with us still inside. Eliza barked "move" and they finally scattered, allowing us to escape. When we reached the office door, I swiped my keycard and held open the door. Eliza walked inside and I followed, locking it behind me.

The sound echoed in the tiny space. If this were the before, she'd push me up against the door, kiss me until I couldn't feel my legs, smile against my mouth, and tell me she missed me. Instead, she walked to her desk, grabbed her chair, and wheeled it opposite mine.

This sixty-four square foot office wasn't made for two desks, let alone two exes. Every inch was crammed full of paperwork, office furniture, and memories of secret kisses and soft moans. I straightened my sweater and stared at my plastic Ficus tree in the corner, which was trying its hardest to lift the mood.

Eliza reached out and touched a petal of my fake orchid. "This is new."

Why did her knowing that feel like a knife between the ribs? "Yeah." I sat, annoyed when her warm cinnamon scent wrapped around me. I set the case on my desk and lifted the lid to reveal twenty-four trackers that looked like clear bandages. "Trackers."

Pride swelled in my chest as I scooped one up. The fingernail-sized, nearly translucent devices were attached to a base that was used to charge and program them. Each charge could last twenty-eight days when in sleep mode, a week in active mode.

"Once charged and programed, we remove the base and attach the business end to an object or person. They're water-resistant for up to three hours submerged at fifteen feet, have a range of thirty miles, and are virtually undetectable."

Eliza sat in the seat across from my desk, and I set a tracker in front of her. She stared at me, an unrecognizable expression on her face. "What?" I asked.

She blinked then shook her head. "I can tell you made these by the way your face lights up."

I smiled and laughed awkwardly. "Yeah, I guess you could call them a passion project. They took years but Miriam never gave me the green light to do rigorous testing."

She frowned, touching the edge of the base and leaning close to examine the device. "Why wouldn't they greenlight this? This would be immeasurably helpful."

"Like most things we make in R&D, it came down to money. Didn't get the testing budget approved. Maybe it was a good thing, in the end. I made them with the best intentions and didn't think about what would happen if someone was able to attach this to a world leader or if a stalker used one to track a victim." My shoulders slumped and I sat down in my chair, letting out a long breath.

"Ah, that would be problematic." Her foot bumped mine, likely accidentally, under the desk and I stilled.

This simple touch was enough to make my stomach

squeeze. How did she still have this effect on me? Why couldn't I break free?

I stared at the way her fingers smoothed the edges of the tracker base, then looked away, shoving down memories of how those fingers felt running along my bare skin. I cleared my throat. "Thank you for bringing a release form. That was smart."

She lifted her blue eyes to mine. "It probably wouldn't hold up in court, but it was close enough for our purposes."

My god, she was so smart. I glanced at her lips, so desperate to kiss her, the back of my neck pricked with sweat. We needed these trackers to work because if we didn't solve this case soon, I was going to lose my mind.

I wanted to dig my fingers into her thick, red curls, gently remove her peacock feather earrings, which were the same blue as her eyes, and kiss the soft skin behind her ear lobe. She always melted in my arms when I did that. I wanted her weight against me when she tilted her chin and leaned into me.

"You need to stop looking at me like that," she whispered.

"What if I can't?" I dared to reply. It had been five months since our last kiss, and I'd felt every minute that passed. Eliza and I clicked in a way I'd never experienced with anyone else. We'd instantly become a team—us against the world—and I could've taken on anything with her by my side. I wanted to listen to her talk for hours, hold her close, bury my face against her neck. I wanted to make her laugh and grab her hand and dance in the kitchen while cooking. I wanted to watch movies with her and Daisy, which was always a hilarious experience.

She was the first person in my life to take my dietary restrictions in stride and not treat them like a defect. It wasn't a burden for her to share a meal with me. My entire life, food had always been a source of conflict, and it didn't help that it played such a significant role in dating. Nearly a dozen people had dumped or ghosted me after our first meal together because I was too "high maintenance." I was so tired of having to explain that yes, my restrictions were real, and no, I couldn't just have a cheat day for their convenience.

"What's your plan with the trackers?" Eliza asked, refocusing the conversation. She shifted, her foot moving away, and I closed my eyes feeling the loss more than I probably should.

I swallowed down all my unsaid words. "I want to put trackers on the vixen in evidence."

She pursed her lips, then handed the tracker back to me. Our fingers brushed as I took it from her, and she yanked her hand away as if I'd burned her. It was my fault we were broken, and the constant guilt I carried over Ben's death sank its claws into me a little more.

"Why the vixen?" She gestured to the case. "It hasn't moved in weeks."

"That's why."

"Your communication skills haven't improved."

"I think they're pretty on par with yours."

She crossed her arms. "What's that supposed to mean?"

"You're all smoke and mirrors. Anything about *you* stays hidden."

"Oh, you're one to talk—"

"I kept one secret. You kept a lifetime full." I set the tracker back down in the case.

"I don't harbor secrets about killing people."

I stood, shoving away the weight of her words. "Involving you was a mistake. I'll do this on my own."

She stood and put her hands on her hips. "Yes, I'm sure you can, even though it took two of us to even get the trackers. Want me to just finish the paperwork and turn it in to Jim? We can wrap up this whole damn case right now and move on with our lives."

My cheeks burned with anger. "I'm not going to flake on a case that hurt so many people just because Jim wants to suck up to some DEA agent. I took an oath—"

"Oh, so you do have morals?"

I slammed my hand on my desk. "Stop. Just, stop. Not everything I do has an ulterior motive designed specifically to hurt you!" I turned and paced behind my desk, even though it was only three steps to the wall and back. "I didn't even know you when…that night. I would give *anything* to change the past, but I can't."

I slumped down in my chair. "This is where we're at. Either you stop purposely twisting my words and actions and join me, or you concentrate on the paperwork and leave me the hell alone."

Eliza gripped the back of her chair, standing still. She stared down at me as if she'd never seen me before. I'd never raised my voice or called her out when we were together. I had been trying so hard not to lose her, I didn't stand up for myself. Not even during the breakup.

But this was too important. The vision of her lying dead in the snow was still all too real whenever I closed my eyes.

A small electronic noise came from the box on my desk, and I stopped breathing. My eyes met Eliza's and I held my finger to my lips. Unlocking my phone, I opened an app I'd developed which could detect even the RD131-T trackers. My camera powered on, a large red circle appearing at the edge of the screen and narrowing down as it located the signal.

Keeping the phone steady, I moved it over the case. *There.* A piece of iridescent film. I gathered a pair of tweezers from my desk drawer, then pried the tracker away from the top left corner.

Switching from camera to flashlight mode, I leaned close to inspect the device. It was modeled after my schematics but without finesse. Someone had used my tech—poorly—then stuck it on something I'd made. *Why?*

Why was there a tracker in the box? Did it only track movement? Was it able to pick up audio? Visual? Was there a heat sensor?

I grabbed a bottled water from the bottom desk drawer, where I hid snacks, and handed it to Eliza. "Open it," I mouthed.

She twisted off its cap and set it down in front of me. I tucked the tracker into the cap and poured water over top, submerging it. After about a minute, it made a dull pop.

I opened my app again and held it over the tracker. No signal. I leaned back in my chair and pulled my dark hair out of its neat bun, massaging the aching skin on my scalp. *What were the facts?*

1) Someone had used my design as inspiration
2) They either couldn't understand the directions or made it in a hurry

3) No waterproof layer to protect it from liquids
4) Based on Miriam's reaction, she didn't know that someone else had created additional trackers. Miriam was many things, but a good actress wasn't one
5) Which meant someone was keeping an eye on these and knows they had moved to my office

In good news, the signal was dead. If they hadn't pinpointed the exact location before I killed it, I was safe. In bad news, it meant we needed to make sure someone didn't have us under surveillance. Not just the cameras in the lobby and the porn blockers on the work laptops surveillance, but *tracked.*

"What just happened?" Eliza asked, voice little more than a whisper.

"Are you in?" I wasn't going to waste my time explaining it if she was just going to accuse me of planting the bug myself to look good.

"I'm in."

I picked up my phone and texted her.

Me: *Go walk around the building twice. Take Clark St. south to Café Eleonora. Meet me there in twenty*

She read the text, put her phone in her pocket, moved her chair back, and grabbed her coat. "Meeting Patty for a coffee break," she said, referring to her old partner. "Be back in a bit."

I nodded as I opened my software tracker on my laptop. Time to make sure this was an isolated incident.

Chapter Eight

Eliza

PARIS SAT IN the back corner booth of the café, a red mug with a tea bag string over the side. She was wearing the scarf I'd given her last Christmas. She'd cooed when she'd opened it, then wore it the entire day, even after hula-hooping with Daisy for an hour, her cheeks pink from exertion.

"It's like a hug around my neck," she'd told me.

"You're ridiculous."

"It's why you love me," she whispered.

"Always."

Why had she been the one to betray me? Sucking in a deep breath, I put one foot in front of the other until I made it to the booth.

When I slid in opposite her, she didn't look at me, but off to the side. Indignation at being ignored heated my chest when I remembered her words from earlier. *Stop purposefully twisting my words.*

I hadn't been twisting anything. She had always been like this. Too quiet, spacey, not looking at me until I practically forced her. It had been cute at first—I loved shy women—

but now I knew it was because she was hiding secrets. "Paris?"

She leaned across the table so close and so quick, I thought she was going to kiss me. *Finally.* A wave of relief washed over me, and I began to close my eyes.

"Did you see the man walking behind you?" she whispered. "Dark navy peacoat, close-cropped blond beard, sunglasses, baseball cap?"

I blinked, caught off guard. Her gardenia scent wrapped around me and buried itself in my nose so I'd think of her the rest of the day. *If she'd kissed you, what would you have done? Would you have grabbed her and kissed her back?* I looked at her lips, my jaw clenching against the desperate longing in my chest.

"Eliza?"

I shook my head then leaned back, trying to suck in a lungful of air without smelling *her*. I looked back over my shoulder. "I...didn't notice." The only person I knew with a navy peacoat was Ben, and I hadn't seen it since he died. "You sure he was following me?"

She looked over my shoulder, scanning the area. "He was really close to you." She scrunched her nose. "He seemed familiar, but I didn't get a good enough look at him to place him. Maybe he works at SHAP."

Her stupid scrunched nose almost did me in. She'd made that exact same face when she'd explain how some technology on a show was impossible, or when we watched a baking show, and someone didn't properly structure their dessert. If this was *before*, I'd lean over and kiss the tip of her nose. I'd tell her how cute she was.

Her eyes turned toward mine as if she were surprised to see me, then lifted her mug. "Do you want a beverage?" she asked before taking a sip.

I shook my head. I unwrapped my scarf then unzipped my coat. "Why are we here?"

"I didn't want to speak in the office." She leaned across the table. "Give me your phone."

"What? No."

She closed her eyes for a beat, as if asking for patience. "Please, just trust me for a minute."

My stomach tightened, but I reluctantly unlocked my phone and handed it to her. She deftly moved through the screens, then picked up her own cell and held it near mine. After thirty seconds of excruciating silence, she slid it back to me.

"What was that for?"

"Needed to make sure we weren't under surveillance. I need to check your laptop too, or I can talk you through it."

"Why would we be under surveillance?"

"I don't know. The tracker we found was a rough prototype. Whoever built it used my schematics but did a half-ass job."

I sat back. "If R&D isn't going to fund the project, and it was relegated to a storage closet, why track it?"

Paris put her chin in her hand. "The question of the day. It was active, and guessing by the workmanship, it had to be fresh. That one wouldn't have had a long battery life."

"So, either they replace them frequently, or someone wanted to know where these trackers were at all times?" I tapped the table with my fingernails. "Could Miriam have slipped it in?"

The line between her brows deepened. "Possibly?" She chewed her bottom lip, then straightened, pressed her hands to the table. "Or someone knows I'd want them?"

"How?"

She shook her head. "I have no idea. No one knows I'm working this case."

"Why do you think tracking vixen is the key?"

She blinked at me. "You're asking for my expert opinion?"

"I…guess I am?"

Her hands wrapped around her mug. "Well…I think that a lot of money was put into this project and even though it caused a lot of deaths, it's still a powerful drug."

I crossed my arms and waited until she looked at me. "Bullshit. People scrap clinical trials all the time. Tell me the real reason."

She raised both her eyebrows in surprise then leaned forward, pressing her palms to the table, as if to keep it from hearing the secret. "Vixen can create a near invincible army. Sure, there's some sun sensitivity and feral vampires to worry about, but if they give vixen to several thousand people and turn them into hybrid vampires with fast healing, plus above human energy and strength, it would change everything. Sell it to leaders around the world and they could rule for five, ten, fifteen extra decades. Market it as a fountain of youth, a cure-all for cancer and disease, the world would go to war for it."

Her words shook me. I hadn't thought about vixen as a weapon so much as a drug. Which made Jim's orders even more concerning. I leaned forward, so close my hair nearly brushed hers. "How do you know someone's coming for it?"

She closed her eyes for one beat, then two, her jaw ticking.

"You had a dream?"

"I did."

Do I trust her? I'd never forget how panicked I'd been when I woke to her screaming, blood streaming from her nose. It took hours to calm her down, for her to be able to close her eyes without the nightmare coming back. I may not trust her, I may still hate her, but I knew in my gut she wasn't lying about this.

I leaned back. "Okay, what's the plan?"

"Every afternoon, an hour after his coffee break, Lance—the agent assigned to the evidence room on weekday afternoons—takes a long bathroom break. He calls down to the main desk and tells them to hold all calls until he's back, which averages twenty minutes."

I lifted my eyebrows. "You know a lot about this man and his bathroom habits."

"This isn't the first time I've broken into evidence," she admitted, barely audible.

My brows climbed higher, practically touching my hairline. I checked my watch. "We have forty minutes."

She grabbed a pen from her bag and a napkin. "This is the evidence room," she explained, sketching a crude map. "The target." She made a star off left center. "There are six exit points." She tapped on five, then circled one and drew a line between it and the star. "But this one is ideal. Least likely to be caught."

"Least likely?"

"In this case, the benefits outweigh the risk." She shoved the napkin toward me. "Memorize it."

I studied the map. It was a straight shot in, two lefts, and a right. It wasn't the map that was tricky, it was dropping my guard long enough to trust her. I pushed the napkin across the table.

She lifted the tea bag out of her cup and dropped it onto the napkin. The ink ran as she soaked it, making the writing illegible. With another napkin, she wiped up the mess. Then she chugged the rest of her tea and stood. "Let's roll. We have a stop to make."

LANCE'S BATHROOM BREAK was like clockwork. He called reception on the main floor and then disappeared down the hall with his cell in hand. Paris, in a white lab coat and blue light glasses, pushed out of the closet then walked in the opposite direction, planning to make a circle. I followed, wearing a white painting jumpsuit from the local hardware store, with my easily identifiable hair meticulously shoved into a large beanie.

I navigated a mop inside a bucket with wheels out of the tiny cleaning closet and dropped a few wet floor signs. Leaving the bucket a few doors down from evidence, I brushed the tile with a dry mop. We were lucky this was one of the floors without carpeting.

Paris rounded the corner holding a tablet she'd somehow acquired in the last three minutes. I continued mopping around the desk outside the evidence room, and when Paris approached, I lifted the mop head to cover the camera. She ducked under my arm and removed a keycard from the back of the tablet case. "Amazing what people leave in their unlocked offices," she whispered, then slid the card through the card reader and entered the code. She pushed the door open, tucked the keycard in her pocket, then wiped off her prints on the tablet with her sleeve before tossing it onto the desk. "Let's go."

I scooted back, removing the mop from the camera, and pulling it through the door.

"The cameras in here are on a different system than the ones outside to make it more secure," Paris explained. "Playback will show a continuous hour loop." She pulled on disposable gloves and then handed me a pair.

"If it's so secure, how on earth were you able to do that?"

"I like computers."

"I would marry my phone, doesn't mean I can shut down a security system with it."

She waved a hand to dismiss the question. "Aisle 65, unit 3, boxes 113 through 120. That's where the supply of vixen is stored. Let's move."

The evidence room was a massive storage warehouse several stories high, with floor to ceiling metal shelving that ran nearly the length of the room. On the opposite side, a perpendicular wall bisected the space, and beyond that, the sounds of banging, thumping, and metal-on-metal clanging. I scooted closer to Paris and gripped her arm, just above the elbow. "What the hell is that?"

"Trust me. You don't want to know."

A loud crash had my heart in my throat. "Is it alive?"

She paused, turned around, and set me away from her. "In a manner of speaking..."

"What does that mean?"

"It means don't go say hi to it or you'll probably be Aplechester's newest ghost agent. Move and stay quiet." Gone was the soft-spoken, shy Paris. Agent Evans had taken her place and my stomach flipped. I pressed my hand to my abdomen. The only other time she took charge and ordered me around was in the bedroom.

She snapped her fingers and pointed down the row, a silent command to follow. Another stomach flip. The room felt larger than the Detroit Metro Airport, which at least had a tram and a moving walkway system. I was used to moderate exercise and always being on my feet with my kid, but the rush of adrenaline and nerves made my lungs too small for my body.

As we passed by row fifty-five, I wondered if any of Ben's information was still here. His death had been ruled an accident, but nothing about it made sense. Why had he driven his motorcycle instead of his SHAP truck? Why had he been on that bridge, sixty miles in the complete opposite direction of both SHAP and home?

Why had Paris been there? What had she seen? Why wouldn't she tell me?

Ben's life had been reduced to one box a SHAP agent handed to me at my front door. Inside had been his grandfather's pocket watch, his engagement band he wore on his right hand, and his wallet, empty except for a water-stained picture of Daisy as a baby.

"He must have not been paying attention while driving," they'd said.

Ben didn't slip up; not with work, not with driving, not with anything involving him and his family's safety. Our phone plans, along with our health, home, and auto insurance all were significantly discounted through SHAP and in our individual names. The deed on the house was in my name only. We kept separate bank accounts. I'd never realized how much space for secrets our relationship had until I tried to uncover them.

His phone records, which were considered part of SHAP's investigation, were classified until the formal report came out two years after his death, four days after Daisy's birthday.

Paris's number stared back at me from his cell phone bill. She'd called him three times after his time of death. The SHAP agents had found her in the freezing water holding onto his peacoat. I might never know what happened that night, but I know she had something to do with it. I could never forgive her for having a hand in destroying my family.

Paris turned right and disappeared down an aisle. I looked up at the sign that read AISLE 65, then followed her to the third section. She pushed the ladder on wheels to the correct bay, and then halted, turning to me.

She nodded. "Climb up behind me."

The bays in this section were large enough to store an SUV and based on the number of vehicles on the concrete floor, this was not an uncommon occurrence. The ceilings here must be nearly forty feet, each of the three stacked bays eight to ten feet high. Paris climbed to the second compartment, with me right behind. She folded into the bay around large storage containers.

I had forgotten she was so flexible. I sucked in a deep breath through my nose to chase away the lingering memory of *why* I knew that intimately. For the millionth time, I despaired that she had turned out to be the woman who destroyed my life because we could've built a beautiful one together. I found my ever-present hot ball of anger in my chest and let it spread, burning away any rose-colored memories.

Paris slid a lid off the box, revealing rows of liquid venom in vials from the Thinner shakes and baggies full of vixen, a pink powder stuffed into capsules. I hurried up the ladder and leaned in to examine the contents. Capsules with a white ring around the middle. Just like the sample in my own collection.

"We have twenty-four trackers, which would cover part of what's here," Paris explained.

"Is there a way to tell which of the capsules have been laced with fentanyl?"

She studied me for a moment, then pulled a flashlight from her pocket, inspecting each bag of capsules. "These are a slightly lighter color and the line around the middle is off," she explained, gesturing to the back section. "My guess is these were tampered with."

I nodded in agreement. "We would have enough to cover the rest of the vixen bags." She stared at me for a long moment, but her eyes were unfocused, as if she were somewhere else. "This isn't the time to zone out."

She refocused on me. "Not zoning out."

"What then?"

"Trying to see possibilities."

I frowned. "Possibilities?"

"Yeah. Sometimes I can guess how different actions will play out." She reached into her bra and removed the case of trackers.

Her words were like a blow to the stomach. "You can see the future and you never thought to tell me?!" I whisper-yelled. I knew about the dreams but not about the visions. How much had she been keeping from me?

"There's nothing to tell. They don't tell the future like my dreams. I can just *sometimes* see different options with varying probability."

"You know that's not just a thing most people do, right?"

She shrugged then gestured to the bag. "Pick it up and hold it steady."

I scooped out the pills closest to her. She removed something that looked like tweezers, with one rounded end and one flat end, from the top of the case. Using the rounded end, she pressed it into the tiny, nearly invisible squares and lifted one off the pile. It flashed blue once, then went completely clear. From a distance, it would be invisible.

She pried a tiny bit of the evidence label away from the back, fit the tracker underneath, and smoothed the edges. Retrieving her cell, she removed her thumb from her glove, then pressed a few buttons and held her phone up to the bag. She set the phone down and nodded. "Next."

"Why didn't you tell me? About the visions?"

"Didn't know there was anything to tell. They're like daydreams, a diet version of my nightmares."

How much didn't I know about her? "Except that's not what daydreams are like at all."

She didn't respond, just kept methodically placing trackers. When her watch beeped, she looked at it, then back up at me. "Time's up." She shoved the four remaining trackers and phone back in her pocket while I pulled on the lid on the evidence. I climbed down the ladder with her nearly on top of me. She shoved the ladder to a different bay, then held perfectly still, her head turned toward the way we had come in.

The clanging and banging that had been our soundtrack the entire mission had stopped. Everything was eerily silent. Paris was completely still. I bounced on the balls of my feet, waiting. I glanced at her a second, then third time. I hadn't realized she was seeing *something* whenever she spaced out.

"Do you trust me?" she breathed.

I didn't, but I was also extremely aware that I didn't have another choice right now. "In this."

She nodded. "Take off your coveralls and gloves. We'll hide them." She moved into a bay and with her back to the wall, squeezed through a small opening and into the next aisle.

I unzipped the coveralls and followed, stepping out of them when I hit the opening. She was already one bay ahead of me and moving a box aside with her leg so we could crawl through. After inching under a parked car, she pulled the transmitters from her coat and shoved them into her bra. She bundled the coat with my jumpsuit and gloves, and then lifted a dusty cover off a bin, making sure not to leave marks. She shoved the items inside and closed it, then stilled.

"Shit," she breathed.

"What?"

She bit her lip and held out her hand. I hesitated for only a moment before I took it. She tugged me through three more bays and to a Mustang that was painted bright red with thick black racing stripes and a crushed front end. She reached around the tire and pulled out a magnet box that held a key, then unlocked the doors. "Get in the back seat."

"What?"

"Back seat. Go." She tucked the transmitters into her back waistband and unbuttoned her shirt until her bra was exposed.

"Why are you undressing?" I couldn't look away from the black lace hugging her curves.

She widened her eyes then glanced at the backseat. I scampered into the car, leaving the door open, and she climbed in behind me, shutting it as quietly as possible. "I think the dogs are coming and they've picked up on our scent. We can't get out without getting caught in any scenario that doesn't involve a big explosion."

"We can make an explosion!"

She waved me away. "You would be injured. This was the second-best idea. We just need to fog up the window and mess up your hair. Hide the beanie under the front seat."

"What?" My voice was little more than a squeak.

She reached out and tugged off the beanie, then tossed it. She pushed her hand into my hair, her fingernails sliding over my scalp. Goosebumps erupted down my neck and arms.

I ducked and shoved her hand away. "I can mess up my

own hair."

"Then do it." She leaned close to the back windshield and pressed her face to the glass, breathing heavily. It fogged for a second, then disappeared.

"That's your plan?"

She breathed out twice more. "Would you rather fog up the windows for real?" She licked her lips and my body clenched.

I shook my head no, even as my eyes fell to her bra again.

"We wanted to find someplace secret," she explained. "Since I had business down here, I brought you with me to impress you with this car. Got it? Start breathing on the glass." She turned to the side window, trying to steam it.

I shifted to the opposite glass and started huffing and puffing. "This isn't working." I started breathing even harder, trying to ignore the dizziness.

"Stop."

I spun to face her, eyebrows raised. "What now?"

She stared at my lips, then glanced down at my chest as I panted. Warmth spread through me at her inspection. She swallowed hard. "We're, um, out of time. Just, lay down. I'll get on top of you."

"You'll what?"

"Next time I'm leaving you on the ladder," she grumbled. She moved so her right leg was between mine, cupped her hands on my upper calves, and pulled me into her. My work pants did little to distract from the pressure of her leg *right there*. "We have to make it believable. Put your arms around me—without strangling me, please."

I rolled my eyes. "You gonna leave me a hickey, too? Really sell it?" I snapped, putting my arms around her neck and only squeezing a little.

Feather-light fingers stroked the side of my neck, and she looked up at me through her lashes. "All you have to do is say the fucking word," she breathed, "and it's no longer acting."

My entire body went liquid at the first sign of her dirty talk and I clenched my jaw against the unexpected feeling. She was always so quiet, so buttoned up, so afraid to speak what she was thinking. Except in the bedroom. Her people-pleasing became her superpower.

She shifted to get a better look out the window, her chest moving directly over my face, and her leg moving and applying more pressure. My back arched and I gasped. I hated my reaction. I wanted to destroy her, but my body remembered how well she fit against me. It had been so long since another person wanted me like this.

Her eyes snapped to mine, so dark they felt like a black-hole. "Eliza…" my name was a plea, a prayer, on a soft exhale.

My brain short circuited at the sound. I needed to kiss her. My hands moved without my permission into her hair. Her breasts pressed against mine as she lowered her head. The anger burning in my chest joined the embers low in my abdomen, causing an inferno. I lifted my mouth to hers, my top lip brushing her full bottom one.

Finally.

A knock at the window made us freeze. All the burning heat in my chest extinguishing as reality washed in.

Chapter Nine

Paris

WHEN I'D ENVISIONED getting Eliza into the back of this car and steaming up the windows, I'd been looking at the car from the outside, and not down at the devastatingly beautiful woman beneath me. For one second, I hesitated. If I kissed her, she'd kiss me back. It wouldn't matter if we were alone or in front of a crowd, she'd always responded to me.

It was almost physically painful to untangle myself from her body, her warmth. She whimpered in protest as the knock came again. I straightened my bra and climbed to the front seat.

I opened the door and stuck my head out, purposely leaving my hair messy and my shirt open. As expected, there were two men, Lance and a security guard with a German Shepard.

The security guard blinked once, then twice, trying to keep his eyes above my collarbone. "The evidence room has restricted access. How did you get in here? What are you doing in this car? Er, besides…"

I tucked my hair behind my ear, then looked down, pretending to be shocked by my shirt being open. I gasped and started to hurriedly close the front, mismatching the holes and buttons. "Oh god, this is so embarrassing," I whispered. "I wanted to impress this amazing woman I'm seeing, and I had to double check some evidence for a case. My date was with me, and I figured I'd show her the Mustang and she'd be impressed, and she *was*. One thing led to another…" I rolled my hand to silently complete the sentence.

I lifted a shoulder and gave my best sheepish smile. "I know we're not supposed to be here, but you understand, right?"

As if on cue, Eliza stepped out of the back of the car on the other side, her hair half hanging from her scrunchie. "What can I say?" she questioned, her tone that of a love-struck teenager. "She knows Mustangs are my favorite." She winked at me.

I stared at her for a long moment, my breath caught in my throat, no longer acting. Her winking made my finger-tips tingle. God, how did this woman still have so much of a hold on me? Touching her again was like returning to a warm, dry home after a year of backpacking during snow-storms.

"This is evidence in a case," Lance argued. "You can be charged with tampering of evidence, and the case could be dismissed because of your negligence! I should have you arrested."

I held up my hands in surrender. "I know, I know. But please don't. I checked that the trial was complete on the log first." I had indeed *not* checked, but by the layer of dust on the outside, it was safe to assume the case was over. Unlike regular human courts, SHAP was filled with supernatural creatures who didn't need much, if any, sleep. Trials ran for twenty-four hours a day, seven days a week.

I looked up at them with my hands in prayer position in front of me. "Please, please just let us off with a warning. Just this once? I promise to never do this again."

The security guard nodded. "You have to be respectful of your woman. Romance her. Take her out to dinner and then go back home, you get me? Don't be messing around in the back seat. That's some high school bullshit right there."

"Of course, yes sir." As a bi woman who was romantically attracted to women, he wasn't telling me anything I didn't already know.

Eliza cleared her throat and shot me a glare that said, *Paris, keep it together. Don't argue.* "Of course," she said out loud. "That sounds so much more romantic."

Eliza's response shook me out of my stupor. "Yes, of course," I added. "You're absolutely right." I threw Eliza a smile. "Maybe I'll take my baby out to dinner tonight."

Lance sighed, "Fine. Just hurry up and get out before someone else catches us."

"Oh, thank you!" I cried. I felt behind my back for the tracker case. It was mostly on my ass cheek, and I pretended to pick a wedgie to shift it. I reached out and closed the door to the car. "Lead the way."

Eliza held my hand, making my knees melted butter. She threw me sly glances every so often, earning a smile from the security guard and a scowl from Lance. They kept us between them, as if preparing to chase if we took off after another back seat. The group walked right past the mop

Eliza had left in the corner. She squeezed my hand when she spotted it and I tightened my own in response, but we didn't dare look at each other.

The moment we exited, I pulled Eliza down the hallway without slowing. We needed to disappear from this floor as quickly as possible before anyone thought about our story too hard. Honestly, I can't even believe they bought it. It was probably just the absurdity of the situation; who breaks into the evidence room to make out in a car?

Someone was stepping off the elevator as we neared, and I slid my arm out to stop the doors from closing. Eliza skated in, let go of my hand, and hit the button for our floor. I followed and slammed the close door button. We stood nearly shoulder to shoulder, the space between us charged with unspoken words and desire.

What if I grabbed her arm right now and pulled her into me? What if I kissed her? What if I—

The doors opened, ending my litany of what if's. I couldn't do any of those things. Running my hand through my hair to try and tame it, I walked as fast as I could without seeming suspicious.

I swiped my keycard hard and nearly yanked the handle off our door. I guided Eliza in by her arm, shut the door, and then locked it. Eliza stared up at me, blue eyes so big they were oceans. *Just like before, when she'd sneak in because she missed me.*

I reached into the back of my pants for the case and then tossed it and my keycard on my desk.

"You still have it," Eliza said.

I nodded, taking a step closer, my eyes on her lips. She

licked them and I took another step toward her.

"Your plan worked. It shouldn't have worked."

I nodded again. Another step. We were almost touching.

"This can't happen again," she warned, but her body swayed into mine.

"It's not technically over yet," I whispered, my fingers tracing beneath her shirt, along the edge of her pants. She gasped. "You know I don't quit until you sigh my name."

She grabbed the front of my shirt, her forehead pressing against mine and her lips parting.

Her cell phone rang.

I stilled, knowing this was it. The moment was gone. All that coiled, ready-to-be-kissed desperation dissipated the moment she lifted her cell and looked at the screen. MOM CALLING.

I stepped away from her, the space between us feeling like miles instead of inches. I missed her, needed her so bad, my body ached, and my temper flared. "Answer the damn phone," I barked, for once not double checking what I said before I said it. "Fix the mess with your parents."

Eliza ignored the call and tucked the phone away. If looks could kill, a grim reaper would appear, ready to take me. "First of all, we're not together. We're not friends. You don't get to have an opinion."

Her words were a knife between each rib, and I felt every one of them slide in. *We're not together. We're not friends.*

"Second of all, it may come as a surprise to you because you're really good at lying, but I have to trust a person to have a relationship with them. Once they screw up, that's it. Doesn't matter if it's my mom, my girlfriend, or the barista at the lunch counter."

"You would never cut out the barista at the lunch counter."

"Fair, but I would ask for a manager."

I searched her face. "What can I do? What can I do to make this better?"

Eliza held herself very still, as if any sudden movement would cause her to crack in half. She swallowed twice, rubbed her palms over the front of her shirt. "Let's just finish the case."

I didn't need to be psychic to spot the evasion. "There's no hope, is there?"

"Hope that I can somehow forgive the last person who saw Ben alive?" Her voice hitched, her eyes flooding with emotions. "Tell me, how am I supposed to move past that when you won't tell me what happened?"

I hastily wiped my own tears away. "You can't."

"*We* can't."

Those two words were an explosion. Jarring, surprising, pain-inducing, breath-stealing, and violent. The office should have transformed into dust, but I was the only one who was destroyed.

I couldn't speak. I hadn't physically pushed him over the bridge, but I might as well have. If I hadn't been there, he might've made it. He might have been okay.

"I'm so sorry," I breathed.

"Why? Why were you even there? What aren't you telling me?"

I opened my mouth and hesitated.

She didn't wait for a response. Just turned around and left the office.

Chapter Ten

Eliza

CRYING IN FRONT of the cemetery was old habit by now. The sun was low in the sky, the shadows of worn headstones stretching past the iron gate. I couldn't see Ben's grave from here, but I still felt its weight.

Or maybe it was just the heaviness of guilt. I missed Ben, but he wasn't why I swiped tears off my cheeks in the corner of the small parking lot. It was the memories of Paris, sitting next to me under that streetlight. Our first hellos in a place meant for goodbyes.

How did I get rid of whatever stranglehold she had on me? How did being in her orbit still make me feel like I'd just gotten off the teacup ride at the fair after too much cotton candy? Five months might as well have been five days, five hours.

The sun sank down behind the trees and the streetlights turned on. I stared at the sidewalk underneath. That's where she'd found me. Crying, scratches down my face and arms, hair tugged out of my ponytail, and a handful of now-tattered daisies my daughter had asked me to leave on Ben's grave. Paris sat down next to me without saying a word and after a minute of silence, handed me a tissue.

I wiped my face and blew my nose before looking over at her. "You just sit next to random crying women in the dark?"

She lifted a shoulder. "Only the beautiful ones. And it's not quite dark yet."

I laughed without humor. "Yeah, it's the blotchy face and swollen eyes look that does it for ya, huh?" An invisible hand tugged at dangling hair, and I yelped.

Paris put her hand on my shoulder and spoke in a low but sharp voice to the spirits. "Leave her alone."

My head quieted, the chaotic voices dissipating to whispers. The fingers and hands that had been shoving and scratching fell away. I stared at her wide-eyed. "How'd you do that? Make it quiet?" I brushed my temple.

"Whatever makes my brain the way it is, I guess." She lifted her own arm boasting its own set of scratches. "I'm not a medium, but they still get me sometimes." She smiled at my gaping fish expression. "I've seen you around SHAP a few times. Put two and two together."

"Ah. Yes." I leaned back against the fence. "I'm Eliza. Dead Letter Office."

"Paris. Transferring from R&D to field agent."

"Pretty badass."

She smirked. "Which one?"

"Both."

"You too. I can't write to the dead."

"It is an interesting résumé entry."

"Would love to see you explain that to a civilian."

I motioned to the cemetery. "So, here for shits and giggles like me?"

"Yep. Favorite Saturday night activity." She kept a straight face for a few seconds, then laughed into the twilight.

I could've floated away on the sound. *This woman is going to change my life.* I knew it like I knew I had red hair, like I knew Dutch processed cocoa powder made fudgier brownies, like I knew I loved my daughter more than anything in existence.

Inherently. Indisputably.

I cleared my throat. "Came to put my flowers on my fiancé's grave. It was the first anniversary of his death this week and our daughter asked me to." I sucked in a breath and let it out slowly. "Her name's Daisy," I explained, gesturing to the flowers. "You?"

Paris sobered, nodding. "I came to see my grandma. Got about halfway before someone tripped me and I nearly busted my head on the corner of a statue. Not the way I want to go."

I cringed. "Dying in a cemetery is far too meta."

"Tell me about it. My grandma Dottie would probably find a way to haunt me if something that ridiculous happened." She spun a ring around her middle finger on her right hand, then held it out so it could catch the light from the nearby streetlamp. The emerald stone looked almost black against the gold band. "This was hers. She swore it helped ward off bad spirits."

"It's beautiful. Is it working?"

"I think so, or at least I hope the truly bad spirits stay away." She smiled. "That's how Grandma lived her whole life. Beautifully and full of hope." She leaned back against the gate, her shoulder brushing mine. "What about your fiancé?"

I held up the gold band on the ring finger on my right hand. "Went to work, didn't come home."

"I'm so sorry. Been a year?"

I reached up and yanked the scrunchie out of my hair then tucked it into a low pony. "Yeah. You?"

"Six months." She turned her head to study me, and I turned to meet her eyes. While she was essentially a stranger, it was almost as if we had known each other for weeks, months, instead of minutes. "Well, Eliza. We better do something with those daisies."

She leaned forward and gathered them, then started twisting them into a chain. "My years of being a Girl Scout are finally paying off!"

"My daughter would lose her mind."

She smiled. "She get the red hair, too?"

I nodded. "For better or worse, it's curly and red and as loud as she is."

"Amazing. You have perfect hair." She finished connecting the last daisy in the circle and held it out to me. "Think Daisy would be okay with hanging this on the gate?"

"I think that's about as close as we dare get."

She stood then reached down to help me up. As her palm slid against mine, tingles ran up my arm. My feet carried me so close, I could feel the heat radiating through her shirt. Without releasing me, she held out the daisies.

I took them and hung them on a fence post. *Thank you for our daughter*, I thought to Ben. "Well. That was a fun adventure for a Saturday."

Paris nodded. "Do you have to get home or…"

"Daisy is at her grandparents tonight. I'm free."

She reached out and grabbed my other hand. "Then, by all means, let's blow this Popsicle stand. Maybe get some tea. Make a whole night of it."

"I'd like that."

Massaging my temples, I closed my eyes and took a deep breath, trying to shake the memory. *Get it together, Eliza. Stop crying in the cemetery parking lot.*

I mostly got it together. I did honk my horn three times on the drive home, then nearly cried after I dropped my keys twice, however. By the time I pushed my way inside my house, my temper had reached dizzying heights.

"You look like you had a fight with a tiger and lost," Jake said in way of greeting when I walked into the kitchen.

"I feel like it," I admitted.

Daisy ran up and hugged me tight around the waist, then returned to her chair. "Mom, we're working on math, and Uncle Jake was trying to teach me how to do this, but he was doing it wrong, so I teached him how to do it the right way."

"You *taught* him, baby," I corrected.

Jake looked horrified. "Did you know they changed math? Why? Why did they change math?"

"Yes, it's the bane of my existence. However, I do have a coping strategy." I reached into the freezer, snagged a box of mint chocolate cookies, and removed an open half sleeve. I popped one into my mouth, then set the rest in front of Jake and Daisy. "One for each problem done correctly," I directed through a mouthful.

"You're my favorite sister," Jake sighed, reverently.

I rolled my eyes. "I need a quick shower. Work was a challenge today. Then I'll make dinner."

"Want me to start something?"

"No. Math. Please, finish the math."

"Roger." Jake gave me a thumbs-up, then looked over a problem Daisy had just completed. They high-fived and each ate a cookie.

They would spoil their dinner, but I didn't care. As long as I never had to do that weird math again, it was worth it. I hurried into the bedroom, locked the door, and turned on the shower to boiling lava hot. I peeled off my clothes and stood under the stream, trying to wash away the feeling of Paris's body pressed into mine. The water eased the tension in my shoulders, but couldn't erase my memories.

Ten minutes later, I gave up and dried off. While massaging lotion into my skin, my phone dinged with an urgent email. I wiped my hands and opened my work inbox.

To: ERobinson@SHAP.net
From: TerritoryDirectorOffice@SHAP.net
Subject: Letter request

Hello Eliza,

Jim has reviewed your request to contact the victims in case #32841B, colloquially known as vixen. It has been denied due to the death of recent client Edward Gardner.

If you have any questions, please bring it up in your next scheduled meeting on November 30th.

Sienna

I stared at my phone. Edward had died and they told me

via email about something else? God, I hated this job sometimes. I closed my eyes. *I hope you're with Rosie now, friend.*

I'd been on probation multiple times before—client death was a hazard of the job—but I'd never gotten an outright denial. Was it just this case? Was it the vixen?

I took a screenshot of the email and opened a text to Paris, my heart beating faster as my thumb hovered over send. "Just send it!" I scolded myself.

> ***Me:*** *This is suspicious*
>
> ***Paris:*** *Jim said he wouldn't review the request until we turned in our weekly summary*
>
> ***Me:*** *Good thing we had an alternate plan*
>
> ***Paris:*** *I'm sorry your client died. You okay?*
>
> ***Me:*** *Part of the job*

I exited my texts and clicked to my timer, selected one minute, and pressed start. Then, I shoved my towel in my mouth as I gave into the urge to cry, again. My face burned as I poured out my constant worries about Daisy, my grief of Edward's passing, the frustration with Jim not letting me do my job, and having to deal with Paris every single weekday. When my alarm when off, I took two stuttering breaths, blew my nose, splashed cool water on my face, then checked my phone.

> ***Paris:*** *I know you don't want to talk to me, but if you need me, I'm here*
>
> ***Paris:*** *What happens if we write letters without Jim's approval?*

I blinked to clear my vision.

Me: *SHAP sanctioned means they pay the postage. I can't afford to take any more years off my life, even for a case.*

Paris: *Anymore? How many have you given up?*

I didn't respond. Because after Jake went home and Daisy went to bed tonight, I was going to add one more year to that pile. I needed to find out what was happening to my daughter.

DEARLY DEPARTED BENJAMIN DYLAN SOMERSET (1988-2020)

D SICK. NEED YOUR FAMILY HISTORY TO HELP. BOTH MEDICAL AND NON-MEDICAL.

MISS YOU

I stared at the message, trying to decide if it made sense. Was he not responding because he was worried for our safety? Was he concerned about an interception? Did I say enough without being obvious? Would he know I meant magic history? Outside of our trusted circle and her doctor, no one knew how powerful Daisy was. I wanted to keep it that way.

PS. WHAT HAPPENED THE NIGHT YOU DIED?

I lit the candle on my nightstand then ran a pin over the flame to sterilize it. I stuck my finger and squeezed out a few drops of blood, pressing the stain onto a separate paper, and smearing it so the fingerprint wasn't legible. Then, I began fire scrying.

Maybe this time, he'd answer. *Please answer*, I prayed.

I sent the message through then burned the postage just as my bedroom door opened. I immediately blew out the candle to seal off the connection and turned to find a pale Daisy slumped against my door.

"I don't feel good," she cried, her hand over her stomach.

I launched over the bed, grabbed her, and made it to the bathroom just in time. *Please be a normal stomach bug and not her getting worse*, I wished.

Chapter Eleven

Eliza

A KNOCK ON my door woke me from a sleep so heavy, I couldn't lift my head. "Yeah?" my voice was mostly croaking. Jake must have come back after taking Daisy to school. She'd finally been puke free long enough to go.

I'd been worried it was her magic making her sick, but twelve hours later I was nearly relieved when I became symptomatic. Dr. Marback had explained over the phone that Daisy likely caught the stomach virus circulating, although it was possible that her magic had weakened her immune system. We were both relieved when Daisy bounced back fast. I, however, still felt like death.

The door opened. "Eliza?"

I groaned, my stomach turning over, but this time not from the virus. Paris walked in the room. "What are you doing here?" The words were smushed together.

"Because you suck at being a sick person and we only have thirteen days left to finish this case."

I held up my middle finger.

"How long's it been since you puked?"

"Time?"

"It's Friday, 10 am."

I took a breath and tried to do the math. "Eight hours maybe?" I licked my lips, but my tongue was sandpaper. "You're gonna get sick." Why did I even care if she got sick?

"Stomach of steel."

I moaned my response. I definitely did not have a stomach of steel over the last thirty hours. "Why're you helping me?" I managed, pushing myself to the side so I could look at her without moving my head.

"Because I know you're dehydrated, you need groceries, we need to work on the case, and Loren's been trying to get ahold of you."

I pushed myself up, then went back down on my elbow as the room spun. "Loren?"

"Easy, babe." She brushed my hair back from my face and my eyes automatically closed.

It had been so long since I'd been soothed. I wanted to lie back down and have her stroke my hair until I fell back to sleep. *No. Don't let her touch you. Don't let her break down the walls you've erected to keep her out.*

"The first call was him worried you hadn't responded to his text. I asked Jake and he informed me that your head was probably in the toilet. The second call was because he had some information for you."

Had Loren texted me? Honestly, the last several days had been a blur. "Did he tell you?"

"Not the specifics. But because of the urgency of the info and him not being able to get ahold of you, I told him I'd pass on a message."

I lifted my hand and rolled it, prompting her to keep

going.

She sat on the edge of the bed and shoved a bottled orange sports drink in front of me. “Sit up and take a mouthful, then I’ll tell you.”

“Uh-uh.”

She stood and I reached out, grabbing her sweatshirt. With a soft laugh, she sat back down. “Come on, let’s get you up.”

As if maneuvering a doll, she practically lifted me until the side of my body was leaning against hers. I forgot how strong she was. For one moment, I pushed away that she was Paris, the person who destroyed my family, and took comfort in being held by someone who had cherished me.

She unscrewed the cap and brought the bottle up to my lips.

“If I puke orange, you’re cleaning it up,” I warned.

“Promise.”

I nearly cried as the cool liquid coated my parched tongue. When she tried to pull the bottle away, I grabbed her wrist and held it in place for one more sip.

“Easy. Don’t rush it.” She took the bottle away and put the cap on, then leaned forward and set it down on my nightstand. “You feel well enough to brush your teeth while I change the sheets?” She pressed the back of her hand to my forehead.

The thought of brushing my teeth was insurmountable right now. “Want sleep.”

“Okay, sleep. Then teeth.” She shifted her arm and I flopped back down into my spot.

“What’d Loren say?” I asked into the pillow.

"He said your target is like a ghost. Can't get farther back than you. Is going to call his old partner Javier to help. Wanted to know if you'd talked to any of the family recently."

"They moved. Changed their number. Disappeared."

She paused. "I'll let him know."

"Not gonna ask?"

"I trust you'll tell me if it's something I need to know about the case. Otherwise, not my business."

My chest buzzed at her words, but I couldn't pinpoint why. I was too tired. I grunted a response.

"Want me to leave?"

Wanting to be soothed when sick was a completely natural response. It was the only defense I had for reaching out and wrapping my hand around hers, just for a moment. I didn't want to be alone. Not right at this moment.

She shifted closer, running her free hand over my hair. "How about this? I'll wait until you're asleep, run to the grocery store, and when you get up, we'll try soup."

I squeezed her hand in response. "Soup," I whispered. Then I fell back to sleep.

I HESITATED OUTSIDE the office door on Monday. *You are an adult. You have a mortgage and a kid and you're old enough to vote. You can drink alcohol and rent a car—not in that order—and fly around the world. Just walk into that office and get to work like an adult.*

It had been nearly a week since I'd been back. The last

time I'd crossed that threshold, Paris's hands had been all over me. Then, she'd held my hair back when I puked up the sports drink. It took another four hours before I was able to drink more.

She'd stayed all day, forcing me to have soup when I could handle liquids, and making me brush my teeth and wash my face while she changed my sheets, making more cracks in my walls. When Jake showed up with Daisy in tow, she said her goodbyes, and outside of a text on Saturday to ask how I was doing, I hadn't heard from her or seen her.

Which was good. Exactly what I'd wanted. Space.

I wouldn't admit I missed her.

I bit my lip, eyeing the office. A hummingbird in my stomach flapped its tiny wings at the thought of walking through that door and being trapped in a room with Paris for the next eight hours. She'd seen me at my worst multiple times when we were dating, but it was different now. Like being in your underwear in front of the whole school on stage, then having to walk down to the hall to class once the adrenaline faded.

"Did you move your desk to the hall?"

I turned to find Sienna carrying a stack of three file boxes. "I just…"

"Keep your excuses. I have eyes. All the better to see you with, my dear."

I laughed. "Did you just make a Little Red Riding Hood joke about yourself?"

"What's the point of being a werewolf if you can't have a little fun with it?" She smiled, her blood red lipstick flashing against white teeth. She shoved through the office door and dropped the boxes on my desk, then smoothed down her perfectly styled black pantsuit and brushed a hand over her tidy hair.

She gave a quick look around. "It's so small, I'm developing hives. Jim really wanted to rattle your cage with this one."

She passed by me and walked down the hall, and I bravely took the last five steps into the office. The *empty* office, which I'd been pacing in front of for ten minutes. At least no one else had been around to see my ridiculousness.

I dropped my laptop bag into my chair and removed the lid from the top box. Unlike the manila file folders I'd been sorting through all month, these were a faded orange. Selecting the first one, I opened the file and rifled through the papers. *September 2006.*

Why had Sienna brought me paperwork from nearly two decades ago? I know Jim wanted to distract us, but I had—maybe mistakenly—thought the werewolf didn't condone his bullshit.

Paris walked through the door and the pit usually in my stomach was missing. Maybe I'd thrown it up last week. I glanced at her, double checking for signs of illness. "You good?"

Her own studying gaze clocked me from head to desk. My body warmed at her concern, and I ground my teeth, trying to push the feelings away. *No, Eliza, do not fall for her again. Don't think about her soft hands or the way her curves fit yours perfectly, or how she took care of you—*

"What's that?" She nodded at the folder.

I frowned. "I'm not entirely sure. Sienna dropped them

off. Nearly twenty-year-old case files about a…" I scanned the top sheet, "wizard. Christian Somerville."

"Sienna dropped them off?" Paris removed her laptop from its case and set it on her desk next to her cell, hung her coat up on a hook by the door, then sidled up next to me to look over my shoulder.

She was in a soft dark blue sweater, and I wanted to reach out and touch it. If she wrapped her arms around me, I could lay my head on her shoulder as she rubbed my back—

Eliza! Stop. She helped you puke. She didn't give you her kidney. She killed Ben. I held my breath, so I didn't get a whiff of her perfume. It reminded me too much of summer sun and stolen kisses.

She stepped back, as if our sudden closeness was also too much for her. "If Sienna gave these to you, she did so for a reason. Unlike Jim, she doesn't tolerate busywork."

I nodded, swallowing against the tightness in my throat. It was as if her taking care of me had opened the carefully crafted box I'd shoved all my Paris feelings into and locked away. *Only nine days left. You can do this.*

Her phone buzzed on her desk and we both sighed in relief. She walked completely around her desk, back nearly sliding along the opposite wall, as if to put as much distance between us as possible. She opened her phone and read the text, then smiled and typed a reply.

Who had texted her? Who'd made her smile? Did she have a partner? Surely, she wouldn't have come over if she did?

"Are you seeing someone?" I blurted, before my brain stopped my mouth.

Startled, she lifted her dark eyes to mine. "I wouldn't

have come over if I was."

My cheeks burned with embarrassment, but the rest of my body warmed at her stupid words. "Just making sure," I mumbled. I set down the folder I was still holding, then set up my computer and turned my chair to the side, so I didn't have to see Paris head on.

Then, I flipped to the second page in the folder and started reading. "Holy shit."

"What?"

I stared down at the page, running my finger along the case overview to make sure I understood. "This describes oral venom experiments circa 2006." I looked at Paris. "What are the chances Jim wanted us to have these files?"

"Close to nil," she agreed, then stood from her desk. "Hand me a box. This takes priority."

A CARDBOARD CUP and paper bag appeared on my desk, and I blinked up to see Patty standing in front of me.

"Caught the delivery kid in the lobby looking for your new digs," she explained. "Figured I'd come visit and drop off your order."

"Thanks," Paris said, lifting her tea in acknowledgement while barely looking up from her reading.

I leaned back, my shoulders and lower back stiff from holding the same position for hours. "You're a sight for sore eyes." I turned over the page I was reading and closed the file. I trusted Patty, but this felt too delicate to share.

"Why'd they move you here anyway? Did you get sick of

writing?"

I waved away her question. "Temporary reassignment to help with a project. I'll be back by the end of the year."

"Promise? Because all I have is Cranky Karl for company. It sucks without you."

I grimaced. Being a hundred-and twenty-year-old vampire who never got to retire would make me cranky, too. "Promise." I held out my pinky and she wrapped hers around mine.

She looked back at Paris, then leaned across my desk close to my ear to whisper. "The last personal letter you sent? Came back return to sender."

"What?" I breathed, pulling back to look up at her. "How? What does that mean?" I looked down at my hands, my body. Usually when a year of life was removed, I noticed a new age spot or a wrinkle. I had a client's hair turn completely white once. I hadn't noticed anything different, but I'd been busy with a sick kid.

"I think it means they don't charge," she offered, as if reading my thoughts. "But I've never seen a return to sender." Patty reached out and squeezed my shoulder. "Sorry, Eliza."

"Thanks for telling me."

She stood. "I'll let you get back to it. Text me soon." She closed the office door behind her.

I shoved away from the desk, needing the movement. Maybe a trip to the bathroom. I moved toward the door, but Paris pushed her chair toward me, grabbed my hand, and stood.

"Maybe the question I needed to ask this morning was

are you seeing anyone?" she asked, voice low, next to my ear. It was the voice she reserved for telling me what to do in the bedroom. Heat unfurled in my stomach. Her palm slid against mine and I closed my eyes.

"None of your business," I managed.

"Eliza," she growled. "Tell me."

My knees were smoke, and I gripped her hand back to keep upright. I loved when she got bossy. "No one," I breathed. "Patty just had to tell me something private about a letter I sent."

Paris stepped away, pulling her hand back as if she'd touched a hot stove. "A personal letter? To Ben?"

My brain was in a fog of Paris-lust and it took me a few beats to catch up. Anger burned away any amorous feelings. I put my hands on my hips. "Why does it matter?"

"Because you're wasting your life on someone who is never going to answer you!" She matched my hands-on-hip energy. "I'm not an idiot. I know you've tried to write him before and the only reason I can think that you're still writing to him is because he hasn't answered."

"And what makes you so sure he won't answer?"

She hit her chest with her hand. "Because I know what it's like to be in love with you, to love Daisy, and if I died and you wrote to me, I would stop at *nothing* to get a message to you. If he hasn't written, it's because something's preventing him. Something unlikely to change. Stop wasting your human years on unanswered letters!"

She was right and I had no response, other than pushing past her and running to the bathroom.

Chapter Twelve

Paris

MY OUTBURST ON Monday had cost us whatever tenuous relationship we'd built over the last few weeks. I'd said what needed to be, but it didn't make it any easier to bear. It was Tuesday afternoon and in twenty-seven hours, the office would close for Thanksgiving weekend. I planned to spend most of my time here, trying to piece together everything we could.

There had been no movement on the trackers and the files were so crammed with reports, we hadn't finished sorting through the boxes. It didn't help that my concentration was shit. My gaze kept flickering to Eliza, trying to soak in as much time in her presence as possible.

I was ridiculous. This wasn't healthy. What was going to happen when the case was over in eight days?

She sighed and put down her papers. "What?"

"Hm?" I looked back up at her.

"I can feel your eyes on me."

I winced. "I was...just wondering what your Thanksgiving weekend plans were."

"Dinner with Jake Thursday and maybe an overnight

thing on Saturday. What about you?"

Overnight thing? What did that entail? I cleared my throat, annoyed at myself. I wasn't her guardian. I had no right to ask questions. "Going to my parents on Thursday then hopefully finishing these files."

She raised her eyebrows but kept her gaze on her work. "Your parents?"

I pressed my lips together and nodded. "Dallas is on assignment and can't make it, so it's just me."

"That's going to be tough for you."

"I'll eat beforehand, just in case. Probably bring a salad."

She set her paper down and looked at me. "I don't understand why your family can't get it together enough to make you a plate. It's not that hard. Some turkey without butter or garlic, a plain potato, some steamed veggies. Maybe some applesauce. I can literally do it with my eyes closed."

God, I loved her. "You make it sound so easy."

She threw her hands in the air. "It *is* easy. Your allergies aren't a burden. They just require a few extra minutes of forethought." She shook her head as she scooped back up her paper. "I should call your mom and talk to her. I'd probably make her cry though."

While I hadn't met Eliza's parents while we were dating—she'd wanted to take it super slow—my mom had surprised us once at my apartment and we'd gone to dinner at their house. Eliza nearly flipped the table when she saw they didn't make me anything I could eat, but I talked her out of it. It was my battle to handle.

"I did give my mom some instructions this year and called her to double-check. She said she'd make me a dish."

Those piercing blue eyes met mine. "Good. You deserve it."

I wanted to preen, bask in her affirmation. I smiled, then looked back down at my paper. I was so lost in an Eliza-haze that I nearly missed it. My eyes widened as I scanned the sheet, then scanned it again.

"A name!" I exclaimed. "There's a name."

Eliza nearly jumped over her desk rushing over. She leaned down next to me, her curls brushing my shoulder. I resisted the urge to wrap one around my finger, and instead pointed at the name. BENNETT SOMMERVILLE.

"Who are you, Bennett?" Eliza asked, reading over my shoulder.

I turned to my laptop and opened the SHAP portal, then navigated to the search bar.

Eliza reached out and put her hand over mine. "Wait."

I looked up at her, then turned back to my computer. She was too close, too tempting. "What?"

"What if searching for him sets off some sort of alert? Let's see what else is in the files first."

I looked at the stack of four folders on my desk, five on hers, and another full box. With each file containing hundreds of papers, there was no way we'd get it done before the weekend.

She looked back and forth between our desks. "I'll tell Jake I'm working late."

Chapter Thirteen

Paris

FOR THE LAST two days, Eliza and I had sat at my desk, facing each other, shifting through stacks of papers and old case notes. We documented everything we knew in a notebook, purposely off the server. So far, nothing made sense, except that this Bennett seemed to be the first—albeit failed—test of the oral venom.

He was male, in his late teens at the time of investigation. He was rescued March 15, 2006, and disappeared from SHAP custody two months later. We were left with more questions than answers, and I still couldn't figure out why Sienna had given us these case files. She never did anything without a damn good reason.

I yawned, my jaw cracking and my neck aching. Exhaustion had not improved my mood. Even though today was Thanksgiving, I'd worked until four, ran home to shower, and immediately driven to my parent's house. Eliza had taken the day off, wanting some time with Daisy. Her absence in the office made the hours twice as long.

It didn't help that my nightmares about the night Ben died were back, probably because it was intoxicating, addictive to be this close to Eliza again. My brain wanted to remind me why we could never work. If I had ignored Dallas's text, would Ben still be alive? Would he and Eliza have gotten married? Would they have broken up and we would've made a happy family?

I took off my glasses and rubbed my eyes, glad I hadn't bothered with my contacts today. When I was tired, they always felt wrong. *Could I have prevented Ben's death?* That was the question, wasn't it?

Two years and counting, and I still couldn't answer it. I had tracked Dallas to a warehouse, where him and Ben were greeted by three men with guns and no fear. I was still in R&D, not used to taking a beat to keep a cool head like I had to do as a field agent.

I grabbed a few smoke bombs I'd shoved in a duffel from an old Halloween stash and slipped out of my car. My hands were shaking as I lit the fuses and threw them. As smoke filled the air, I grabbed Dallas and pulled him out.

"What the hell are you doing here?" he'd whisper-yelled. "Shit, P, you're going to get all of us killed!"

"You texted me 'if anything happens, you were always my favorite sister' and you don't think I'm going to find you?!" I whisper-yelled.

"I thought you'd use common sense and stay out of whatever shit I was caught up in!"

"You're my twin, asshole. You jump, I follow so I can catch you."

Gun shots had ripped through the night air, and he shoved me toward my car. "Move. Get out of here!"

Ben emerged from the smoke and spotted us. "Paris! You

can't be here."

"I'm not leaving without my twin."

"Get in your car and get the fuck out of here!" Dallas ordered.

When I refused again, Ben had picked me up and carried me away, locking his arms around my flailing body. "He's in more danger with you here!" Ben warned, and I stilled. "Get in your car and go. I'm right behind you in case they decide to follow."

Worried my presence might put Dallas in more danger and charged with enough adrenaline that I was nauseated, I dove into the driver's seat and took off with Ben's motorcycle's headlight steady in the rearview.

Why had he been on a motorcycle? Where was his SHAP-issued truck, with the bulletproof glass, strengthened roll cage, and the ability to float for twice as long as a normal car? Why had Dallas gone back into the warehouse and not Ben?

After a few miles, I noticed another car behind Ben. Then, the sound of crunching metal as Ben's bike went over the bridge. The other car had sped off in the opposite direction.

I went the wrong way down a one-way street, trying to call Ben, but no answer. I parked on the river's edge, my high beams barely illuminating the dark water. I could see the headlight of the motorcycle as it sank and I dove in, swimming to where Ben's body should've been.

Over and over I dove, until my fingers brushed a shoulder. I began pulling. He was too heavy, and I was too oxygen deprived.

With one last herculean effort, I kicked my way up to the surface, dragging Ben with me. Except, when I looked down, I only had a sodden peacoat in my hands. "No, Ben!" I'd screamed. I had him, I swore I had him. How could I only have a coat? Where had he gone?

I tried to dive back under but was rushed from behind by a team of SHAP agents. I'd been pulled to shore and detained for questioning. How had they known about the accident? How had the team gotten there so fast? There were so many questions and no one had the answers.

When I first met Eliza, I hadn't known she was *Ben's* Eliza. All I'd known was that the moment I saw her, I knew she was going to be a part of my life. We didn't really talk about our past after that first night, and she wanted to wait to introduce me to her family. She was still raw from her fiancé's death, and I had been burned enough to be cautious.

For seven beautiful months, we kept our relationship between the two of us. Then at Christmas, I met Daisy. When she took me into her room and I saw photos of her and Ben, I almost passed out.

How was I supposed to tell the woman I was madly in love with I was the reason her fiancé was dead? If I hadn't been there…if I hadn't only grabbed his coat…I couldn't tell her. I kept my mouth shut and pretended that she wasn't Ben's, that she was just some other Eliza.

I glanced at the clock. I had to be sociable and pleasant and not piss off my parents for two hours. Alone.

You can do this, Paris. Get out of the car and get in the house. Now. Right…now. RIGHT NOW. Why are you still buckled in?

I stared at my phone, wishing I had someone to text. Why didn't ghosts or demons have cells? What I wouldn't give for Belphegor to tell me "get the fuck over yourself" right now. Maybe I could drive home really fast and track him down…

My stupid heart wanted to text Eliza, but thankfully my mind knew better. I couldn't begin relying on her again. My phone buzzed and I startled, then silently admonished myself. I was an agent now. I couldn't freak out over a text message.

Jake: *I hope you're having some delicious Paris-safe food!*

I smiled. Jake had been an awesome partner. I'd been terrified that he'd forget me once he transferred into the role of Daisy's mentor—or if Eliza told him about my role in Ben's death—but his text reassured me he still cared.

Me: *Just got to my folks. You?*

Jake: *Eliza cooked and gave us a history lesson on each dish*

Jake: *I'm watching Christmas movies with Daisy while Poppy and Eliza dig out the surprise pink tree she bought*

Jake: *Daisy's going to scream when she sees it*

I laughed out loud, imagining Daisy's eyes going wide, her hands going to either side of her cheeks, and her high-pitched, excited scream filling the room. I pressed my lips together at the thought of Eliza begrudgingly buying a pink tree, even though I know she didn't like "unnatural looking" ones. The Christmas we'd been together, we went with Daisy to the tree farm and spent over an hour searching for the perfect one.

The memories pressed heavy on my chest.

Me: *Please get video!*

Jake: *Will do*

Jake: *Have a good dinner* ☺

Someone tapped on the passenger window, and I screamed, dropping my phone. I looked up to see my twin peering in. The asshole was smirking.

I pressed my hand to my chest to hold my heart in, then unlocked the door. "What are you doing here? I thought you were…" I frowned, I didn't know where he'd been, "not here."

"Just got in." He fell into the seat, all folded arms and long legs. He took after our dad, who was well over six feet, except where Dad was wiry, Dallas was muscle.

I'd inherited my mom's body, which was tall, but with shoulders and hips that required a visit to the tailor whenever I bought clothes. I was lean muscle where Dallas was bulky. The difference between us is that I learned to fight for safety, and he learned to fight because he loved it.

I flicked his ear. "I've missed you."

"I know." He turned to face me. "Why're you hiding in the driveway with the doors locked?"

"I'm a woman. I was taught to lock my doors the moment I was old enough to sit in the front seat."

"You sure it's not because you didn't call Mom?"

I narrowed my eyes. "No. Because I *did* call Mom. See? You're not always right."

He snorted, but then tilted his head. "And you're afraid that she still didn't make you food?"

I was silent. He knew the answer. I didn't usually press the issue. When my family had meals and celebrations, I always brought my own food. My mother would act offended the entire night, my dad would take her aside to try and placate her, and Dallas and I would exchange looks from across the dinner table.

My uncle would make some "you can eat a little and it won't hurt you" remark, my aunt would say something ridiculous like "faith over fear" and then I would go home feeling terrible about myself.

"Well," Dallas said, "there's some homemade pumpkin pie with my name on it, and don't worry, I'll have your slice, too."

"Do they know you're coming?"

He flashed me his biggest grin, the one that charmed *everyone*. "Nope."

"At least that'll take the attention off me."

He flicked my nose. "You're welcome."

I play hit his arm, but then turned serious. "Hey, the fingerprint…everything okay?"

"Yeah. I was able to cover."

My head rushed with a vision, the world blurring out, but no image solidified.

"You okay, P?"

I blinked back to present day. When the vision was blurry and jumbled, it meant whatever was going to set off this particular chain of events hadn't happened yet but would soon. My gut churned with a warning. *I can't stop it if I don't know what it is!* I told my brain, as if it could do anything.

"Paris?" Dallas asked again.

I waved my hand and unbuckled my seatbelt. "Warning vision."

While Dallas didn't have the same gift as me—his was the ability to talk his way into and out of anything at a preternatural level—he understood mine almost as well as I did.

"You know why?"

"Wasn't clear enough." I tilted my head. "But it didn't happen until I saw you."

He laughed as if I'd told a joke. "Ah, I see. Daydreaming whenever I'm around."

If I wasn't his twin, I would've likely been charmed, but his joke had the opposite effect. "You'd tell me? Right? If something was wrong?"

There was a beat of silence before he smiled. "Of course, little sis!"

I pinched his hand. "Good."

He looked down at his hand then up at me. "Hey, how are things going with Eliza?"

I laughed once, even though it wasn't funny. "Wrapping up a case."

"What case?"

I opened my mouth to share, but something stopped me. "Just something with some letters."

He was silent for a beat. "She still just a work partner?"

I looked out the windshield, the shadow of a vision still in the corner of my eyeline. "Hard to be with someone when I killed their fiancé."

He grunted. "It wasn't your fault."

"Doesn't change that he died because of me. If I hadn't been there, if he hadn't followed me, if I had pulled a little harder in the water..."

The front door opened, and our mom stepped out onto the porch, waving her hand over her head.

"Busted," I grumbled, grabbing the salad I'd made from the back. I should've fought harder to bring a dessert. Eating my feelings with lettuce just wasn't the same.

The moment Mom saw Dallas, she started crying and calling for our dad. I shoved him ahead of me and he stuck his tongue out before greeting her. She acted as if he were coming home after five years of battle instead of five weeks in a cushy hotel.

"My babies are home!" she cried.

I rolled my eyes. "I literally saw you Saturday to help hang lights, Mom."

She ignored me and shoved Dallas into the house then fussed over him, rearranging his hair, and pressing his cheeks with her palms, scolding him for his week-old scruff. "It's a holiday! You should've shaved."

"Turkey doesn't care if I shave," he argued, letting her pull his coat off his shoulders. She removed his scarf, then hung them up.

He kissed her cheek and accepted a hug, then gestured to the living room. "I'll go find Dad."

"He's in the den with Orlando."

My mom's grandparents had started the naming us after cities they loved tradition. My mom's mom had been named Cecil, after Cecil, Pennsylvania, where her grandparents had settled after immigrating from Poland. Mom's parents moved to Florida after they married, where they had my uncle Orlando, my aunt Dayton, and my mom, Kissimmee, who went by Mimi. I was named after Paris, Maine, where some cousins lived, and my twin got Dallas after Fort Dallas in Florida.

I obviously told everyone I was named after Paris, France, to avoid ever hearing "Oh, I didn't know there was a Paris, Maine," again.

Mom took the salad from my hands and set it down on the hall table as I removed my coat. "Come help me in the kitchen while the boys catch up," she said. "You can explain to me why you decided to wear this sweater"—she picked at the sleeve and pursed her lips—"and your glasses."

She turned, very pointedly leaving the salad on the table. Mom was someone who wanted to cook all the food herself or it was an insult to her hospitality. I didn't care about hospitality, I just wanted to make sure there was at least one thing I could eat tonight.

I refrained from rolling my eyes, then grabbed the salad and followed. The house smelled so incredible my mouth watered. Roasted meats, vegetables, three kinds of pie, and warm cranberries. Hope fluttered in my stomach. Maybe I would get to eat something delicious. I smiled, proud of myself for having a conversation with my mom about setting aside some food for me, before she added things like gravy, butter, or flour.

I had suggested plain mashed potatoes—a scoop before she added the milk and butter—and possibly a plain chicken breast. If she was up for it, maybe some steamed carrots and cranberry sauce. Something she could manage easily without having to alter her cooking too much. I dared to hope for the first time that she listened to me, that we could take this step to mending the food-rift between us.

When I pushed through the door of the well-loved kitchen, I found my mom making cranberry sauce while Aunt Jane pulled a casserole from the oven. She smiled at me as she set the glass dish on a hot pad and opened her arms. "Tada!"

I clapped. "That smells delicious. Mom let you bake a casserole today?" My mother was notorious for sticking to her holiday menu with no deviation. Turkey at thanksgiving, roast beef for Christmas, ham for Easter.

"This is for you, dear!" Aunt Jane explained. "How you managed to convince your mom to add something to the menu, I'll never know. Of course she had to do a lot of extra work, but I came early and was happy to help out."

The little bit of hope glowing in my chest faded away. I looked down at the dish, spotting shredded chicken, slices of potato, and carrots, interspersed with what looked a lot like cheese, bread chunks, broccoli, and likely some kind of butter or cream.

I took a steadying breath. "What do you mean it's for me?"

My mom nodded toward the dish. "It has all the things you asked for. Chicken, carrots, white potatoes, and sweet potatoes!"

"What else is in it?"

Aunt Jane huffed indignantly. "Honestly, this question every time. I'm sorry, Mimi, but your daughter is just ungrateful."

I pressed my lips together and held my breath to keep from screaming, or worse, crying. When my throat loosened enough to talk, I turned to face her. "I'm not ungrateful. I just need to be careful with my dietary restrictions."

"I don't believe in allergies." She flicked a towel at me than threw it over her shoulder, turning toward the sink. "What you have is a lack of faith."

I didn't dignify this with an answer. My belief or disbelief in a higher power wouldn't change my digestive tract. My aunt's ability to blame people for their health issues based on how often they went to church was legendary.

I walked over to my mother. "Mom, what else is in it?"

She concentrated on her pot. "You know, some celery, some spices."

"Is there milk? Cheese? Bread? Broccoli?"

She waved away my question. "Just a splash of skim milk and some chunks of bread and cheese on the top. A few heads of broccoli. It's good for you! Anyway, you can just eat around it."

"Mom—"

"It needed something to hold it together. I couldn't just put chicken, carrots, and potatoes in a bowl for you! This way, everyone can enjoy it."

"You should have called me. I told you I'd bring gluten-free bread and dairy-free milk and cheese. I could've made the casserole instead of the salad and we could've shared with everyone!"

She pointed her wooden spoon at me, dripping cranberry sauce on the floor. "Jane and I went through a lot of trouble to make you something special. We can't conform all our meals to your needs. Do you know how selfish that is?" She sniffled.

In the past, I would wrap my arms around her and tell her it was okay. I would eat a granola bar in the bathroom and pile food on my plate, then move it around to look like I ate something. Then, I'd go home and make myself something quick and easy.

This week, however, I had reached my breaking point. Eliza may hate me, but she never made me feel like a burden the way my own mother did. *I don't understand why your family can't get it together enough to make you a plate*, she'd said. *It's not that hard.*

This time I didn't step forward and placate my teary-eyed mother. I thought about how Fenton had gone out of his way to make me something spectacular to eat when Jake and I were in Hayvenwood for the case. I remembered how Eliza's mom had made me my own plate for family dinner, and then walked me through every ingredient and the way it was cooked.

I cherished the memory of when Jake asked me to text him the list of foods I couldn't eat because he wanted to be a good partner. I fell into the dozens of memories of Eliza making sure I had something when we had been together. Hell, it's probably why I fell for her so hard and fast.

I stepped back. "Mom, Aunt Jane, thank you for making the casserole. I appreciate your hard work. Unfortunately, I can't eat some of the ingredients. Next time, I will come over early and help you cook. I'm sorry I couldn't do that today. I'd be happy to make something for myself when you're done with the stove. That way I can still enjoy a meal with you and not get sick."

My mother threw down her spoon and pointed a finger at me. "Your sass is not welcome here."

The kitchen door opened, and Dallas poked his head in. "Everything okay?" He had asked the room, but his eyes were on me.

"Just a food misunderstanding," I explained. "I offered to cook something myself."

Dallas came fully into the kitchen. "What kind of misunderstanding?"

Mom turned off the burner she was using. "I made Paris her very own casserole with the ingredients *she* requested, and now she's saying she won't eat it."

"Honestly, she should be ashamed of herself for that attitude," Aunt Jane mumbled while drying a pan.

My brother grabbed a fork, stuck it into the dish, and took a bite. He looked at Mom, who'd gasped. It was an Evans Family Rule to never touch a dish that wasn't on the table. "This is delicious," he started, making Mom beam, "But P can't eat this. This could put her in the hospital."

Mom huffed. "Now you're being as dramatic as your sister."

Dallas walked over to the sink and set his fork down next to a pile of dirty utensils. He met my gaze and I nodded once.

"You're doing the twin thing again," Mom huffed. She hated when we silently communicated with each other and left her out.

"Mom, the reason I can't eat food isn't because I don't

like something. It isn't a personal preference. It is because my body physically cannot tolerate it. I can't stop these allergies and intolerances by praying or wishing or eating more of whatever makes me sick."

She put her hands on her hips and I held mine up to stop her before she interrupted.

"I love you. But until you start respecting me and my needs, I will not be sharing any meals with you, for my own safety." I grabbed my salad. "I'm going to leave before something is said that we both regret."

And with that, I turned around and walked out of the kitchen. I waved goodbye to my dad and uncle, who were so engrossed with the football game that they didn't even acknowledge me, grabbed my coat, and made it out the front door. My hands were shaking so hard from the confrontation that I dropped my keys twice on the way to the car.

I climbed in and shoved the salad onto the passenger seat. At least I had that for dinner. I buckled my seat belt and started my car, then paused as I saw the front door open and Dallas walk out.

I lowered my window, and he ran over. "Figured you had enough salad for two," he said.

"Dallas—"

"My twin sister isn't going to eat alone on Thanksgiving because our family is stubborn as hell."

I nearly cried again. "You sure? It won't be anywhere near as good as mom's dinner."

He lifted one shoulder. "But the company will be infinitely better. Come on, it's cold and I have to piss."

"Mom's crying, isn't she?"

He cringed. "Yep, but we can't keep coddling her. She's gotta respect your boundaries."

The corner of my lips turned up. "Still protecting me."

"You know it. Come on. You can give me the Applechester gossip."

"Hey, Dal?"

He leaned on my car door. "Yeah?"

"I need to know what happened the night Ben died."

All levity disappeared from his expression. "I can't tell you, Paris."

"I don't even know what you were doing. How could it affect anything?"

"Because you'd tell Eliza. And if the wrong person found out? That you saw what you saw, and that Eliza knew?"

"What did I even see?!"

He looked back at the house, likely double-checking that our mom hadn't followed us out. "The less you know, the safer you are. Don't involve Eliza." He tapped my roof. "Let's roll. I'll follow you to your place and then you can feed me." He turned and moved toward his car.

I blinked away my emotions and shifted into reverse. Not telling Eliza meant there would never be a chance of us moving past it. Maybe when this case was over, it was time I did some investigating on what really happened that night. I was an agent now with far more resources than I had in R&D.

I looked for Dallas's headlights in my rearview as we drove, double- and triple-checking he was still there. I hoped Reggie and Clint were in the foyer when we got back to the apartments. I couldn't wait to introduce them to Dallas.

As I pulled up to the stoplight in the center of town, that same blurry vision dashed in front of me. “Not now,” I commanded. It dissipated. I glanced again at Dallas’s black truck in the rearview. I wish I knew the real reason he was in town and what he was working on.

Chapter Fourteen

Paris

THANK GOD ELIZA had called me. She'd been upset and asked me to come over. Somehow it was like it had been before she shut me out. She'd pulled me into her arms, kissed me until I whimpered, then we practically ran to her bedroom.

We had fallen asleep in each other's arms. Her lips to the base of my spine, moving higher and higher. "I've missed you," she breathed against my skin.

"I've missed you so much," I admitted, my eyes stinging from the confession.

"Promise you won't leave me like he did." Her hand smoothed around my hips and between my legs, pressing into me as her mouth climbed higher.

"Never," I swore. "Don't you know I've always been yours?"

Her phone started ringing on the nightstand, but she ignored it, her fingers moving faster. "Hurry, before I answer that."

The tension in me wound tighter, but the phone grew louder with each ring. I wrapped my fingers around her wrist, trying to keep her hand in place, but she pulled away. "Too late." She grabbed the phone and checked the screen.

BEN CALLING.

She gasped and answered the phone. "Who the fuck is this?"

I heard Ben's voice come through the other end. "It's Ben."

"But you're dead."

Someone knocked on the window and the curtains opened by themselves. Ben stood there, looking at us. He had a gun in his hand, and it was pointed at me. "Not anymore. Just need to tie up some loose ends before we live happily ever after."

I reached under the pillow, grabbed a gun, and shot up from the bed, fully naked. The gun shook in my hands. A cold brush of metal at my back made me freeze. Eliza had her weapon pressed into my side.

"A life for a life," she whispered.

Ben shot first, Eliza crumbling to the bed, the gun tumbling onto the carpet. Red pooled on the blue duvet. "NO!" I screamed, pulling the trigger of my gun, but nothing happened. Ben turned his gun to me.

The sound of a second gunshot in my head woke me up, and I sat bolt upright, the gun from underneath my pillow was in my hands and directed at my door. My damp sheets fell off my upper body and pooled at my stomach. Blood stained my pillowcase.

I scrambled out of bed, ripping the sheets off. *Eliza wasn't bleeding out on my bed. It was just my nose. It was just a dream.*

I sucked in a breath, my mouth filling with the coppery taste of blood. Turning to the mirror on my closet, I stared at the disheveled, bloodied woman with a gun in her hand. It took me a long moment to realize that it was me.

Post-nightmare nosebleed. Those were always the most fun to explain to my bed partners. I rarely spent the night with people unless we were serious. Waking up to a terrified woman covered in blood wasn't anyone's idea of romantic.

I set the gun down and hurried to the bathroom, then wadded tissues and pinched my nose. I regretted wearing my new pale blue nightgown to bed. I never bought pastels for a reason, but it was so soft.

After the bleeding subsided and I washed my face and hands, I walked back into the bedroom and froze. Eliza was lying across the bed, her lifeless eyes staring up at me. I screamed, running to the bed and clawing the sheets off. Eliza disappeared. I sat on the floor, the sheets half stripped, sobbing.

"Paris?" Reggie called tenderly, coming into my bedroom, presumably through the wall.

"We're here," his boyfriend Clint promised.

I didn't look up, but I knew they were there by the ghostbumps running over my skin. They always dropped the temperature ten degrees when they were sitting next to me. Panic oozed out of me with the tears. I grabbed the already bloodied sheet and wiped my face. When I pulled it away, it was spotted light pink.

"I just want to be normal," I sucked in a shaky breath, the tears still running down out of my eyes. "I want to eat normal food and have a normal girlfriend and normal dreams. A normal life. I don't want to be broken anymore."

Reggie murmured something soft in Spanish and Clint responded before switching to English. "I get it," Clint said, scootching closer so his shoulder was nearly touching mine. "But you're not broken. There's nothing wrong with you."

Reggie added, "If you were different, you wouldn't have ghost friends comforting you after a nightmare."

I almost smiled and rubbed my nose with the back of my hand. "Put that in the negative column."

"If you were someone else, you wouldn't be changing the world," Reggie added.

"How does me not being able to eat bread change the world?" I hiccupped.

Clint tilted his head, studying me for a long moment. "Your restrictions give you compassion and empathy. It teaches you to be cognizant of people's needs in ways others often miss. It's why you're my favorite human," he explained.

I rolled my eyes. "And the nightmares?"

"Hell if I know. I was a rock star, not a psychologist."

I laughed, the sound congested. "Fair enough." I leaned my head against the bed. I closed my eyes for a long moment, but the image of Eliza, dead, was still waiting behind my lids. A burning desperation to make sure she was okay pierced my chest and radiated throughout my body.

I pushed myself off the ground, grabbed a pair of joggers and a sweatshirt draped over my chair, and slipped them on. I tossed the bloodied nightgown in the corner and secured the gun in my waist holder. I couldn't stay in this room anymore.

"Where are you going?" Clint asked, standing.

"For a drive."

"Be safe."

I hurried from my room, shoved my feet into shoes, and grabbed my keys. "Thanks for the company."

They were still standing in the hall, looking worried, when I ran out the front door.

IT WAS BARELY four in the morning and sleet had started to fall the moment I walked outside. The day after Thanksgiving and already winter was here. The streets were empty, except for a few exhausted drivers who left extra space in between cars as a precaution. The asphalt wasn't super slippery yet, but in another half hour or so, it would be a skating rink. I'd passed the defensive driving course at SHAP on my first try. A little sleet didn't scare me.

The salt trucks weren't out yet, but then Applechester was a sunrise to sundown town, even in the winter. The businesses and city council kept small town hours despite growing into a moderate metropolis several decades ago. The major Black Friday sales could be found at the mall two cities over. The stores in Applechester would open at their normal time but offer free gift wrapping.

This town, rumored to be founded by a werewolf, had been lauded for its proximity to the old railroad. Even when the train changed routes, the quaintness of this place carried on and annual festivals made it an ideal tourist attraction for those who liked the small town feel mixed with city amenities like a dry cleaner, movie theater, and chain restaurants.

The town's decorators must have come out in droves after dinner last night, since every lamppost lining the sidewalk downtown was newly wrapped in silver and gold garland. Custom light arches over the roadway, which were only on from dusk until eleven at night, displayed a wolf in a Santa hat howling at the moon. The forced festiveness was in stark contrast to the panic clawing at the top of my stomach. I pressed the accelerator down a little more.

Eliza lived on the edge of town, past the train tracks. The neighborhood of small ranches and bungalows had been built to accommodate an influx of workers needed first for the railroad and then for the car companies. While every house was nearly identical with a brick base and siding, decades of improvements included bold colored vinyl siding, tiny but extravagant gardens, freestanding enclosed library boxes on front lawns, and second floor or new garage additions. The city had fought hard against the tear-down-build-bigger concept, preserving the charm.

The homes were worn but cozy, many of the houses draped in twinkle lights or with candles in every window, and deflated inflatable snowmen and menorahs on lawns. No one here half-assed a holiday. Eliza's had a collection of plastic figures from a 1964 *Rudolph the Red-Nosed Reindeer* musical, which was Daisy's favorite holiday movie.

Turning off my headlights, I coasted to a stop in front of her house, then looked at every door and window to make sure they were secure. Everything was dark, except for the small glow of a nightlight in the kitchen window.

I eased out of my car, closing the door as quietly as possible, and moved down the edge of the driveway toward the back of the house. As I neared the garage, my sneaker hit a patch of ice and my leg shot out from under me. My arms flapped as I tried to keep my balance. Falling face first onto the asphalt and needing stitches would make this night even worse.

Grabbing the edge of Eliza's car, I steadied myself. When I was confident enough to let go, I managed two steps before the motion detector light over the garage went on. I winced.

While Eliza's bedroom was on the opposite side, she could more than likely see the light from her window if she wasn't sleeping. My suspicions were confirmed a few moments later when the porch light when on. *Shit.*

With my hands up in apology, I walked across the driveway. I slipped, my left knee hitting the pavement. I bit back a yelp as I pushed myself up and then slid to the porch, while clinging to the railing.

Eliza was leaning against the open door, the storm door cracked between us, her cell in one hand, gun in the other. She was wearing only a long black T-shirt, and it took everything I had not to glance down at her legs. Her stare was nearly lethal, but the tension in my shoulders eased just a little to find her alive and in one piece.

"What are you doing here in the middle of the night?"

I pressed my lips together, trying to figure out what to tell her. *I saw Ben, who killed you. Then, he killed me. I can't close my eyes without seeing your lifeless body.* I couldn't say that. It was ridiculous, even in my head. Ben was dead and he'd left enough collateral damage for a lifetime.

I cleared my throat, feigning nonchalance. "I, uh, wanted

to come check on you."

"And it had to be at four in the morning during an ice storm?"

I rubbed my upper arm with my hand, not sure what to say. "I didn't check the forecast." I pointed to my car over my shoulder. "I'll just…" I turned away from her and started down the stairs. "I just wanted to make sure everything was okay."

She opened the storm door wider. "You had a nightmare." A statement. She knew.

I paused, not turning around.

"About me."

This time I did turn. The first night I stayed over at Eliza's, I'd had a nightmare complete with nosebleed. I thought we'd be over, but she just cleaned me up and made us a cup of peppermint tea. Then, we changed the sheets and she held me as I fell back asleep. *Fuck, I missed her.*

"How can you tell?" I asked.

"Because I know you. And you've still got a little blood under your nose."

I tilted my head down as if it would hide my face.

"Should I be concerned?" she prompted.

I paused, then shook my head. "It was nonsense. Something that couldn't actually happen." Not only because Ben was dead, but also, I would never have Eliza in my bed again.

She tilted her head toward the house. "I'll make some tea."

"I should get home before roads get worse."

"Wasn't giving you an option." She turned around and walked inside.

I hesitated. The dream was over, I'd seen Eliza was hale and whole. I should leave, keep my distance, talk to Clint about getting another message through the ghost network to see if anyone else had heard anything about vixen.

Knowing I'd probably regret it, I took small, rapid steps back to the porch and walked inside. My heart was already aching, but so were my nose and fingers from standing in the yard as the sky threw ice at me. Eliza was waiting there with a towel. I kicked off my shoes and wiped the cloth over my face, then wrapped it around the ends of my long hair and rubbed.

"Come on," she said and walked away.

I hurried after her on the balls of my feet, avoiding the squeaky floorboard. When she crossed the threshold to her bedroom, I froze. Her bed, that same blue duvet from my dreams, was folded over, her pillow mussed. A cold sweat broke out on the back of my neck and between my shoulder blades. I pressed my hands into the doorjamb and closed my eyes, inhaling deeply.

Eliza's warm cinnamon scent washed over me, and the image dissipated. When I opened my eyes, it wasn't the nightmare I remembered, but the nights she fell apart beneath me, the slow kisses in the dark, the whispered stories.

"You always fit in these." She handed me a pair of sweats and a thermal.

I stepped onto her plush carpet, so soft on my freezing feet, and that was my breaking point. This whole thing felt too much like coming home. When she'd been sick, and I'd come over during the day, I had managed to block out the memories. The vomiting had helped. But now, I was too exhausted to fight, and everything felt more intimate at night.

"You can change in the bathroom." She gestured to the door as if I hadn't been here more often than at my own place in the end. "And here." She tossed me a pair of thick, fuzzy socks.

I hurried to the bathroom and locked the door.

Chapter Fifteen

Eliza

I STARED AT the bathroom door, wondering both what the hell I was thinking and what the hell did she dream? She had been so pale, her eyes flat and haunted. She'd worn the glasses she didn't like, not bothering to put in her contacts. Whatever she'd seen had freaked her out enough to come poking around my house before most people were awake.

Anxiety and exhaustion weakened my mental defenses, and the white noise of the dead grew louder. I took several calming breaths, trying to push the voices away. I couldn't understand them, not without paying for an open line. It was like the static on a radio station just out of range. Blips of word symbols popped through in nonsensical ways.

I pressed the heels of my hands to my forehead, trying to ward off the impending migraine from so much noise. My anxiety was spiraling into a panic attack. I truly didn't think anyone could go through as much death as I had and not have an anxiety or panic disorder.

The bathroom door unlocked, and I grabbed a pair of pajama pants and pulled them on before Paris walked out. I deliberately didn't look at her, knowing she'd recognize my turmoil. We had always been able to read each other's moods. *Why did it have to be her?* Why did my friends get to be happy, but my life kept falling apart?

I kept my head down as I moved into the kitchen and filled the electric kettle with water, setting it to boil. Ignoring my shaking hands, I focused on grabbing two mugs, then opened the tea bag canister on the counter. Empty.

My eyes stung in frustration and my chest tightened. I opened the pantry and stood on my tiptoes, using the edge of my fingers to try and snatch the box of tea. I swore. *Why did I even use this shelf?* The box edged back farther.

"Why do you even use that shelf?"

I stiffened as Paris walked up behind me, placed her hand against the cabinet next to my shoulder, and reached over me. The heat of her body soaked into my thin T-shirt, and the hair on my arms stood up, as if trying to reach out and touch her. The golf ball in my stomach grew into a basketball.

I turned around, nearly knocking the box out of her hand. Neither of us moved. "Déjà vu," I whispered, not even realizing I said it out loud until her eyes widened.

If this were *before*, she'd move into me, wrap her arms around my waist, bury her head in my neck. She always needed touch after a nightmare, and I craved it desperately when I was panicking. She used to say my touch kept her anchored in reality.

If this were *before* and she were making the tea, I would wrap my arms around her waist and rest the side of my face on her back between her shoulder blades. She'd hum a song, and the vibrations would chase my anxiety away. I opened and closed my fists, trying to control my breathing. The last thing either of us needed were *visible emotions.*

Paris turned away, moving quickly to the counter, and dropped the box near the kettle. Then, she moved to the opposite side, and turned to stare out the kitchen window. I added the tea bags to the mugs, filled them with water, and refilled the canister while they steeped. I shifted my focus completely to the task.

"Honey?" I asked.

"Yeah?"

I cringed. While I didn't like pet names, I'd started calling Paris 'honey' after a very eventful, kid-free night utilizing some farmers market honey. I cleared my throat. "I mean, do you want any honey in your tea?"

She blinked away from the window, her cheeks burning bright pink. "Sorry, I was—"

"It's okay," I rushed.

"No honey."

I handed her a mug and took my own. Neither of us moved.

"Why are you taking care of me?" she asked, so quiet I wasn't sure I heard her at first.

My back straightened. I wasn't taking care of her. I was just making sure my coworker was safe until we solved this damn case. I would do the same for anyone. "Because you saved Jake's life."

That part was true. It didn't make up for what she did to Ben, but it meant I could be civil to her.

She nodded then picked up the string from her tea bag, wrapping it around her finger, then releasing it. "But a life for a life isn't enough."

I averted my eyes, taking a long sip of my brew. "What happened to me in your dream?"

"How do you know it was about you?"

I lifted my mug to silently indicate I could tell as she was standing in my kitchen before sunrise.

The corner of her mouth lifted. "Fair." She took a long sip. "It wasn't a prophetic one. Or if it was, I didn't understand it. It was probably just a stress dream."

"What was it?"

"Doesn't matter."

"Paris, tell me!" I nearly shouted, my anxiety making my voice shake. "Was Daisy—"

"Daisy wasn't in it." She laughed without humor. "It was you, me, and…Ben. It was violent. Okay? Not going to happen, obviously."

I bit back asking if she was sure. Of course she was sure; Ben was dead. It was probably symbolic of everything that was going on. The sharpest edge of the panic eased, although my body was still overly warm and sweating, and the damn *noise.*

"Why is it always so hard for you to tell me the truth?" I asked my mug.

"It's not hard…" she trailed off. "When we started dating, I loved that you had such strong convictions and boundaries." She turned back to the window, even though it was too dark to see anything except us mirrored in the glass. "But there's no room for a small mistake or a bad day with you."

"Having a hand in my fiancé's death isn't some small

mistake or bad day."

"No, it's not. And you've made it clear there's nothing we can do to get past that, which is completely understandable."

I set my cup on the counter and straightened. "You can tell me what happened and who you're protecting, then I'll decide if I can get past it." The basketball in my stomach was now on fire. How dare she come to my house, wake me up, and then list my faults.

She took a bracing sip of tea. "I can't."

"I can't trust people who don't tell me the truth."

"I am telling you the truth!"

"Shush!" I whisper-yelled, gesturing to Daisy's closed door. "You're telling me a half-truth." I dumped the rest of my tea out, leaving the bag in the empty mug to use at breakfast. "Why does it matter anyway? We just need to get through the job, and we can go back to ignoring each other like we've successfully done for the last five months."

I was so tired of the voices, the drama, these shit choices, vixen, this job. I wanted to quit, go into a regular office building with regular humans. It was as if I were trapped in a pinball machine, bouncing off work, Daisy, my family, Ben's death, Paris, my broken heart.

The spirits grew so loud, my ears started ringing.

Shut up, shut up!

Paris set her mug down, turned toward me, and slid one hand into my hair, the other over my hip. She pressed her forehead to mine. "How loud are they?"

I stiffened at her touch but didn't pull away. "Not bad."

"Now who isn't being honest?"

This time, I did try to step back, but she tightened her grip. "Breathe. I've got you." She pulled me into a hug and made big circles on my back with her hand. She paused to tug off her glasses, set them on the counter, then buried her face against my neck.

The voices faded, as if she had reached over and turned down the volume on the radio. I sank into her. A basketball moved into my throat, then dispersed into tears. I hated crying and my jaw ached from trying to hold it back. "You could've called or texted," I whimpered. "The alarm woke me. I got scared."

"I'm sorry," she said against my skin. "I should've called. I just wanted to check to make sure all your windows and doors were good. I forgot Jake added cameras. I'm sorry. I'm so sorry."

I knew she was apologizing for more than just tonight, even though I couldn't think about it on a deeper level. Not yet. Instead, I just wrapped my arms around her waist and fisted the back of her shirt. "I'm so tired of missing you." My voice broke on the last word.

She held me tighter. "Me too. It kills me every time I see you sitting across from me and know you're not mine."

My aching head subsided, as did the panic. I wanted to stay here in her arms, pretend that the things between us didn't matter. Figure out a way to look past it all. That, however, only worked in the movies. So I shoved away thoughts of the future and just marveled in her closeness.

Why wasn't it enough? Why couldn't it be enough?

We clung to each other, desperately trying to stop time, until my soft sobs turned into slow breaths. She lifted her head, kissed my cheek, and reached for a piece of paper towel. She dabbed at my face, then brushed away the hair that had clung to my damp skin. "Better?"

"They're quiet," I admitted. "Thank you."

She kissed my forehead. "Go wash your face and try to get some sleep."

"If Daisy gets up before me, wake me up." Daisy, even now, was still asking when "mommy's work friend" was going to come back over. They had bonded so quickly. The guilt of introducing my daughter to someone else who would just disappear from her life like her dad still weighed heavy. I pressed my fingers against my forehead, not wanting to bring Paris back into Daisy's life for a short time only to have Paris disappear again when this case was over.

She swallowed hard, glanced at Daisy's door, and nodded. I could see the pain written all over her face. Daisy was such an easy kid to love, and if Paris and I had separated for any other reason, I would've asked her to stay in Daisy's life. But how could I, knowing she was part of the reason my daughter didn't have her father anymore?

I gestured to the hall closet. "The blankets—"

"I know where they are."

I turned to walk to my bedroom, then paused. "Night, Paris." She didn't respond.

Easing the bedroom door closed, I hovered, listening. There was no sound for a few minutes, then the sink turned on and off. The linen closet opened and closed, then the squeak of the floorboards in the living room.

I wanted to open the door, to invite her to come in, to pull her into my arms and fall asleep with her warmth and softness surrounding me. I hated sleeping alone. No, I hated sleeping without *Paris*.

I missed her in a different way than I missed Ben. He and I had been together so long, I constantly forgot he wasn't around to share things with. It hurt the most when our daughter did something amazing and I couldn't tell him, we couldn't stand back and be proud together.

Missing him was an ever-present ache. He should be here. Daisy should know her father. We had planned to be one big happy family and I'd loved him for so long, I didn't remember my heart not loving him. When he died, my heart stopped beating.

Then I met Paris, and it was as if she resuscitated me. She didn't replace Ben but instead carved out a new space for herself that only she fit into. Our relationship had been different from the start.

Ben may have been my first love, but I truly thought Paris would be my last. I sometimes laid awake even now wondering if Ben had lived and I'd met Paris at work, what would've happened? Would it have been the catalyst for the official end of Ben's and my relationship? We had tried so hard to make it work for Daisy, for our families, for us, but the last year together had been more struggle than not.

Ben was my first serious relationship, my first in a lot of ways. Even in the early days with him, I was exhausted trying to figure out why we couldn't get on the same page. He'd promise to call or come over for dinner, then get busy with work and forget.

It wasn't until Paris that I realized things could be different. She always called when she said she would, shared the mental load of decisions with me, and was extremely affectionate. It was as if I had made a wish list and she'd stepped out.

Intimacy with her wasn't always sex, but also included midnight talks with our foreheads touching, secret moments in our offices where we just held each other, and video chats until we both fell asleep.

It was her anticipating my needs, like getting done with work before me and making dinner so I could help Daisy with her homework. Running a bath for us after Daisy was asleep and spending an hour adding more hot water while we held each other. It was the confidence in knowing that I could tell her anything and she wouldn't try to fix it.

Until it all came to a screeching, soul-crushing, flaming-pile-of-shit, gut-wrenching halt.

I sat on the end of the bed, then laid back across the foot, looking up at the stack of pillows on the right side I never used. I should throw those off the bed. I should sleep in the center and not save a space for someone who couldn't come back. Maybe I'd stop reaching out every time I woke up, only to find the pillow cold and me alone.

Chapter Sixteen

Paris

I WAS SO physically and emotionally tired that I nearly cried when my phone vibrated on the couch cushion next to me. The sky was slightly lighter than it had been when I'd finally been able to close my eyes without my nightmare still behind them. I swiped to answer and moaned a greeting.

My twin responded, "Are you sleeping?"

"No, I'm performing in Cirque du Soleil."

"I'm serious."

I pulled the pillow over my face to muffle the sound and whispered into the phone, "What do you think? It's…" I checked the time, "five thirty-seven in the morning. Of course I'm sleeping."

"Well, wake up and get your computer. We have an emergency."

Adrenaline burned through my head and chest, chasing away any immediate thoughts of sleep. "Are you alright? The parents? What's happened?"

"Someone is accessing Ben's files."

"Okay? And you can't take care of it?"

"Not at this level. Whoever it is has a higher security

clearance than me."

I rubbed at my left eye, trying to get my too-tired brain moving faster. "You're a higher clearance than me."

"You're a better hacker."

Fair. "Are they only looking for Ben?"

There was a long pause.

"Dallas?"

"What are you working on? Why is someone accessing your and Ben's files?"

"Mine too?" I sat up, turning toward Eliza's door. She was the only person I could think of who was looking for Ben and me together, but she was sleeping. Wasn't she? She always slept hard after a panic attack.

Plus, she definitely wasn't a hacker, and her clearance wasn't higher than mine. But who did she know that had access to both? Jake? Poppy? I ran the list in my head when I snagged on a name. *Loren.*

"Paris?" Dallas asked. "Whoever this is searched for the report on Ben's death, then they searched your name. Talk to me."

"I think I know who it is. Not a direct threat to me."

Dallas grunted. "Maybe not yet. But if they're digging this deep on Ben, it's only a matter of time before..."

"Before what?"

"Before we're all at risk."

"What the fuck does that even mean?" I threw my hand in the air. "Who are we at risk from? No one except you and our parents know Eliza and I have a personal connection. I already scrubbed any connection between Ben and Eliza. What else is there to find?"

"I can't believe this. Are you drunk?"

"No, you asshole, but I'm not at home. I don't have my computer."

"Fuuuuck," he breathed, adding two extra syllables to the word. "Where are you?"

"I can walk you through it?" I suggested, more of a question than a promise.

"I'm on a case and can't get away."

"You're always on a case and can't get away!" I knew we were in this together, but it felt like I'd been frantically swimming below the surface while he floated around on a life preserver, not helping.

"Where are you?" he asked.

"Not answering that."

"Does this mysterious place have a computer?"

It did, but I wasn't going to use Eliza's computer to hack into the system. "I need a few hours. I'll have it done by lunch."

"We could all be on a hit list by lunch!" he whisper-shouted.

"Whose hit list? Dallas, why are you so paranoid?"

"Because the case I'm on is dangerous and I don't want you caught in the crossfire."

I rubbed my right eye, removing my sleep gunk. I had three options: The first was leave and drive home. In this weather, it would probably take me well over thirty minutes, plus I didn't know how to disarm the alarm without waking Eliza. The second was to try and hack the system from my cell—nearly impossible without a real keyboard—or someone else's computer. Or three, ignore my twin and hope that he was bluffing.

"I hate you right now," I grumbled. "So much."

He sighed in relief. "I love you, too."

"Go away. I need to figure out how to do this without a laptop and I've had a bad night already."

"P—"

"Bye." I hung up and grabbed my glasses. Looking around the room, I spotted a tablet with a glittery rainbow case charging on the coffee table, in front of the unlit pink Christmas tree. This had to be Daisy's. I could not use Eliza's daughter's tablet to do something illegal, no matter the justification. Rolling off the couch, I moved around the living room, then the kitchen, then by the front door hoping to find Eliza's computer but found nothing. She must keep it in her bedroom.

I put my glasses on the top of my head and scrubbed at my face with my hands. My eyes stung from lack of sleep and my body ached with my earlier Ice Capades routine. Hating myself with every movement, I replaced my glasses and picked up Daisy's tablet. If the keyboard was Bluetooth, I should be able to make it work with my phone.

Opening Bluetooth on my cell, I searched and connected the device, then got to work. I doubled check my app that provided me with a secured virtual private network was active. Then, through the login portal for SHAP, I opened the fake employee account I'd created. If anyone ever caught me, I would be in SHAP prison for a long time, especially for tampering with files. Good thing no one was going to catch me.

I searched my name, trying to find a digital trail of folders being accessed. This would be so much easier on my laptop, where I could run the program I'd created that would've highlighted all files with my name in them. In one swoop, I could move them to a different classified folder and break all the current connections. I was going to have to move individual files via my phone, which made it much riskier. Someone could catch me in the system, or Eliza could wake up early.

I started with the file on Ben's death and checked when it was last accessed. Six months ago. Good. Whoever was looking hadn't found it yet. Using a series of keyboard shortcuts, I sent the file to a new subfolder that I locked with an encryption that only Dallas or I could break.

Dallas had wanted me to permanently delete everything about Ben's death, but I disobeyed him. If I were ever put on trial, I'd need access to these. While I knew what really happened that night, the investigation had cleared me of all charges and these documents proved it.

The SHAP system was incredibly complex, developed over decades by supernaturals who never slept. If I hadn't help create the login system, I wouldn't have been able to break in. Still, someone more experienced than me could unravel my work with a hard tug. This was all meant to be a bandage until Dallas figured out a new plan.

I loved my twin more than anyone on this planet, but right now I wanted to scream at him for involving me. What was I supposed to do? Not take his calls? Not follow his orders? What if he was right and someone was after Eliza and Daisy? I couldn't risk it.

The sun creeped up as I located folders I'd hidden, but

apparently not well enough. I created a new file, deep in a twisty maze of locations, and began rearranging the data. Five folders left, four, three, two, one... I clicked and tried to move it. THIS FILE IS BEING ACCESSED BY ANOTHER USER.

"Shit," I breathed.

"Uncle Jake said I should start a swear jar to pay for my retirement."

I startled, locked my phone, and shoved the keyboard between the couch cushions. Flipping the blanket off my head, I looked over the back of the couch to find a smiling Daisy.

"Daisy!" I pressed my hand to my chest trying to slow my racing heart. "You're up early."

She shrugged. "I told my brain to go back to sleep, but it didn't listen. It thinks we have school today."

"I hate when that happens." My attention was split between worrying about the file left behind and taking in Daisy. She'd changed so much since I'd seen her last. Her curly red hair was longer, and she was a little taller, but she had dark circles under her eyes and her shoulders slumped. Her gaze was more assessing, and I suspected that had something to do with her witch training.

"Did you and Mom have a fight? I missed you but she wouldn't tell me when you were coming over again."

Her little kid observation had enough power to knock the breath out of me. "I missed you, too. Sometimes adult friends can't see each other, but even when I'm not here, I still think you're pretty cool."

She smiled shyly and then jumped over the back of the couch to come sit next to me. "Want to play?"

I glanced at the clock above the entertainment center. It was just after six. "I'll make you a deal. If you go back to bed and rest for one more hour so your mom can sleep longer, I'll make you breakfast, and we can play whatever you want before Uncle Jake comes over. Deal?"

She kicked her feet against the couch, looked at the clock, then nodded. "Okie dokie." She jumped off the couch. "You'll be here when I wake up?"

I nodded. "Promise."

She reached over, wrapped her arms around me, then scooted off the couch and nearly sprinted into her bedroom. As soon as she'd gone, I went back to my phone, logged in a second time, and moved the remaining file. I logged out, tossed my phone aside, and returned the keyboard to its place.

Me: *It's done*

Dallas: *Longer than normal, everything ok?*

Me: *Fine. On cell. Got interrupted.*

Dallas: *By who?*

Me: *I'm going back to bed.*

I put my phone on silent and pulled the blanket over my head. I just needed a few more minutes of sleep.

"MOMMY, CAN I wake Paris?" Daisy whispered, which was barely quieter than her full volume.

"Let her sleep, munchkin," Eliza said.

"But she promised she'd make breakfast."

"Did she?" Plates were removed from a cabinet, something sizzled, and then the faucet went on and off. I inhaled deeply, resigning myself to being awake. I glanced up at the clock. It was almost seven-thirty.

I sat up, brushing my hair back from my face. "I did promise."

Eliza looked over and nodded, her face devoid of expression. Daisy beamed as if she'd won the lottery.

"That one woke up at six and I promised if she tried to sleep for another hour, I'd make breakfast and play with her," I explained.

Eliza nodded. "Well, breakfast is about done, but you can set the table."

"Sounds good." I detoured to the bathroom to splash water on my face and used my finger as a toothbrush, then returned to the kitchen to set the table. My stomach tightened as I laid out place settings and filled three glasses with water. It was a glimpse into the life I'd wanted more than anything.

It was silly to add a plate for myself since I wouldn't be eating. I'd forgotten to grab food from my house, and I doubted Eliza still had any of my food in her freezer or cabinets. Even if she did, it'd be expired by now. It would be nice to sit with them and pretend for just a little, anyway.

Eliza brought over a frying pan and put a scoop of eggs mixed with vegetables and cheese on Daisy's plate, then the rest on hers. It smelled so good, my mouth watered. I loved the smell of red peppers, despite not being able to eat them.

I looked up when Eliza moved back to my side, a smaller

frying pan in her hand. "I didn't have your normal stuff, but I made you scrambled eggs with spinach, used water instead of milk, and my spray oil instead of butter. Is that still okay?"

I nodded in shock that she remembered what I could eat, then blinked down at my plate as she put the eggs on. She set the pan back on the stove and brought back a bowl of fruit. "It was frozen. I threw in half a banana too." She then grabbed a stack of toast for her and Daisy and sat down.

I opened my mouth to say something, but my throat was so tight I couldn't get the words out.

Daisy smiled at me and took a giant bite of her eggs, which made me laugh.

"You're such a goof," I told her.

She puffed out her cheeks, then turned to her plate and took a huge bite of jam toast. I just shook my head. Daisy was very theatrical, which was exactly what this moment needed.

"Everything okay?" Eliza asked, glancing at my untouched food.

"Yes, yes," I rushed out. "Just...you know. You went out of your way to feed me and that means a lot."

She frowned at me and lowered her fork. "Just because we—" She cleared her throat, seemingly remembering that Daisy was listening intently. "I'm not going to invite someone into my house and then not feed them simply because their diet is different than mine." She scoffed, offended. "Your restrictions aren't a burden. You know that."

God, how did the Robinsons say things that so frequently tore up my heart? Eliza used to repeat that phrase when I'd apologize for being an inconvenience. My diet meant a lot of home cooking, since there were only a few restaurants in the area that could accommodate me.

She nodded and pointed her fork at me. "Eat."

I ate. And I pushed away all the fear and exhaustion and heartbreak, and just enjoyed Daisy's antics and Eliza's conversation. I tried to memorize every single moment, so I could carry it with me. Jake walked in a half an hour later, looking rested and limping less than when we had worked together, and the morning was complete. He startled to find me there but didn't ask. He just rested his cane on the end of the table, dropped into a chair, and stole some toast.

For one morning, I could pretend everything worked out. A beautiful partner, an incredible kid, a trusted friend for a brother-in-law, a family whom I supported, that supported me and filled my days with laughter. It was one of those moments where I was so happy, so content, it was like a scene in a movie. They were so rare, so special, and so fragile.

Then Eliza's phone chimed and the movie screen shattered.

Chapter Seventeen

Eliza

THIS MORNING HAD been a mistake. It reminded me how much I missed Paris, her quiet, steady presence sitting next to me. She had been my anchor, my companion, and a role model for Daisy. One meal shouldn't feel like coming home, but it did. For a little while, I'd forgotten how much pain she'd caused this family, how I couldn't trust her.

Then my text alert went off and it was like someone had thrown a rock, shattering the snow globe around this perfect but precarious morning. Reality flooded in, souring everything.

Loren: *Call when you can talk*

I responded with a thumbs-up emoji and put my phone away. "How're the roads?" I asked Jake, who had been laughing at something Paris said.

He was leaning back, his chair on two legs, but straightened when he heard the tone of my voice. "Salt trucks are out and it's stopped sleeting. Go slow and you should be okay. Already had Poppy, Mina, and Carma out Black Friday shopping."

"How'd that go?"

"They're going to have to build a second bed and breakfast just for storage."

I laughed. "Sounds about right."

"You coming tomorrow night? Carma said you didn't respond to her text."

"We'll talk after work about it. Paris and I have a case we need to wrap up." I glanced at the clock on the stove. Just after eight. I looked at Paris. "You good?"

For one moment, she looked like I'd punched her in the stomach, then her expression was normal again. I fisted my hand to keep from saying *I know, I understand, I didn't want it to end, either.*

Paris stood and started gathering plates. "I'll grab these, you go get ready for work."

I shook my head. "You have to drive home, change, then drive to work. It'll take you longer. I've got this."

"Did you cook?"

"Well, yeah—"

"Then stop arguing with me."

I opened my mouth, then closed it, hands up in surrender. "Okay, you win. Thank you."

Paris carried the plates to the sink and started rinsing them, then placed them in the dishwasher. Jake looked between us for a long moment, then turned his attention to Daisy. "Munchkin, go change into daytime clothes so we can do some work."

She crossed her arms and groaned. "But it's vacation."

"Ah yes," he lifted a finger. "Which means once we finish our lessons, we can go play hide and seek with Reggie and

Sebastian." He lifted his finger to his lips. "We don't even have to tell your mom if we have ice cream for lunch." He winked.

She nodded, completely serious. "I'll get dressed," she whispered.

He nodded back with the same level of seriousness. He watched until she ran into her room and shut the door, then turned to face me and Paris. He gestured between us. "We finally going to talk about what's going on here?"

Paris dropped a pan into the sink and grimaced. "Nothing," she said, more to the sink than Jake.

I crossed my arms and looked down at my brother. "What makes you think something's going on here?"

He laughed once. "You mean besides the fact that Paris clearly spent the night?" He leaned forward, putting his forearms on the table. "Because I used to be a professional investigator?"

"And you still think you are?" I shot back, a sibling habit.

"Paris is doing the dishes in the exact same order you do them. She knows how you prefer your pans to be washed. And the two of you keep looking at one another when the other isn't looking. The tension is so thick, I could cut it with a knife. You tell me."

I glanced at Paris over my shoulder, who had fixed her gaze intently on handwashing a frying pan. Her cheeks had turned pink in the dim gray of the morning. I pushed my tongue against my teeth then sighed. "Paris and I…spent some time together. Unfortunately, we weren't compatible long-term. Since we're working together, we decided to keep our history private."

Jake slapped the table. "I fucking knew it. Mina owes me a twenty."

"Jake!"

He leaned back again in his chair. "Remember your fifteenth birthday party? You're just a tad more subtle than I was." He lifted his thumb and forefinger, a tiny space between them.

I pursed my lips but didn't respond. We weren't *that* bad. Poppy and Jake had shown up late to the party, hair mussed and clothes in disarray. I'd pulled Poppy in the bathroom to fix her makeup and smooth her hair.

Despite Jake and Poppy sitting across the room from each other that night, it was impossible to ignore the electric charge between them. Their eyes were always searching for each other, their bodies leaning toward each other, their silent conversations all but shouted. Our parents had pounced the moment the party ended, reminding him that they were not allowed to be together in *any* capacity as more than friends.

The reminder that they knew Poppy was a grim reaper made the memory sting even more. They could have told us, prepared us, helped us grieve. Instead, they told Jake it was because he was seventeen and Poppy was too young.

"I'm going to get changed." I spun on my heel and nodded to Paris. "Thanks for cleaning up. See you in a bit." It was such a casual goodbye for what had happened in the last few hours. From whispered confessions of mutual pain to "see you in a bit."

I hurried through my morning routine, and when I returned to the kitchen, Paris was already gone. Good. We needed the space, needed to find our equilibrium.

Daisy was at the table, turning on her SHAP issued computer. She looked up at me with sad eyes, deep sea blue, a mix of Ben's hazel and my sky blue. "Mom, when can Paris come back? I missed her."

Shit. This was exactly what I didn't want to happen. "She's really busy on a case right now, but I'll let you know when she can."

Jake's eyes bored into mine, clearly wanting answers I couldn't and wouldn't give. I walked over and kissed Daisy on the head and then squeezed his shoulder. "Thanks for coming today. We're trying to get this case done as fast as possible."

"Best job in the world," he said. "I threw some salt on your sidewalk so you should be good. Also, if you think I'm going to forget about this—"

"Yeah, yeah. See you later." I palmed my phone as I went out to my car. I navigated out of the icy subdivision before pulling into the back of a parking lot. I couldn't wait any longer to call Loren. He answered on the second ring.

"Lynch."

"It's Eliza."

"Hold on." He whispered something and then clearly moved into another space, punctuated by the closing of a door. "You alone?"

"Yeah."

"Had Javier poke around Ben's old records, trying to find any family ties. While he was searching, someone was moving the files. He was able to get some information before they disappeared."

"Whoa."

"Eliza, Javier has the highest clearance available outside of his boss. These files are only accessible from his clearance or higher. Which means either this runs deep or someone's covering up something."

I tapped on my steering wheel, trying to ignore the swooping of my stomach. I'd known this was an inside job, but it didn't make hearing it any easier. "What'd he'd find?"

"Somerset, your fiancé? He was in something. Super off record. Project didn't even have a name. His partner's name was redacted. Javier was able to do a workaround and view the edits. Name Dallas Evans mean anything to you?"

"Paris's twin." I shook my head. "Impossible. I know for a fact Paris was involved. And Ben was working in research. Why would he be teamed with an active agent?" *And why had I been paired with an active agent?*

"Had the same questions. Had Javier look up Somerset's and Evans's keycard swipes the month before Somerset's death. They checked into the labs multiple times a day until the last four days. Then, nothing. No record of them even being in the building. Couldn't get any security footage dating back far enough."

I tugged my hand through my hair, my breath coming faster as my chest tightened. A memory of Ben coming home after midnight two days before he died. He hadn't been home in nearly forty hours, claiming a work emergency. His clothes were wrinkled, his stubble was thick, and his left eye black and blue.

"Where have you been? What happened?" I'd asked,

running over to him.

He'd brushed me off. "We were working on a new gun in the lab and the kickback took me by surprise. I'm fine."

I'd crossed my arms. "Good, I'm glad you're fine. I'm not."

He ran his hand over his face. "Can I please get in the door before you lose your shit? I'm fucking exhausted and haven't eaten since god knows when."

"You couldn't call me and let me know you were alive?" I moved quietly but aggressively through the kitchen as I put together a plate of leftovers. I didn't want to wake Daisy, so I had to really concentrate on not raising my voice or slamming the cupboard.

"I texted."

One time, thirty hours ago. I didn't respond as I set the plate in the microwave.

"You know what this job is like, Eliza."

And I did. It had always been work first, Daisy second, us third. The life of a SHAP employee. This time, however, felt different. Maybe I'd been at the end of my rope, or maybe I'd known something was wrong. A deep sense of foreboding had nestled into my gut and wouldn't leave me alone.

"Have you ever thought about leaving SHAP?" I asked.

He crossed his arms and leaned against the wall. "Why?"

"Because I think it's going to be the end of us. This job takes and takes and what does it give back?"

He shushed me, walked over, and wrapped his arms around my waist, kissing my neck. "It gives us this life together, okay? I'm sorry. I'm sorry I didn't call. I'm sorry."

He punctuated each sorry with a soft kiss.

Someone honking on the street brought me back to the present. Ben had told me he'd been in the lab, but he hadn't even been in the building. He had stood by his lie as we argued, even when I threw my engagement band at him when he wanted to postpone the wedding again because of his schedule. He'd lied when he kissed me goodbye for the last time.

"Eliza, you okay?" Loren asked.

I shook my head, even though he couldn't see it. "Just…a lot to take in."

"I can imagine." He hesitated, then added, "I did get a lead on your biological father."

I sat up. "What'd you find?"

"Ricky Jenson, age fifty-nine, currently residing at Texas State Penitentiary for tax evasion and domestic abuse. Had a buddy of mine get a bio sample—don't ask me how—and found a recessive supernatural gene for mediums, but no one with magic. Ricky's full human."

"Wow. He was a real winner."

"I'm sorry."

"Nah, don't be. I already knew he was a piece of shit. My mom dropped him the moment she figured out he had a second family." As mad as I was at her, at least she wasn't scum of the earth like my bio father. "Well, guess that means the magic is definitely from Ben's side. How is that possible? That it's only from one side of the family?"

Loren shifted the phone to his other ear. "I think the 'magic on both sides' is an outdated philosophy. If the magic is strong enough from one line, it would be enough. Especially when paired with a medium gene."

"So we're not any closer. And no luck with Ben's family?"

"No, it's like he's a ghost. Both his parents were closed adoptions, but I can't find the adoptive parents either. Their birth certificates are blank, their birth names erased, their marriage license has a witness who is deceased. Their old house was turned into a Walmart."

"How is this possible?" I whispered, shaking my head in disbelief.

"It's highly improbable in the age of computers and DNA tests. Someone's hiding something." He sighed. "Give me some time. I'm going to have Javier look again and see if he can find the missing files. I'll be in touch."

"Thanks, Loren."

"Give my best to Jake."

"Will do."

I sat there for a long time after the call ended, trying to reframe my memories from Ben's last few days. Late nights, derailed conversations, pushing me away, picking up Daisy early from school to spend the afternoon together, even though I disapproved. If he was postponing the wedding so our names wouldn't be linked in any case reports…

He knew. He knew something was wrong. He didn't tell me. He didn't trust me enough to tell me.

My phone chimed with a text, my fingers shaking as I read.

Paris: *Tracker activated. Meet at office when you can*

Me: *Be there in eight minutes*

Chapter Eighteen

Paris

IT WORKED. THE trackers worked! The little green dot moved across my map, the perpetrator already out of the building and making their way through downtown Applechester. While it would be easy to jump into a car and trail them, there was more of a risk of being caught. I could control everything in my office in a way I couldn't control it on the street. Besides, once I had a face, we could go hunting.

I grabbed a pencil and a sticky note. The tracker sent a signal as soon as it was jostled for more than one minute. Assuming the perp was on foot, was not using any mobility devices, and they were average height with an athletic build—like most SHAP employees who could also access the evidence room and climb a ladder—would mean they would've been in the building between roughly 9:46 am to 9:55 am.

After opening my laptop and launching a program to block my identity, I logged in the SHAP database and accessed the security system. I glanced at the clock. I had about three minutes before someone noticed me poking around.

I scrubbed through the recorded footage, scanning for something, someone that didn't belong. In a second screen, I piggybacked street footage from traffic cams and security cameras in SHAP-friendly businesses. My eyes shifted to my phone. Perp was still moving at a steady pace. Applechester wasn't a small town, but it was a quiet one, and someone aggressively walking the morning of an ice storm was rare.

They paused at the corner. I pulled up cam footage from the intersection. A man with a dark coat, aviator sunglasses, a baseball cap tugged low, short beard, and a black shoulder bag was crossing the street. Something twinged inside of me.

Fear.

No. *Dread.*

This was the man following Eliza at Café Eleonora. And that coat…I swear I could feel the texture of it in my memory. I jumped back over to the SHAP footage, scanning for the same man. *There.* Walking through the back entrance and getting into the service elevator. I switched to the evidence room floor cameras.

The elevator doors opened, he took one step out, and then he disappeared. "What?!" I whisper-shouted. I paused the video, toggling between the two frames. He was holding a tablet, and his hand swiped the screen before he disappeared. That meant he could get into the system.

I'd expected an employee with access to the evidence room would be the one to steal the venom and vixen, someone with a plausible excuse to be there. This was so far beyond. I only knew two people who could hack the SHAP security cameras from a tablet—me and Dallas. So who was this guy? And why did he look so familiar?

I toggled back one more time. He slipped his sunglasses on the second before he stepped out of the elevator car. Zooming in on the black and white footage, I let out a single laugh of disbelief.

Wow, Paris, you need more sleep. I shook my head and looked again. My gut clenched, my chest filled with cement, making my lungs unable to suck in oxygen.

Impossible. I had to be hallucinating.

I snatched my phone and checked on the trackers. The signal was gone. Completely gone. I refreshed the signal, pinged the trackers, and restarted the app. Nothing worked. Which meant either someone had found them and removed them, or they had blocked the signal transmission.

Dallas was the only other person alive who knew both how to disable the security cameras for the evidence room and how to detect and block the trackers I'd made, information I'd kept out of both the manual and official report.

But Dallas could have told someone.

Holy shit. What the hell was happening? What I thought I knew was battling what I was seeing with my own eyes. My brain rejected the possibility because that would mean…

A cacophony of expletives whipped around my head as my shaking fingers moved—seemingly independent of conscious thought—to delete the footage. I didn't trust anyone else with this knowledge. Dallas had to be involved, and until I got answers, I couldn't risk exposing whatever he was working on.

Not again.

My heart was thrumming so loudly, it blocked out all

other noise in my ears. It was impossible. The man standing in that elevator was impossible. The trackers disappearing were impossible.

After deleting the footage, I closed my laptop with shaking hands. Grabbing my phone, I dialed Dallas and paced aggressively. Directly to voicemail. I called again. This time it rang five times, and then went to voicemail.

"I can do this all day," I told the phone as I dialed again, then a fourth time.

On the fifth, Dallas picked up. "What?!" he hissed. "I'm *working*."

"I put some trackers on the vixen in evidence. They were stolen this morning."

Silence.

I pulled the phone away from my ear to make sure he hadn't hung up. "Do you want to explain to me why a dead man was on the security footage before he looped the cameras?"

He swore.

"Dallas, where the fuck are you?"

There was rustling and the sound of an engine starting. "Meet me at the gym in an hour, okay? We'll talk then. And Paris? You can't tell a soul."

"Fuck you."

"Promise me! I'll explain it all later."

I hung up then let the phone drop. I fell into my chair and put my head between my legs, breathing in and out. Black spots danced at the edge of my vision.

He was alive. *Ben* was alive! He'd dyed his hair and grown a beard, but he was wearing the same coat I'd dragged out of the water.

A knock at the locked door shot my heart back to racing. *Eliza.*

Chapter Nineteen

Eliza

MY FIST CLENCHED around the strap of my bag, anxiety and anticipation making my legs feel like springs. I was bouncing in place, waiting for the door to open. It was impossible to forget the day we placed the trackers and now, we were finally getting answers.

Paris's office door opened, but only wide enough to stick her head out. "False alarm," she said. "They ripped off the trackers and threw them in a trash can just outside the building. No clear footage. I'm sorry, I just figured it out."

My body deflated as if I were one of the flailing inflatable guys and someone had pulled the plug. "What's our next step? Why are you blocking the door?"

"I'm not feeling great, incoming migraine." She rubbed at the center of her forehead. "Can I text later? I think I'm going to work from home."

Paris didn't get headaches in the center of her forehead. She got them up the back of her neck and over her left eye. I studied her shaking fingers, the perspiration around her hairline, the way her chest rose and fell. She was having a panic attack and was trying to hide it.

Was she having one because something happened with the trackers, or something *didn't* happen with the trackers? Also, we'd agreed not to take the files outside of the office, just in case, so how would she work from home? None of what she was saying made sense.

"Let me in," I ordered.

"No, I—"

I crowded her. She was taller and stronger than me, but she stepped back, as if it were too much energy to force me out. I moved fully in and then closed the door behind me, locking it.

The moment we were alone together, all the feelings from last night, the vulnerabilities, the longing, the desperation crashed over me like a wave. I pressed my hand to the door for balance. "I'm going to ask you a question and I need the truth."

She didn't answer, just stood in profile, staring at the wall, lips pressed together. Her right hand was picking at the cuticles on her left.

I reached out and grabbed her hand, smoothing it in mine. "Was Dallas working with Ben when he died?"

Paris's entire body tensed. I had my answer.

"On what?"

"I don't know." Her voice was barely above a whisper.

"What *do* you know?"

A sharp breath broke from her chest, and she pulled her hand away, covering her face for a long moment before continuing. "No one's connected you to Ben, at least no one who didn't know you personally. The HR file with Ben's address and paycheck information has been deleted. Daisy's birth certificate was altered so his name's not on it. You never married. You're not linked in the SHAP system."

My hand fell away from the door, my chest empty, achy. "It was you? You were the one who was hiding the files while Javier was looking?"

"Whether or not you want anything to do with me, I'll always protect you. I'm not going to let anyone hurt you."

I staggered back, hitting the door, the confession still swirling between us. "You changed Daisy's birth certificate?"

"I'm sorry—"

"Why? Ben's death was ruled an accident." I didn't believe it, and clearly neither did she.

She swallowed hard. "I don't know who was after Ben and I don't know what they were looking for, but I do know Dallas is still working on that case. I figured if they got desperate, they may do some digging, leading back to me." She hesitated, then added, "Or worse, leading back to you and Daisy. The more barriers, the better."

Had she been protecting me and Daisy all this time? "How long have you been covering things—how have you been?"

She stared at the wall behind me, as if trying to decide how much to share. "A while."

My stomach had crawled into my chest cavity and seemed content with staying there. "So, it wasn't just an accident." A statement, a confirmation.

Paris blinked and refocused on me. Her look was clear. *No, this wasn't an accident.* "I knew Ben before I met you. Not well, but through Dallas," she admitted, quietly. "I didn't realize you were his Eliza until after...well, you know.

When I made the connection, I started to make sure you were safe."

"How? How have you been able to do it? SHAP's security system is supposed to be hackproof."

"I helped build the system. I know the back entrances and exits."

I blinked at her. "You? Built the security system?" How had we dated for nearly a year and I didn't know this?

She slumped against my desk, as if her legs couldn't hold her upright. "As much as we talked, we didn't *communicate.* At least not more than 'yes, please,' and 'right there.'" Her smile was bitter. "You're so charming, so adept at turning the conversation away from you, and I...wanted us to be on the same level. So, I kept my cards close to my chest, too."

I blinked, cheeks burning from the call out. Keeping people out was a trauma reflex, one that had proven useful time and again. But useful didn't mean healthy. "What a great couple we were."

She released a watery laugh and stood, walking the four steps to the window, staring out across the parking lot. "Yet your claws are still sunk in me so deep, it hurts to breathe."

I leaned against her desk, wrapping my fingers around the edge. "You're not easy to get over either," I admitted. "I can't believe you built the security system."

"Helped. I don't have the expertise to build it from scratch. For that you can thank all the supernaturals. But I worked on programing portions of it, like the employee log in system. I got my masters in both software and electrical engineering."

"You're only thirty-three. You had to come to SHAP

right out of school."

She stuck her hands in her back pockets, still not looking at me. "Graduated high school a year early, spent my summers at computer camps, then sped through undergrad. Computers come easy. It's everything else that's hard." She looked over her shoulder and gave a brief, self-deprecating smile.

I began to reframe how I thought of Paris after the last twenty-four hours. She was used to feeling like a burden, which probably had something to do with her home life. She sped through school and graduated young into a male-dominated field. She didn't seem to have a huge circle of friends but would do a lot to protect people she cared about…like drive to their house during an ice storm.

I could picture a shy, quiet Paris, glasses on, staying home alone with her computer, striving to be the best at what she did, to prove she was worthy of love. Now, adult Paris was using her knowledge and skills to protect me and my daughter. Warmth eased across my chest, and I took a shuddering breath.

I still love you, I didn't say. *Tell me there's hope.*

She removed her hands from her back pockets and wrapped them around her middle. I didn't miss their shaking. I pushed off her desk and walked over to her, sliding my arms around her waist. I pressed my head into the spot between her shoulder blades.

Finally.

"Paris, tell me what happened that night. Please. *Please*," I pleaded. *Tell me so we can somehow move past this. So, I can hear more about your childhood and have more breakfasts together, and spend nights in your arms again.* I hadn't spoken the words aloud, but she'd heard them anyway.

Her hands covered her face for a long moment, and I wondered if she was looking for a future scenario. She gasped, her shoulders rolling forward. She was crying.

I turned her around and pulled her into my arms like she did to me the night before, running my hands through her hair and rocking her gently back and forth. "Talk to me, honey," I begged in a low voice.

She fisted my coat at the use of her nickname. Then, she sank into me as if she'd given up the fight. "Dallas texted me 'if anything happens, you were always my favorite sister'. I tried calling him, but he didn't answer. I broke several national security laws finding his location."

I held her tighter. If Jake ever texted me that…I didn't know what I would do. Thank god Paris had been there to save him. I kissed the top of her head, a secret thank you as she continued her story.

"I found him, cause I'm fucking great at computers."

I laughed softly. "You are."

She sucked in a broken breath and let it out slowly. "I followed him and…" She shook her head.

Her voice was barely louder than the sound of my breath, so I held it, desperate for answers. I squeezed her tighter, hoping to encourage her to continue.

"I don't even understand what I saw."

The weight of her words slammed into me like a cannonball, knocking all the breath from my body. "What did you see?"

"I was at an angle and couldn't see anyone's faces. It was

an abandoned warehouse. I recognized the backs of Dallas and Ben, and they had three guns pointed at them. I didn't have a lot of weapons, but I had smoke bombs. I threw two then grabbed my brother, and Ben ran out after us."

"You threw smoke bombs at people with guns?" I asked, incredulously.

"Simple but effective." She swiped at the tears on her face with force. "Ben carried me out, refusing to let me help. Then, he followed me to make sure we weren't tailed, but we were. I saw the headlights. As soon as I got past the bridge, I heard crunching metal." She paused, her body shaking. "He was just gone."

I was crying now, and we both gripped on to each other as if an ocean was trying to tear us apart.

"I tried to get to him," she promised. "The water was so cold. I thought I had him, but it was too dark and I was out of air. I-I only came up with his coat."

Each word slammed into my chest with the force of an air gun. Ben had died trying to protect her, trying to make sure his friend's sister was safe. It was heroic, and it proved just what an amazing man he'd been. And Paris dove into a freezing river in the dark to try and rescue him.

"If I hadn't been there, he wouldn't have—" a sob cut her off.

"You didn't ask him to follow you? You didn't know he was there until you showed up?" I had to know.

She shook her head.

Everything I thought I knew about that night had been wrong. I assumed Paris was the one who'd led him there, had targeted him specifically. That she'd somehow arranged for him to be on the bridge with her. But it was Dallas and Ben who'd made the decision. Paris was only trying to do what she did best—protect her loved ones.

The truth washed over me in a wave so unexpected, I lost my breath. *She hadn't killed Ben.* And she likely saved her twin's life, too by giving him the upper hand.

I sucked in air, and it felt like the first breath I'd taken in five months. "You didn't kill him. If you hadn't been there, it's likely you would've lost Dallas, too."

She pulled back and stared at me, face splotched red and damp with tears. She was still the most beautiful woman I'd ever seen. "What did you say?"

Her expression was contorted in misery, but not deception. I raised my hands to cradle her face. She closed her eyes and pressed a soft kiss to my right palm. Using my thumbs, I brushed away the newest tears. "It's not your fault," I whispered.

Her eyes opened and she searched mine for a long moment. Then, she reached out, dug into my hair, and brought her mouth to mine.

Finally, finally, finally.

The missing piece of my heart snapped back into place with a jolt. I cried out when her lips moved against mine. Relief flooded through me, extinguishing the ball of anger in my chest and making my head spin. This wasn't a sexy kiss, but a teeth-mashing, sloppy, desperate reconnection. I fisted her shirt, desperate to be closer, futilely wishing we could somehow go back in time and not waste nearly half a year apart.

"Why didn't you tell me?" I asked, sucking in air and

then kissing her again for a long moment before moving my lips to the soft skin below her jaw. She tasted sweet, like honey, like hope.

She tilted her head back and sucked in a sharp breath. "How could I tell you I was the reason your fiancé was dead?"

"But you're not." I kissed her lips again. "And we've lost so much time."

"We did." She wrapped her arms around my back, lifting me a few inches off the ground as her lips returned to mine. She parted me with her tongue, kissing me deep.

Moments led to minutes led to memories, with our hands gripping and caressing, our mouths only separating for desperate gasps of air. I'd never forget this homecoming. Panting, she set me back on the ground, burying her face in my neck.

"What changed?" I asked when I'd found oxygen again.

"This morning."

"Tell me we're not too late to fix us."

She kissed my neck then raised her forehead to mine. "I don't want to be without you anymore. But maybe we should take time to recover."

I pressed my lips against hers. "We've had five months."

"Let's not rush this," she whispered, her voice shaking.

"Why not?" I asked, my nose bumping hers.

"It's too much at once." She leaned back, those few inches more like miles. "I just need some space."

Space from me. Some old, familiar hurt resurfaced. Ben's voice bounced around in my head. *I just need some space. This family, this job, it's suffocating sometimes.*

He'd wanted space. Just like Paris did now.

I smoothed down my shirt and rubbed my hands on the front of my pants. "Okay. Whatever you need." *Please don't do this*, I thought, but it was too late. I could see it in her face. She had put back up her walls.

I knew better than to let anyone in, yet I kept making the same mistake over and over again. Drop my guard, get hurt. "I'm going to take the weekend off, then, if you have this under control."

I turned around and left, closing the door hard behind me. The lock sliding home nearly brought me to my knees.

Chapter Twenty

Paris

MY BOOTS PUNCHED the ground as I crossed the parking lot not caring that it was slippery. Surely, my rage would melt any ice that dared get in my way. I finished wrapping my knuckles and then opened the back door, practically ripping it off the hinges.

The gym was closed the Friday after Thanksgiving, which meant I could kick Dallas's ass without witnesses. Or at least the ones who would call the cops. He'd taught me how to fight. He was expecting my right hook if he asked me to meet him here.

The smell of sweat, disinfectant, and body spray filled the hall, a usually comforting scent that just stoked the fire. Our older cousin, Juno, poked her head out of the manager's office. Normally, I'd be excited to see what color she dyed her hair this month, but right now I couldn't even recognize any color.

"Oh shit," she said.

"Where's Dallas Theodore?"

"Not you calling him by his full name? Oh *shit*!"

I didn't have the patience for this. "DALLAS THEO-

DORE!" I shouted.

My cousin pointed in the direction of the boxing ring. "He's with Pete."

I kicked off my boots and tossed them near her office door, then pulled off my socks. My coat dropped somewhere behind me. Juno was hot on my heels. I ignored her.

Pete and Dallas looked up as I approached, and Dallas held up his hands. "P, let's talk about it."

I spread the ropes and stepped in. "Why? So you can figure out another convincing lie?"

"Oh shit!" Pete said, then whistled low.

"That's what I'm saying!" Juno returned.

Dallas backed up. "You don't know the whole story."

The rage of heartbreak, the phone calls where he asked me to drop everything drove me forward. The calm, forgiving, quiet Paris had been replaced by a lion who had just spotted her prey, and she wasn't going to give up until her teeth sank into his neck.

I lifted my arm and punched him in the jaw. "One hundred and sixty-two days since my girlfriend left me because she thought I had something to do with her fiancé's death. And all this time, it was *a lie*?" Even in my anger, I was smart enough not to use names, just in case.

"Oh *shit*!" Juno and Pete said together.

He swore, throwing his arms in front of his face like an amateur. I went for his stomach. He doubled over. "Calm down!" he wheezed.

"That's throwing gasoline on the fire, cuz," Juno warned. "Never tell a woman to calm down.

"I lost the woman I wanted to spend the rest of my life

with because of your bullshit," I growled, "and you couldn't be bothered to tell me the truth."

He recovered and blocked my next two hits but didn't throw a punch. "It's not like that."

"It's exactly like that." I danced around him, throwing out a kick and dropping him to his knees. "Why don't you hit me? Too scared to fight your sister?"

"Because you're hurting enough," he admitted, bouncing back up.

"And you caused it." I released a series of punches and kicks, some legal, some downright dirty.

"Paris, Paris!" Dallas reached out and grabbed my arm, bending it behind my back and locking it in place by putting his other hand on my elbow. "You're going to hurt yourself before you hurt me."

Twisting from my waist, I used my core strength to knock an elbow into the side of his neck, causing him to stumble back and gasp for air. He recovered too quickly, rushing me and wrapped one arm around my shoulders and one around my waist.

I threw my head back, trying to hit his nose, but he leaned back in time. He had taught me how to fight and knew all my moves. I tried to kick him, swing my feet so I could topple us over, but he held tight, shifting his stance to keep me locked down.

"Paris, I'm sorry. I'm so sorry."

At his apology, the anger in my chest splintered into grief and my body ached with the exertion. I burst out crying.

"Oh shit," he sighed, out of breath. He staggered under my weight as I slumped, and slowly lowered me down to the mat. "Stop crying, Paris. You don't cry," he pleaded.

I did, I just usually didn't let anyone see because I didn't want to be a burden, didn't want to affect anyone else with my off-kilter emotions. Today, he could witness what he caused.

"I hate you," I whispered.

I curled my knees up to my chest and rested my forehead on them, letting the sobs wreck me. I hated crying, and I had already done it more this week than I had in months. Ben was alive, and as soon as Eliza knew, she'd stop at nothing to get to him, leaving me behind. The joy of holding her, kissing her today had evaporated into despair. I should scold myself for wishing that he was actually dead, but in that moment I didn't care.

I just wanted this to be over, wanted the heartbreaking blow to be over with. Maybe I'd move out of the country and work for a different SHAP offshoot. No, fuck that, maybe I'd just start an alpaca farm and do like llama yoga or something. Somewhere without snow.

Dallas knelt next to me, hand on my shoulder. "Sis, breathe."

I sucked in a ragged breath. "I deserve to know why."

"You do."

"You can use the office," Juno said, voice so quiet, I could barely hear her over my sobs. "Pete and I are going to go wash towels. On the opposite side of the gym."

"We are?" He made an *oomph* sound as if he'd been elbowed. "I mean, we are. Yeah."

I wiped my snot and tears off my face with my sleeve, not caring. Dallas helped me roll onto my feet and I stood on wobbly legs. My ears were plugged and my face throbbed with the pressure of crying so hard. I'd lost my left contact and the right one was cloudy. Awesome.

Dallas held the ropes apart as I climbed out, then I scooped up my coat, socks, and boots. When we got to the office, I slammed the door, pulled out my phone, and checked for trackers. While I trusted Juno and Pete, there were dozens of people who walked in and out of this gym daily, most SHAP agents. And it'd become increasingly clear that I couldn't trust other agents.

Dallas sat, but I remained standing in the opposite corner. "Speak," I ordered.

"Ben and I met in college, did you know?"

I shook my head. I thought they'd met at work. But he'd had several college friends named Ben, and I never thought much of it.

"He introduced me to SHAP, got me an interview. Even though we were in different departments, we'd still hang out. Grab lunch or a beer after work. One day Celine—one of Ben's lab partners—came along and admitted that the moment her daughter hit puberty, they discovered she was a werewolf. And it was *rough.*"

"Teen hormones and a werewolf gene? Ouch."

"Right? We started bullshitting solutions which eventually turned into playing around in the labs. One night, Ben suggested we look at vampire venom, claiming vampires were the opposite of werewolves, so maybe there was something there. Turns out, there was."

I blinked at him. "You made oral venom?"

He nodded. "We made *successful* oral venom."

I slid down the wall, my legs no longer able to hold me up. "Holy fuck, Dallas." Whatever Glen Somerville had been doing wrong, Dallas and his team had corrected.

"I know." He threw his hands out in front of him, fingers wide, and tensed. "We could have done such amazing things with it. The ability to ease not only werewolf transition but to cure chronic and debilitating illnesses—" he broke off, swallowing hard. "But we knew as soon as we made it that it needed to be destroyed. That the technology would only be perverted and lead to a global crisis."

"People are terrible."

"Yeah, they are." He rubbed hard at his eyebrow, as if he could erase whatever happened next from his mind. "We'd thrown everything into the incinerator and swore we'd never share anything about what happened. We made a pact."

I scooted across the office to sit next to him, my shoulder resting against his knee. Tension eased out of his stance, and he tilted his head back to look up at the ceiling.

"One of the other R&D guys, Russell, didn't come in the following day, or next. After a week, I started searching for him and got jumped for my efforts. Then, got word he was meeting a potential buyer at a warehouse."

"That's when I showed up."

"Yeah." He blew out a long breath. "Should've known you'd find me."

"Why did Ben go over the bridge?"

"He knew the buyer and was worried they'd go after Eliza and Daisy," he admitted. "He never talked about his family at work, always paranoid someone would hurt them. He realized until we silenced Russell and anyone surrounding the venom, his family could always be used as leverage. So he faked his death. It freaked out the buyer, and they ran before the sale was complete. Russell took off with the venom, and we made a plan to track him down."

My chest ached at every twist and turn. "It's like a bad movie."

"A movie would've had a happy ending." He blew out a long breath. "He knew he had to cut Eliza and Daisy off completely to keep them safe."

"And you?" I raised my head to study his face.

He pressed his lips together, a habit we both shared. "Been teaching Ben what I know. He's launched an entire counter operation to gain control of the venom. No one knows his full name. Just goes by Somerset, and there are plenty of those around."

I rubbed the heal of my hand across my chest, trying to ease the ache. "What's the end game?"

"We'd recruited Fletcher, gave her the idea to blow up the warehouse, decimating Russell's main supply. We just needed to get all the remaining venom off the street and destroy it. Then, go after Russell."

"The evidence room."

He nodded. "Assuming you're the only person who caught Ben, all that's left in our plan is eliminating Russell."

"Then it's all over?"

"God, I hope so."

I gripped his knee. "I'm going to be right by your side, okay?"

"Know you will, sis."

"And you're destroying the venom?"

"Yes. It's caused enough harm."

I nodded. "It has."

"And…I'm sorry."

I couldn't tell him it was okay. It wasn't. But it wasn't his fault, not completely. It didn't matter anyway. Nothing changed the fact that when Eliza's dead fiancé came back, she'd be united with her first love, and I would be alone. Again. Still.

"I'm thinking about transferring somewhere far away," I admitted. "Maybe starting an alpaca farm."

"I'll come with you as soon as this case is done. You jump, I jump."

I hugged his legs and nodded. "I'd like that."

Chapter Twenty-One

Eliza

JAKE SAT AT the kitchen table, arms crossed, staring at me while I kneaded the gluten-free bread dough. It had taken me a long time to figure out the best way to work with the sticky substance, but I was a pro at it now. I figured I should have a loaf on hand for Paris just in case she decided she didn't need any more space.

I'd also stocked up on some of her other favorite foods. It definitely wasn't because I was rushing into anything. I liked being prepared.

I knew we both needed time to adjust to this new information, but I wanted more, *needed* more. The anticipation of reconnecting had me climbing out of my skin. I'd cleaned both bathrooms, the inside of my car, the refrigerator, and all the floors today already.

"So, you're just going to skip Mina's birthday party instead of talking to our folks?" Jake prompted, reaching out and snatching the invitation, then holding it between his pointer and middle finger.

I slapped the dough on the counter, pushed the heel of my palm through, and then repeated. Kneading bread was a great way to relieve stress, as long as I didn't throw it at my brother's head, which was becoming harder by the minute.

"I'm not skipping it. I just can't take Daisy, ergo I cannot go."

He tossed the handwritten invitation back onto the table. Carma clearly had a blast creating them, all fancy calligraphy on thick, sparkling cardstock with embossed skulls. She had invited Mina's closest friends to a soft grand opening of the bed and breakfast for Mina's birthday, before the official launch. She "needed time to work out the kinks" she explained.

The only catch was no one under eighteen was permitted. She had called me a few days ago to explain it was an adults-only evening, which I totally understood. But because of Daisy's powers, there were only a few people who could safely babysit her and all of them were going, except my parents. I wasn't in the mood to make amends.

"Call them," Jake ordered.

"No."

"You're just going to burn a good thing because you're stubborn?"

"Sorry I can't forgive and forget like you."

"Haven't forgotten. Just came to terms with the fact they thought they were doing the best thing for us."

I threw the dough down and pointed at him. "They lied to you—to us—for twelve years, probably longer, and you're okay with it?"

"Didn't say I was okay with it."

"You went there for dinner last Sunday, didn't you?"

He nodded once. "Poppy doesn't have any living family.

I'm not going to deprive her of people who care about her—whom she cares about—because of a mistake. A big one, I'll admit. It'll take more than one dinner to heal."

"Are you shitting me right now?" I sucked in a deep, shaky breath, trying to control my volume. Poppy and Daisy were in the next room, and I didn't want Daisy to hear. "Jake, they let you suffer for over a decade."

"I know."

"And that's fine with you?"

He threw his hands up in frustration. "Of course it's not fine with me, but it's done. None of us can go back in time. I'm not going to waste now because of a mistake they made back then. They're not the same people they were when they made that decision, and neither am I. Neither are you."

"And Poppy's fine with this?"

As if summoned, Poppy danced into the kitchen and leaned against the doorframe, the movement so fluid, it was almost ethereal. It was still nearly incomprehensible to have her standing here, in my home, as a human. Well, mostly human. She'd been a grim reaper for so long, I kept expecting her to disappear any moment.

She gestured over her shoulder. "Daisy's engrossed in that show about a ghost band again."

"It's a staple in this house," I admitted.

She gathered her long, dark hair into a top knot and pulled a purple scrunchie around it, then turned her gray eyes to mine. "And Jake's right. We're working through it. You're my only living family, and your parents only ever wanted to protect you. I can't say that I wouldn't have done the same thing in their shoes."

I put the bread into a baking tin and pulled plastic wrap over it, setting it aside to proof. I grabbed my spray bottle and kitchen cloth and started cleaning the gluten-free flour off the counter. My teeth were chomping down on the sides of my cheeks, trying to keep my temper from exploding and creating a bigger mess.

"I know they hurt you," Poppy said. "And you have every right to be upset. You can take all the time you need. But this isn't an all or nothing, black or white situation. Everything is gray."

"It's not fair to keep Daisy from her grandparents," Jake added.

"I have to trust the people who watch my kids," I shot back.

"Outside of this, have they ever given you a reason not to trust them? Especially with Daisy?" Poppy asked.

I scrubbed harder at the countertop, even though it was probably cleaner than it had been since installation. "It only takes one lie to destroy everything. And yes, lies of omission count."

First, my bio dad had lied to my mom about being single when he had another family in another city. Then, my folks had lied about Poppy. Ben lied about his work and wanting to marry me. And then Paris had lied, and it destroyed us. If she'd told me what had happened that night, we wouldn't have lost everything.

Poppy walked over and gently rested her hand on mine, forcing me to stop scrubbing. "Does that mean you're angry at me, too?"

"Why on earth would I be angry at you?"

"Because I lied by omission. I didn't tell you I was a reaper."

I pulled my hand away and walked to the sink to rinse out my cloth. "Please. You weren't allowed to tell me."

"It was still a lie. The same lie your parents told."

"It's different."

"It's not." She rubbed my upper arm. "It's just another gray area."

I threw my cloth into the sink, wiped my hands on a towel, then placed them on my hips. "Fine. Daisy can stay at her grandparents, but," I pointed at Jake, "you're calling and arranging it, and you're dropping her off."

"That's fine with me," he agreed. "This time only."

"How about we take Daisy to spend the night tonight? Give you some time to yourself," Poppy offered.

I dropped my hands from my hips. I didn't want to be alone, didn't want to sit here and think too hard about what Poppy had said. My stubbornness is what got me through the hardest years of my life. But I was in a terrible mood and didn't want to take it out on Daisy. "Sure, fine. She'd love that."

Poppy went to help Daisy pack. Jake pushed away from the table and walked over to me. He wasn't leaning as heavily on his cane as he had been a few weeks ago, and the dark circles under his eyes had receded. He no longer looked like he was about to shatter into a million pieces if hit by a soft breeze. I was so happy for him, but also envious. Whatever was holding me together had cracks covering the surface.

"Just want you to be happy, sis," Jake said, wrapping his

arms around my shoulder.

I wrapped mine around his waist. "I know."

He squeezed before he let go. "Tell Carma you'll be at the opening. I think it'll do you good."

"Yes, Mother."

He pinched my arm. "You're annoying."

I poked his side. "Ditto."

"Mom, Mom!" Daisy called, running over to me. "Aunt Poppy says that her and Uncle Jake have a brand-new couch that can turn into a bed! And they got me *purple* sheets and blankets. Purple is my favorite color. And probably pink. And blue."

"Purple sheets sound very exciting."

"I bet I'll have the best sleep of my life. No, of all time!"

I laughed. "I hope you do."

She hugged me around the waist and was outside before Jake had even walked down the hall. They took all the good feelings with them when they shut the front door.

I stood in the middle of the kitchen, trying not to think about what Poppy said, until someone knocked. "What'd you forget?" I asked, opening it.

Paris held the storm door open and leaned heavily on the doorframe, as if standing was too much. Her hair was damp and tangled, eyes swollen, and a desperate expression on her face.

My entire body clenched at the sight of her. I wanted to wrap her in my arms, kiss her until her eyes softened and the corner of her lips curled.

"Can I come in?" she asked, her voice rough.

She didn't even need to ask. I pushed the door open wider and she stepped inside.

Chapter Twenty-Two

Paris

COMING HERE WAS a terrible idea. I'd been crying since I left the gym. I was so angry at Dallas, even though none of this was his fault. I attempted to take my emotions out on a punching bag instead of his rib cage, but it didn't help. I cleaned my entire house, went on a five-mile run, showered, and made dinner, but still, the rage throbbed against my ribs.

I shouldn't be here. It wasn't fair of me to pretend I wasn't carrying more secrets. But there was only one thing that could take the rage away and she was standing in front of me, with her blue eyes round and bottom lip between her teeth.

The news of Ben's resurrection weighed heavy on my chest, and it took a conscious effort every breath not to blurt out the news. She'd never forgive me for keeping the secret, and I had no doubt she'd figure it out. I needed to tell her, explain the risk of anyone finding out, with Dallas still on the case. She had a right to know and keeping secrets from her always ended badly.

But what if I told her and she went after Ben and got

caught in the crossfire? What if she told Jake or Loren and something happened to one of them? What if Russell caught wind of Eliza and hunted down her and Daisy? What if I couldn't stop something bad from happening to the people I loved?

What if I lost her forever?

"Paris, what's wrong?" Her fingertips stroked my cheek and I nearly cried out at the touch.

I swallowed so hard, it felt like razor blades. I didn't know how to tell her, not yet. "Had a fight with Dallas. Was still pissed, so I tried to take it out on a punching bag. What about you?"

She lifted a shoulder. "Had a fight with Jake."

I nodded. "Brothers," I sighed.

"Yeah." She twisted the bottom of her shirt around her fingers. "He and Poppy took Daisy for the night."

I straightened. That admission shouldn't have changed anything, but it did. The charge that flared between us was proof. I reached out and touched her arm and she didn't push me away. I ran my palm over her skin, moving until I had wrapped my hand over her elbow, and then pulled her closer to me.

"Let me take care of you tonight," I whispered. "It doesn't have to mean anything." I needed to get lost in her, needed to feel her hands on me, needed her soft pants in my ear to chase away the spiraling thoughts. "Please, Eliza."

Her chest rose and fell, nearly touching mine. She lifted her head to stare into my eyes. I let her see all of me; the way I still loved her, how lost I was without her, and how much I still wanted her.

She raised her hand and brushed my hair behind my ear, letting her fingertips trail down my jawline. The touch radiated throughout my entire body, and I closed my eyes. She brought her other hand up and slid it around the back of my neck and I held my breath, scared this was somehow all a dream.

A timer went off in the kitchen and Eliza jumped back, then shook her head laughing. "I'm sorry. The bread's done proving. I just—"

I gestured her toward the kitchen. "By all means." I shrugged off my coat and hung it on a peg by the door, then followed her.

She uncovered a loaf pan and turned on the oven. "Normally, you proof bread twice, but gluten-free can only handle one time. Hopefully, this works."

I leaned my hip against the counter. "Gluten-free?"

She waved away the question. "Wanted to be prepared, just in case."

"You're making me bread?" She was hoping I'd come. She'd been waiting for me. She made me something.

She lifted one shoulder. "Yeah. I figured—" Her words morphed into a squeak as I grabbed her around the waist and pulled her toward me.

"You're making me bread."

She rolled her eyes. "The bar is on the ground if this is what you're freaking out over."

"Eliza?"

"Hm?"

"I'm going to kiss you." Her eyes focused directly on mine before closing. I breathed a sigh of relief at the silent permission and sealed my mouth over hers.

Her lips were warm and soft, so pliant and ready. She had the best lips in the entire world. Her hands went around my shoulders, then one sank into the back of my hair. I eased back then tasted her top lip, nibbled her bottom, sank into her mouth. When her tongue swiped mine, my knees turned to jelly.

I kissed her like she was the most important person in the world. I wrapped her thick curly hair around my hand and pulled it to one side. She made a noise of pleasure that went straight to my center. I broke away from her lips and tasted the soft, sweet skin of her neck. Her head tilted back, exposing more of her throat to me. "It's only bread," she laughed.

"Do you want me to stop? Or would you like me to continue showing you my appreciation?" I asked against the skin of her neck.

She shivered. "Keep going." There was no laughter now. Her hands went under the edge of my shirt, her palms on my back fanning the flames growing in my stomach.

"Do you want my lips all over your body?"

Her hands slid down and cupped my ass, pulling me tight against her. "Everywhere."

I smiled. "Good girl."

She gasped at the phrase, and I felt like a queen. She always loved when I got bossy. I nibbled on her earlobe, then kissed away the sting. "I was tested during our annual physical, and everything came back negative. Haven't been with anyone since."

"Same." She kissed me quickly. "Negative tests and

there's been no one else."

I reached down and pulled off her sweatshirt and shirt in one motion, then immediately unhooked her bra, shoving it down her arms and tossing it away. "God, I've missed these."

My mouth and tongue took over as I followed the curve of her breast with my lips, circling but not reaching the peak before shifting to the other side. I moved up to her collarbone then down to her ribs, teasing her with the pads of my fingers and soft lips. Her breathing sped, her hands gripping my waist even harder.

I inched toward her nipple, ready to pull her into my mouth and stroke her higher, when the oven beeped. I paused, just over the taut skin. "Do you need to deal with that?"

She whimpered in protest. "If I don't, the bread will be ruined."

I licked my lips, the underside of my tongue brushing the sweet, pink skin. "Pity, because the only thing I want to ruin tonight is you."

Her grip didn't loosen, and I held perfectly still, waiting to see what she wanted to do. I didn't care about bread nearly as much as having my mouth on her. With a groan she released me and moved to the oven, opening the door and tossing the bread inside.

She aggressively set a timer and then stomped back over to me. "We have thirty minutes."

I smiled at her, grabbed her by the hips, and moved her to the counter. I picked her up and placed her on top. "We better stay in this kitchen then, so we don't miss the timer." I spread her legs and stepped between them, lowering my head to suck on her collarbone.

"We can't—we can't—on the counter," she panted, as I caressed her breast, then lowered my mouth to lavishing one, then the other.

"Every time you're in this kitchen, I want you to think about me making you come apart," I growled into her soft skin. When all this was over, after the truth came out, and Ben came home, I wanted her to think of this moment. I wanted her cheeks to burn every time she made bread.

Was it selfish as hell? Yes. I may not have been her big love, but she was mine.

"Take off your pants," I ordered. I grabbed a kitchen chair as her hands unbuttoned her jeans.

I was dizzy with anticipation as I helped her tear them off her body. "God, you're so beautiful," I breathed reverently as I kissed her ankle and moved up her legs with my hands and mouth. "I've missed you."

I nipped her thigh and she sucked in a sharp breath. "Now then, I wonder if I can make you come at the exact same time the timer goes off."

Her eyes widened. "That's like twenty-six minutes!" her voice went higher, betraying her excitement. This wasn't something we got to do a lot of with Daisy down the hall, usually it was as fast and quiet as possible, but tonight we were alone.

"I'm going to enjoy making you beg," I promised, sucking the skin inches away from where she needed me most, leaving a hickey.

She moaned. "Just give me a small orgasm first, please."

I licked her once along her seam, as if she were my favorite ice cream on a hot summer's day. "Fuck, I've missed how you taste. My favorite meal." I repeated the motion.

She reached down to touch herself, but I knocked her hand away. "My turn."

I put her legs over my shoulders and took my time exploring, tasting, savoring her. My hands moved up and down her body, trailing fingers over her skin, cupping her breasts, and massaging her ass.

Her fingers threaded through my hair and held on as I brought her close, then backed off. She whimpered as she got *close, so close*, then I moved back to kissing her thighs, her stomach, her lips. A third time, a fourth.

Her skin was flushed pink, her thighs squeezing tight around my ears, her hands tugging almost punishingly at my hair. It was the most erotic thing I'd ever seen and my body ached with need.

She tossed her head back and forth. "Please, please, please, honey, please." She sobbed, tears at the corner of her eyes.

I glanced at the timer. Perfect. "Call me honey again," I ordered.

"Please, honey. I need you, honey."

I moaned against her and slipped my fingers inside. She arched at the new sensation, her pants turning into desperate pleas. I put my other arm over her hips to keep her anchored as I brought her up one more time.

Her skin was damp, her words coming out in nonsensical phrases, "please" and "honey, I need" and "only you."

I lifted my head to check the timer. Close, so close. "You have less than a minute. If we miss it, I'll just have to stop and try again."

"No, no, please." Her words were more breath than voice.

"Then come," I ordered, sucking her favorite place into my mouth and curling my fingers in exactly the way she needed.

Her legs trembled and her entire body tightened around my fingers. I needed air, but I didn't dare let up. If this was how I died, that was fine with me. She ground into my mouth, and I just kept giving. Then, she detonated.

She screamed so loud, the wine glasses in her cabinet rattled. I kept sucking and licking as she grabbed at anything and everything, her entire body tensing and releasing, arching and throbbing. She tried to push me away but I shook my head.

"Again," I ordered.

She shook her head. Tears of pleasure ran down her cheeks and she covered her face with her hands. "There, there, there, right there, honey. Don't stop. I can't. I can't. Don't—don't—"

I smiled. I knew her body. Knew exactly what she loved and needed.

This time, it was a deep, low moan, from the place of euphoria where she could no longer talk. She drowned out the ring of the timer and I couldn't take my eyes off her. I tried to memorize this moment for nights where it was just me and my showerhead. This beautiful woman, wrung out on the kitchen counter, completely bared and unselfconscious in front of me.

I didn't want to stop, couldn't bear the thought of pulling away now, but I didn't want to be the reason the bread burned, especially after she went through the trouble of making it. Besides, we were going to need sustenance when I was done with her.

With a groan, I lifted my head, licked her off my hands, and kissed the tops of her thighs. "Let me get the bread out and we can continue."

I grabbed an oven mitt, removed the bread from the oven, and placed it on top of the stove. I made sure everything was turned off, then returned to her.

She was resting on her elbows, watching me. "We need to let it cool for a few, then turn it over on a cooling rack and—"

"It'll be fine." I walked over, grabbed her chin, and kissed her like the world was going to end and this was our last goodbye. For me, it truly felt like it. "Do you still have your favorite toy?"

Her breathing sped. She nodded.

"I want to see if I can make you lose your voice from screaming my name."

She shook her head and fisted my shirt in her hands. "Later. It's my turn." She slid off the counter, slipped her hand into mine, and led me to her bedroom.

As I lost myself to the feeling of her mouth, her bare skin against mine, the sound of my name on her tongue, I forgot about everything except this moment. Tonight was about us. Tomorrow could wait.

Chapter Twenty-Three

Eliza

IT WAS STRANGE waking up next to someone who wasn't Daisy. The first thing I noticed was a soft hand on my arm. I opened my eyes to see Paris, dark hair spread over the pillow, her pink lips parted, the constant frown between her brows relaxed. She was on her stomach, face toward mine, her left hand on my upper arm.

I smiled. The right side of my bed wasn't empty. It had *her*.

Paris always was in contact when we slept. Her hands or legs or feet stretched out toward me, as if she couldn't stand to be apart. I pressed my fingertips against my swollen lips. I shifted, wincing at my stiff muscles. The counter sex had been amazing, and a night spent making love had been worth it, but I should've stretched my back and neck before bed.

I turned on my side to face her. *I would give anything to wake up next to you every morning. Can we try again? Are we too late?*

She stirred and opened her eyes, then smiled. "You watching me sleep, you creep?"

I stuck my tongue out at her. "You look happy when you

sleep."

"I'm happy when I'm awake, too." She reached out and pulled me into her until our breasts pressed together and our legs entwined. She kissed my neck and skated her hand lower, cupping me between my legs. "Too sore?"

I winced a little at her touch. "Yes, but I'm willing to give it a try anyway."

She smiled against my skin and my entire body shivered. "Good girl."

Those two words brought me to the edge. My hand moved down and mirrored hers, and as the sun rose higher, we did too. While the landing was more subdued than last night, it was still delicious.

"I don't want to leave this bed today," I admitted.

"Me neither." As if on cue, her stomach grumbled. "Think a delivery person would bring us food in bed?"

"Maybe if we tip extra," I teased. I kissed her slowly, savoring the feel of her lips. "I'm going to the bed and breakfast tonight for Mina's birthday. Come with? I'm allowed to bring a plus one."

"What about Daisy?"

"Adults only. Daisy's staying with my folks." I kissed her again. "Plus, I bet we'll get one big bed."

She laughed and brushed my hair away from my face. "I'm glad Daisy's with your family. Did you talk to them yet?"

I pressed my finger to her lips. "Don't ruin the morning. But no. Jake is handling it."

She didn't say anything, just kissed the tip of my finger.

"I know," I sighed. "I'll try."

She opened my hand and kissed the palm. "Good." Another kiss. "And yes, I'll go with you tonight. Even though I should probably be working."

"Fuck the case. Let's just have a night together and we'll deal with it on Sunday."

"Okay. Deal." With a groan, she sat up.

"No, don't do that." I tried to tug her back down.

"But if I get up, I can make us breakfast."

"Hmm. I'm listening."

"Then we can shower. I need to run home and pack a bag, but we can tag-team all the chores, and then we're free."

It sounded like the Saturdays we used to share. So simple and ordinary but perfect. Paris called when she said she would, showed up when she promised, and wasn't constantly looking at her phone or sitting around waiting to be told what needed to be done. She was by my side, ready to work or play or relax with me. She enthusiastically wanted to share her time with *me*.

I reached out and touched her wrist. "Hey, wait."

She turned to face me. "Hmm?"

"I don't know what this is," I gestured between us, "and I know it's probably way too early to talk about but…I would be open to trying things again. But we can't keep secrets, not like last time. It has to be all or nothing."

She searched my face for a long moment. "Can I ask you a question?"

Not the answer I was expecting, but I nodded.

"If Ben hadn't…" she trailed off, "and we'd met. What would've happened?"

I chewed on the inside of my lip, unsure how to answer.

"I think that it's a moot point because there are too many unknowns," I finally explained. "Ben and I weren't perfect, but he was Daisy's dad, and I would've done anything to make sure he was in her life."

She nodded but didn't meet my eyes.

"But you love me in a way he couldn't," I added. "We fit together perfectly."

Her smile lit her face. "We do."

I kissed her. "It doesn't matter what would have happened. This is what did happen."

"Okay." She scooted out of bed and threw on one of my shirts. "I'll be back with breakfast soon."

IT WAS ONE of those warm hug days. The kind where everything just works, where you don't want the day to end because these moments were so rare. Breakfast—and the bread—were delicious. We used up all the hot water in the shower as Paris and I washed and savored each other. We had moved to the bed shortly after and been so enthusiastic, we'd knocked my lamp off my side table and broken the bulb.

After vacuuming and cleaning up, we went to Jake and Poppy's for lunch, where Sebastian was teaching Daisy how to reenact Titanic. My girl looked exhausted but happy. The ghosts tried to get Paris and me to reenact the door scene, but we kept laughing too hard and Reggie told us we were "disrespectful to the creative process."

"How's she doing?" I asked Jake.

"Went to bed early, slept late," he admitted. "Otherwise, no change."

I watched her laugh as Sebastian melted through the floor, pretending to sink into the ocean. "Hopefully the vitamins help until we can find something more permanent."

"I hope so, too."

When Jake left to drop Daisy at our parents, Paris and I headed back to my place to grab our stuff. Then, it was time for Mina's birthday weekend.

The bed and breakfast had been draped in twinkle lights and every window had a battery powered candle. Carma opened the new ornately carved front door and gestured us in. I stopped two steps in and stared.

I'd been visiting since they started remodeling the bed and breakfast, but I still wasn't prepared for the magic. All the drop cloths, paint buckets, toolboxes, and dust were gone. A large fire roared in a stone fireplace, pouring heat and a soft glow into the main entrance. The foyer had a Christmas tree so large, I couldn't wrap my arms around it. Black and gold ribbons cascaded from the treetop to the bottom branches, and matching rhinestone skulls of various sizes had been hung with precision.

An ornate, polished reception desk, decorated with green garland and black bows, had been fitted with computers and sleek phones. Two employees with black suits waited for guests, while two more moved through the large foyer offering cups of hot mulled wine. The scent of cloves and orange trailed behind them. The glittering chandeliers that dangled from the ceiling bathed everything in a soft glow.

"It's like a fairy tale," Paris breathed, looking around in

awe.

"It really is," I agreed.

Loud male laughter cut through the peacefulness, and we looked up to see Sebastian and Reggie sliding down the banister of the winding staircase. Well, Sebastian was sliding down. Reggie was more sliding through.

"We gotta keep practicing, Mano," Reggie said, reaching the bottom. Sebastian slid off and stumbled through him, making them both laugh.

"This is what Carma gets for not specifying what *kind* of haunted bed and breakfast she wanted," Mina teased, coming into the hall. "Maybe we should've gone with a circus theme."

"What did you expect, mi Minita?" Reggie called.

Mina sighed and shook her head. "My mistake for forgetting ghosts act like twelve-year-olds!"

"Please. I did this until I was sixteen," Sebastian defended. "Made two butlers quit before my mother put a stop to it by installing decorative globes at regular intervals."

"Smart woman," Mina shot back, before turning to us. "Welcome, friends, to the chaos." Her blonde faux hawk had been curled and her brown eyes sparkled under the chandeliers. She glowed, rosy cheeks on fair skin.

"Happy birthday!" I wrapped her in a quick hug, smoothing my hand over the red velvet tuxedo jacket she wore over a black jumpsuit. "This is lovely."

She smiled and tugged at the coat. "This one has some memories attached to it." She turned to Paris. "So glad you decided to join us."

"How much is it killing you to not ask eight-hundred

questions about why she's here?" I asked.

Mina closed her eyes. "So much. So, so much." She opened them and winked at me. "You only get a reprieve for the next twenty-four hours. Just an FYI."

"Will you make it?" I teased.

She nodded solemnly. "It's a sacrifice I'm willing to endure so I don't risk upsetting Carma's perfectly scheduled evening." She glanced at her phone. "Which I am about to do if I don't get my ass in gear." She waved at a person behind the desk. "Jasmine, check in for Eliza Robinson and guest."

"Yes, Mina," Jasmine replied and turned to us. "I have your key right here. Do you need help with your luggage?"

We only had one suitcase and a backpack of snacks for Paris—traveling without a child required so much less stuff—so I shook my head. "We're fine."

Mina took the key from Jasmine and gestured for us to follow. "Come on. You're on the third floor. Paris, you're going to love the view."

"I'm sure I will," Paris replied, grabbing the suitcase in one hand, and entwining the other around mine.

I nearly tripped up the stairs at the casual way she slipped back into my life, as if she'd been gone for a day instead of half a year. That warm-hug-day feeling washed over me again. I pulled out my phone, opened the camera, and tugged Paris to a stop. "Quick selfie."

I took the picture then looked up to find Mina staring at me as if she'd seen a dinosaur.

"Twenty-three hours and fifty minutes," she warned. "Expect a call. Consider it my birthday present."

"I already emailed you a Café Eleonora gift card on your actual birthday."

"Yes, thank you, I loved it, but this is better," she rushed out as if it were one word instead of an entire sentence.

I stuck my tongue out at her and Paris laughed. I lifted her hand to my mouth and kissed her inner wrist. Her smile deepened, her gaze holding mine.

"Okay, keep your bras on until you get to your room," Mina laughed. "This has my favorite bathroom. Make sure to tell Poppy how much you like it. She's nervous as hell."

Mina slipped the skeleton key into the thick wooden door, then opened it wide. Paris and I both gasped. It was a stunning white marble, dark wood room, with a deep green floral-print canopy bed, matching green seating area near a large picture window, and gold furnishings. A glass-front gas fireplace burned in a white stone hearth across from the bed. While the fireplace was original to the house, they'd changed to a gas insert for guest safety.

Paris set down the suitcase next to the bed and followed me into the bathroom, where we stood shoulder to shoulder in awe. The entire room was cream with decorative white molding. Three thin, tall windows covered in lace sat behind a sparkling claw foot tub in the center of the room. A chandelier hung over a damask cream and dark wood chaise. A gold cart hosted rolled, plush towels, baskets with toiletries, and a vase of fresh white roses.

Opposite the chaise was an ornate cream and gold two drawer dresser that had been turned into a sink, with a large gilded mirror on top. To the right of the sink, a cream and dark wood screen separated the toilet from the rest of the room.

I turned to look at Mina, who had her phone out, clearly recording. "I'm glad I have you speechless on video. No one would believe me otherwise."

"I would throw something at you, but I'm busy ogling," I retorted.

"Love you back." She put her phone away and set the door key down. "Key's on the dresser. You've got an hour before cocktails start in case you wanted to test the tub. There's hypoallergenic bubble bath in the bottom of the cart." She laughed as she let herself out the door.

Paris immediately turned and tugged me into her using my beltloops, then kissed me as if I was oxygen itself. When she finished, she dropped a peck on the tip of my nose. "Shall I run us a bath?"

I'd forgotten what it was like to be cherished, and in less than twenty-four hours Paris had completely turned my life upside down. Again. "No, I'll run us a bath. It's my turn to take care of you."

I kissed her quick, then turned on the tub's faucet. She left the room and returned in only a robe, hair pulled into a clip high on her head, a few tendrils caressing her neck. "I hung our dresses for tonight and set an alarm for forty-five minutes." She dropped her phone on the chaise.

"Always so smart," I cooed. My gaze landed on the belt of the robe. The bow she'd tied at her waist made her look like a present, and I couldn't wait to unwrap her. I turned off the water and walked over to her.

My hands tugged at the tie, releasing it, and spreading the robe wide. I pushed the cloth off her shoulders, letting my fingers follow down her entire back until I reached her hips. Her mouth parted with a soft inhale and I sucked her bottom lip into my mouth.

"Get in the tub," I ordered.

She looked a little dazed until I guided her forward. She eased into the hot water, the bubbles gathering around her. My breath escaped me as I took in the scene. It was like something out of a movie, a dream.

She let out a breathy laugh. "What?"

"I've never seen anyone so beautiful," I admitted. I know I'd gone from zero to sixty in less than a day, and I didn't care. Tonight was for dreams.

She bit her lip and looked down, the tops of her ears turning pink. I tore off my clothes, leaving them in an ungraceful pile next to the robe, and climbed in behind Paris. The water was the perfect temperature—just shy of lava hot. I leaned against the back of the tub, then wrapped my arms around Paris's waist and guided her to lean back against me.

I ran my fingertips all over her skin. Down her neck, across her collarbone, down her arms, over her palms. She hummed, closed her eyes, and turned so her forehead was against my neck. I kissed her, then continued administering soft, soothing touches.

"I could stay like this forever," she whispered.

"Me too." Another kiss. "How did we end up back here so fast?"

She smiled. "I've always been here, waiting for you." She opened her eyes and looked at me. "Just took you a minute to catch up."

My hands stilled. "I wish you would've told me what had really happened sooner."

"Me too. I just...I'd promised Dallas I wouldn't."

"It's okay. We have now." I kissed her softly. "God, I've missed this."

"Baths?" she laughed.

I rolled my eyes. "No, just being with you. Taking care of you." *Loving you.* I didn't say the last one out loud, but I swore she heard it anyway.

"Me too." She pressed a light kiss to my neck. "Being able to touch you whenever I want is a gift I'll never take for granted again."

I rested my head against hers as my heart drummed a joyous beat. This was my happy place. Warm bath, Paris in my arms, soft conversations. These were the moments where I felt treasured, even if I was doing the treasuring. My heart reached through my chest and wrapped around Paris's, and my entire body relaxed. Muscles I didn't know I had released the tension and anger they'd been clinging to for the last six months.

It had never been like this with Ben. We never just stopped to hold each other, to soak each other in. We sure as hell never took a bath together. Intimacy with him had been only about the physical. I pushed the thought away. I didn't want to think about him anymore.

Not tonight. Not with Paris in my arms.

She scooped up a bubble on the surface and held it in her hand. "Bubbles are so cool."

I grinned against her shoulder. "You're about to explain how bubbles work, aren't you?"

"Yes. I absolutely am."

As she spoke, I sent thoughts to whoever was listening. *Please let me keep her.*

Chapter Twenty-Four

Paris

IT TOOK EVERY ounce of willpower to put clothes back *on* and head downstairs to the party. I wanted to stay in this room, this little cocoon Eliza and I had made. We were safe here, safe from the case and the outside world and impending heartbreak.

I knew, however, that tonight was important. Not only for her, but for my place in the group as well. When Eliza discovered Ben was alive and broke things off, I'd like to keep Jake as a friend. Working so closely with someone in such an intense situation really bonded two people.

After helping Eliza dry off, we changed. I pulled on a simple long-sleeve black dress.

"I know it's December," Eliza said, "but this dress is too cute for a sweater."

I looked up and stared. She wore a dark blue sleeveless dress with a generous V-neck and thick straps at her shoulders. It hugged her from her breasts to her knees. "You…I…"

The corner of her mouth lifted. "So, you like it?"

I ran my hands over her hips and pulled her close so I

could whisper in her ear. "When we get back upstairs, I'm going to get on my knees and show you how much I like that dress." She shivered when I pressed my lips behind her ear.

"What if you just show me now?"

"Because we'd never make it downstairs." I kissed her gently, too gently. I wanted to mess up her lipstick and have it smeared all over my mouth. With a growl, I forced myself to take a step back. "We need to leave this room, like now."

She laughed and opened the door, and I followed her out. I slipped my hand in hers like it had every right to be there.

Mina spotted us first, checked her phone, and grumbled, "Twenty-one hours and forty-five minutes."

Carma was dressed in a black lace long-sleeve dress with green embroidered flowers, a sharp contrast to her pale white skin. As a vampire-hybrid, she couldn't spend a lot of time in the sun. Her long, thick brown hair was artfully pinned in an updo, with matching green flowers—the same color as her eyes—threaded through. She rubbed Mina's back and kissed her cheek. "I know. It's torture."

Carma walked over to us. "You both look so beautiful." She hugged Eliza, then gripped my hands and kissed my cheek. "Jake sent your dietary restrictions ahead. Has anything changed?"

I caught my breath. These little kindnesses were continually surprising me. It was such a strange feeling to be taken care of, instead of being the caretaker. "No, uh, nothing has changed," I managed after an awkward silence.

She looped her arm through mine. "Good. I had your meal prepared first, so there was less risk of cross contamination." She led me into the front room. "Everything on the small round table is for you. Chef typed out what was in each of the dishes and how it was prepared. If you need anything, she's still in the kitchen. Just find me, okay?"

I looked at the table, which had soup, salad, small triangled sandwiches, desserts, and snacks. I was silent for a long moment, taking in the printed cards in front of each dish with all the dietary information. "I—" My throat had tightened past the point of making complete sentences.

Carma squeezed my arm and dropped it. "You're part of the group now. We look out for our own." She turned to Eliza. "You're welcome to anything here or on the main buffet." She gestured to a long table on the opposite side of the room. "Just use a fresh plate."

"Of course, thanks," Eliza returned.

I hesitated and then asked, "Are Amber, George, and Belphegor coming?"

Carma smiled. "Belphegor didn't want to have a sleepover like he's 'a damn human child' when he can sleep in his 'perfectly good cave'. He promised to bring the Andrews by tomorrow morning."

I smiled. "That sounds like him."

Carma laughed and agreed, then excused herself. I turned and faced the table of food made just for me.

Eliza pressed into my side and wrapped her arm around my waist. "You okay?"

I wanted to keep things light tonight. Make it a good night without bringing in the darkness from the outside world. Yet, I found myself confessing, "I haven't talked to my mom since Thanksgiving. Not really. A few texts only."

She squeezed my waist. "It didn't go well."

"Nope." I sighed. "Not at all."

"I'm sorry."

"It's nice to feel welcome."

She leaned up and gave me a quick kiss.

"Well, well, well." We turned around to see Poppy smirking. "Would you look at that."

Eliza rolled her eyes. "Stop."

Jake walked up and slipped his arm around Poppy, then threw Eliza a shit-eating grin. "Unlike Mina, I have zero problems giving you shit tonight." He nodded at me. "Paris, I'm so glad you could make it. You're welcome to come hang with us when you're tired of Eliza."

Eliza eyed a cracker on the end of my table then eyed Jake.

"It's okay," I whispered. "You can throw it."

She beamed, then picked it up and chucked the cracker at Jake. He stepped forward, shifted to the left, and caught it in his mouth, then winked at me.

I burst out laughing. Eliza stuck her tongue out at him. Poppy just shook her head but gazed at him with adoration. "He'll be impossible to live with now."

"You love me," he teased.

"I do," she responded.

As if sensing someone behind her, she turned and looked over her shoulder. I followed her gaze to see Loren and his wife, Raine, enter the room. I tensed. I knew they could be here for a social visit, but something in my gut told me otherwise.

Loren walked over and hugged Jake then pulled me into

a tight hug, too. "Glad to see you," he said.

"Likewise," I agreed, the smile on my face genuine, despite my stomach tightening. "Let me introduce my date for the evening, and Jake's sister, Eliza."

While they spoke, Raine greeted Poppy and me with tight hugs.

Then, Raine pulled out her phone and took pictures of the food table. "Fenton will love this." She laughed at my expression. "You look a little overwhelmed."

I laughed in return. "I guess I am. I'm so used to being alone."

"I understand. They just kind of suck you in. I got two brothers the moment I married Loren."

"Ah yes. Brothers. My twin is everything to me, even when I plot ways to smother him in his sleep."

She laughed harder. "It's one of my favorite pastimes." She looked around the room. "This place is breathtaking. I bet the acoustics are amazing, too."

Mina walked over, a smile on her face but her eyes serious. "It's nice to finally meet some of the Hayvenwood crew." While Loren had assisted on the venom case during Mina's tenure, they hadn't yet met in person.

She turned to Raine. "You're the musician, right?"

"That's me."

"Carma just brought in a beautiful pianoforte from the 1800s. The instrument also came with a friend. We haven't been able to get the ghost to talk, but I'm hoping you playing something may bring them out of their shell." She leaned closer and stage whispered, "And none of us can play."

Raine's eyes were practically hearts. "That would be pretty awesome. Would love to give it a go."

Loren moved close to me and tilted his head for Jake to join. Loren's face was a mask, and I couldn't tell if he was about to share he'd scored tickets to the Super Bowl or the sun was due to explode next week. He tucked Raine into his side and she smoothed the front of his coat, but her jovial expression had vanished.

Shit.

Jake had his gray cane tonight, the one with the recording device and small sword inside. We exchanged a look, and I knew immediately we were thinking the same thing. This wasn't a vacation. This was business *disguised* as a vacation.

Jake held up his cane and Loren nodded, giving silent permission to record the conversation. Jake twisted the top of the cane and placed it in the center of our small huddle. I wrapped my arm around his waist to provide him with balance, in case he needed it. He leaned into me just a little.

I looked up at Mina, who stepped away from the group to talk with an employee. It was clear she was doing this for show and would be listening to every word.

"I have an update on things in Hayvenwood," Loren said. "Met with August, head of the werewolf pack, before we drove down. Had asked them to keep me posted on any changes with the hybrid wolves. They'd been keeping to themselves since the explosion, hunting deer and other forest animals, but not moving closer to town, which was good."

"But?" I prompted.

"No one has seen a hybrid wolf in eight days," Loren continued. "No tracks, no animal kills, no excrement, no sound. Nothing. They've vanished."

I swayed on my feet, the vision of wolves roaming through the piles of dead bodies of almost everyone here as fresh in my mind as when I woke up the first time. The sour tang of blood filled my nostrils. If they weren't in Hayvenwood, it meant they were on the move.

Eliza slipped her arm around my waist and squeezed. "Breathe, honey. It's okay. You're safe here."

"What's wrong?" Jake asked.

"She's been having nightmares," Eliza explained. "My guess is about the wolves."

I nodded, unable to open my mouth without a scream coming out.

"When you're ready to talk about it, I'm here," Jake added.

Again, I nodded, but that was a lie. I would *never* be ready to talk about it.

"Don't worry, Paris," Loren continued. "I requested the pack expand their borders and keep looking. They've agreed. My brothers are combing through satellite images. Wanted to come tell you in person, so when Carma extended an invitation to us, it was the perfect opportunity."

Loren looked around the room, then returned his attention to the group. "Hazel's working the bar, keeping her ear to the ground, and reporting local gossip. She's been spreading the word that they're looking for information through the supernatural side of town. Grayson's on the hunt. Fenton and Romi are heading toward Applechester, stopping in the smaller towns along the way to check in. Raine and I are going to the west side of the state tomorrow morning to follow a tip."

Jake turned the knob of his cane, turning off the recorder. "What would you like us to do?"

"You protect your family." He turned to me. "Same to you. Don't know what any of this means, but I suspect it's something to do with the venom."

Jake turned to Eliza. "You and Daisy are moving in with us. Or us with you. Take your pick."

She opened her mouth to protest, based on her frown, but I squeezed her hand. "I'll stay with her, okay?"

He eyed me. "You're one of the only other people I trust to take care of my sister."

"Excuse me, I can take care of myself," Eliza grumbled.

Jake pointed at me. "She's got better aim and can fight dirty. It's her or me, Eliza."

"Fine! Her."

"Sorry to ruin the night," Loren said. "I was afraid if I didn't say something now, I'd miss my chance." Raine whispered something in his ear, and he nodded. "I think that's a great idea."

She kissed his cheek then turned to the group. "Let's try to enjoy the rest of the night. Mina, will you show me to the pianoforte?"

Mina turned to face the group with a nearly believable smile. "It's just across the hall." She linked arms with Raine and led the way.

"I should find Sebastian and Reggie," Jake surmised. "Activate the ghost network. If the hybrids make it to populated areas, we could have major casualties."

"Last I saw, they were sliding down the banister," I mentioned.

"None of what you said should surprise me," Jake said. "And yet..."

We all walked out of the door and into the hall, glancing up at the stairs. It had been nearly two hours since check in, but Sebastian and Reggie were still having fun. Sebastian slid down on his head, top hat and all, then somersaulted off the end, landing on his feet. We all clapped. With a big grin, he turned to face us and then bowed.

"Show off!" Reggie called, completing his turn on his stomach.

"Pizzazz!" Sebastian returned.

The airy music of a pianoforte filled the hall. Sebastian stilled and tilted his head toward the sound. "I have not had the pleasure of hearing this instrument in decades. I didn't realize Carma had acquired one."

We crowded around the parlor, Raine practically becoming one with the instrument. She swayed as she played a popular Sorry Charlie song, one of the group's favorite bands. It sounded entirely new on this instrument. The light melody was reminiscent of a harpsicord over a modern piano.

Then, without warning, the mashing of high notes and a high-pitched shout. Raine jumped up from the stool with her hands in the air.

A ghost of a woman in a blue gown appeared, scolding Raine. "You should have asked first."

"You're right. I'm so sorry." Raine stood and gestured to the bench. "Would you please play something for us?"

The ghost hesitated then sat down, immediately sliding

her fingers over the keys in a tune she'd clearly been playing for a very long time. Bitter cold went through me as Sebastian moved between us, moving to stand in the center of the room, mouth agape.

He pulled his hat off, his face slack with shock. As if she could feel his gaze, the ghost looked up and shot upright, her song ending mid-stanza. "Sebastian?" she gasped.

"Evie?" he breathed. "My Evie."

THE ENTIRE NIGHT had taken a nosedive after the conversation with Loren, but then jumped back into the stratosphere as Sebastian reconnected with the one who'd gotten away. Sebastian was already on his knees, begging for forgiveness by the time we all shoved out of the room and closed the door. Reggie paced outside, clearly wanting to support his friend but knowing he needed to give them space. I'll admit, it was hard to walk away.

"As Sebastian tells it," I explained to the group, "he was a notorious rake, and she was his best friend's little sister. He compromised her in the gardens at her coming out ball, and to distract her brother from discovering the betrayal, Sebastian challenged him to a race, where Sebastian had his accident."

Carma shook her head in disbelief. "I can't believe…what are the chances?"

"I'm not a big believer in fate, but it sure seems like it in this case," Mina replied.

Carma agreed, then straightened her shoulders. "Let's go

eat and give them some privacy. I'm sure we'll hear something from them soon." She looked at her girlfriend. "Maybe this is a good time for our announcement?"

"Announcement?" Jake prompted. "What didn't you tell me? Am I not family?"

Mina smiled at him. "Go look out the front at the sign." She gestured to the window. "Everyone, go."

We all moved. Two employees went out the front door and crossed the lawn to the sign, which was covered in a tarp. They released the binding and pulled the tarp away.

CARMINA'S HAUNTED BED & BREAKFAST

FREE BREAKFAST, WI-FI, AND FRIENDLY GHOSTS

"Carmina?" Jake asked. "Like Carma and Mina?"

Mina smiled. "Look at you, exercising those detective skills."

"You're both disgusting," he said, pointing at Mina and Carma, before breaking into a huge smile and wrapping them in a group hug. "And I love you for it."

Poppy joined, her and Carma squealing in delight. They separated, and Mina walked over to Eliza, wrapping her in a hug.

"Honestly, I'm surprised the U-Haul wasn't out front two months ago," Eliza told Mina.

Carma joined us. "I mean, if Mina were a lesbian, it would've happened. It's the bi-chaos that slowed her down."

Mina turned around and kissed her nose. "You love my chaos."

Eliza made a face. "Gross."

Mina stuck her tongue out, then glanced down at her watch. "Twenty-one hours and nineteen minutes until payback."

We all moved into the dining room and piled our plates high. Carma hit a spoon on a glass and suggested everyone take a tour of the completed inn instead, excluding the occupied rooms. Then, we sang a very boisterous rendition of Happy Birthday for Mina, who blew her candles out on an apple pie. Carma rolled out a buffet to the delight of everyone. She made sure I had four single-serving ramekins of dessert. They were so good, I nearly wept.

While we indulged, Poppy, Jake, and Eliza shared their childhood memories of the house.

"I can't believe you locked Jake in the butler's pantry!" Mina snorted.

"At least I had good company," he teased, looking at Poppy.

"That was one of our first kisses," she said, brushing a lock of hair behind his ear. "Because you were afraid of the dark and I wanted you to stop complaining."

Mina nearly wept with laughter.

Jake looked indignant. "Excuse me, it was because I was charming, and you were in love with me."

Poppy shrugged and made a "whatever you say" face.

Eliza leaned back in her chair. "Listen, it was his own fault. If he hadn't waited behind that couch to scare me, I wouldn't have retaliated."

I kissed the back of her knuckles, trying to hang on to this precious moment. But time refused to slow, and by midnight, we were all glancing at the still-closed parlor door while heading to our rooms.

"I've never wished to be a fly on a wall more," I admitted. "I want to know what's going on!"

"Well then, I'll need to distract you," Eliza teased.

And she did. She'd brought a feather with her, tracing it over my skin until I was vibrating with need. Then, we made love by firelight until our bodies were damp and wrung out, whispered pleas and sighs lost between the sheets. She laid sprawled across me, her head just above my chest, running her fingers up and down my arms. I played with her hair, fingering her curls, then smoothing them. My body relaxed and my brain quieted.

"I don't want to go to sleep," she admitted.

I leaned down and kissed her forehead. "Why not?"

She left a lingering kiss on my skin. "Because then today's over, and it was nearly perfect. Good days like this are too rare."

"It was a really good day, wasn't it?" I sighed. "But days with you are usually good, even when they're messy."

She smiled. "Even when I'm angry with you?"

"Even then, especially because make up sex with me is excellent."

She poked my side and I laughed, brushing her hand away from my most ticklish spot. She left me another kiss and I felt it down to my bones. "I'm scared," she whispered.

"Of what?"

"That something will happen, and it'll destroy us again."

My hand stilled. This was the worst part about secrets; they grew in the spaces between truths until they suffocated everything good and honest. "Don't think about that tonight, okay? We'll figure it out."

She lifted her head. "Promise me we won't screw this up. I don't know if I can take another loss. It's just one after the other, after the other. Every time I'm happy and—"

"Hey, hey, shh, shh," I wrapped her tightly in my arms. I lifted up her chin and kissed her until her chest was moving faster. I slipped my fingers down between her legs and she gasped, more than likely still tender, but she let me continue.

"I'm obsessed with your body and your whimpers and how you taste. I'm not going anywhere until you chase me away, got it?"

"Yes," she breathed as her entire body tensed, then sagged against me. She left sloppy kisses on my chest before closing her eyes. "Thank you."

"Anything for you," I promised.

Her breathing slowed, her mouth parting. I smiled. I'd forgotten if I got her off just the right way, she'd fall sleep immediately. Just one of the thousand things I missed about being with her.

Ben was such a fucking asshole. How could he leave Eliza and Daisy like that? Fake his own death? I knew if he had given Eliza the choice—fight or fake his death—she would've fought with every breath left in her body.

Selfishly, I was glad he left. She was mine, even if just for a little while. Just for now, I was going to pretend that I got to keep her, that I would win this ultimate battle for her heart. That somehow, she would choose me, and we would solve this case and I'd be able to keep her alive. A lifetime of holding her in my arms every night, years of hearing her breathe my name as she fell apart, thousands of nights cooking together, weekends cleaning together. Terrible school plays and soccer games and sleepovers.

I wanted to be there for all the events—big and small—in both Eliza's and Daisy's lives. I closed my eyes and decided tonight I would believe. *Please no nightmares tonight*, I prayed to whoever was listening. *Let me have this one night.*

Chapter Twenty-Five

Eliza

BREAKFAST WAS DELIVERED to our door, and we ate wrapped in robes, constantly touching each other. "What do you want for Christmas?" I asked.

"I don't need anything," Paris said, popping a grape into her mouth. "You're my present."

I threw a grape at her. "Stop. For real."

Something changed in her expression, but then it was gone. "Okay, how about this. Buy me your favorite book, okay? And I'll do the same."

I smiled. "That is the perfect idea." I leaned over the food tray and kissed her. "Should we have the defining the relationship talk now or next weekend?"

She swallowed hard and cleared her throat. "We already covered a lot of ground this weekend. Let's save some memories for next week, huh?"

I stuck my tongue out at her to cover my unease. Her answer was completely logical, yet there was something discomforting in the way she said the words. I was probably overthinking things. She wanted to be here. If she didn't, she wouldn't be. Right?

After we finished breakfast and packed, we headed downstairs to socialize for the last hour of the party. Jake and Poppy were walking out of their first-floor room and glanced up the stairs as we crossed the landing.

"Did you hear anything about Sebastian?" Jake prompted.

I shook my head. "Just came down. You?"

The front door opened, and Belphegor lumbered in, with Amber and George in either arm as if they were infants and not fully grown humans. "The ghosts are losing their minds," he boomed. "Saying Sebastian found Evie."

He looked over at me and Paris. "This your 'situation'?"

Paris's cheeks went red.

Situation? I was going to have to ask her about that later.

"That's what I thought," the demon responded. "I want details, after I find out what's going on with the duke."

Jake nodded at the parlor door. "They've been locked in there since last night. He actually left us alone."

"I honestly didn't know it was possible for him to be this quiet," Poppy added.

"You're all being dramatic," Sebastian said, poofing in next to Jake. Evie stood next to him, arm resting on his. "I leave you alone often. I just try to prevent you from making my same stupid mistakes."

"Didn't work," I whisper-coughed and gestured to Jake.

He shot me a glare. "My mistakes were well-calculated risks, thank you very much."

"Does this mean you've made amends?" Paris prompted, gesturing between Sebastian and Evie.

"Yes. Evie has somehow found it in her heart to forgive me." He patted her hand on his arm.

"I did have a century and a half to come to terms with

it," she admitted. "But yes. Your past transgressions are just that. Past."

Paris looked at me, as if the words were meant for us. Her silent question, had I forgiven her for what happened? And my silent, *I think so*.

Belphegor grunted, as if he had understood our conversation, too.

As soon as Sebastian was done making introductions, Reggie appeared, speaking in excited, quick Spanish. Poppy replied and quickly translated for us that Reggie couldn't wait to see how Sebastian handled being in love. Sebastian responded in Spanish, something that made Reggie laugh and Poppy snort, but they did not share.

With the threat of the real world waiting for us, everyone dawdled a little longer than planned, and Carma put out yesterday's leftovers for an early lunch. No one wanted to break the seal and be the first to leave, knowing as soon as that front door opened, it was over. It was so rare as adults to be able to have one big giant sleepover with your friends.

Carma clinked a spoon against a glass and waited for quiet. "I must say, this was an even bigger success than we could have dreamed. If you're open to the idea, we'd love to make this an annual thing. Same time next year?"

Everyone cheered in agreement.

Then my and Jake's phone went off simultaneously.

It was like slow motion. I knew the moment before I even looked at the screen the perfect-day bubble was popped.

"Mom," I said, looking up at my brother.

"Dad," he responded, eyes wide.

We answered at the same time.

Chapter Twenty-Six

Paris

ALL I HEARD was "Daisy" and "hospital" and I was out of my seat. Sebastian handed Poppy Jake's keys, and she had the truck pulled up to the door before Jake even finished relaying the entire story.

Daisy thought she saw Ben at the park and wanted her mom. Before they could call, she started crying. She shattered the windows on two cars, broke the slide, fell off her swing, and went unconscious.

"It's her magic," Jake confessed, voice shaking.

Loren stood. "I'll call Javier. See if he's made any progress on finding out Ben's history."

I grabbed Loren's arm. "What do you need to know? I can get the info."

Eliza ran past me. "I'm going with Jake!"

"I'll meet you there!" I promised, then turned back to Loren, who was having a silent conversation with his wife.

"Yes," he confirmed.

She kissed Loren hard but quick, then was out the door.

He turned back to me. "Eliza asked me to dig into Ben's history to try and find his family lineage. They need to know what kind of witch she is before they can do a ritual to help."

"And Raine?" I asked, knowing there was a reason she went.

"Raine gave up her own magic and survived. It's a last-ditch effort."

Jesus. Pulling magic this strong from a kid would likely kill her. "Have you made any headway with Ben?"

He shook his head.

"You got a vest and weapons?"

He nodded.

I held up my finger and dialed my brother.

He answered on the first ring. "What's up, P? I'm about to head back to work."

"I need to come by. Can you wait ten?"

He sighed. "Only ten."

I hung up and looked at Loren. "Let's suit up." I pointed at Belphegor. "You in?"

"Is it for Daisy?"

"Everything I do is for Eliza and Daisy."

He glanced at Amber, who waved him off. "We'll be fine here. George already found a chair to fall asleep in."

"What can we do?" Mina asked.

"Call Javier for me," Loren ordered. "Tell him we may have a lead on Ben."

Carma came rushing down the stairs holding my backpack and a duffle bag. "I hope you don't mind. I grabbed your backpack and added a few snacks. I know it's hard to eat on the go." She handed me the bag and then turned to Loren and gave him the duffle. "Your keys are in the side pocket."

"Thank you for everything." I gave her a quick hug,

which seemed to startle her. "Let's go," I ordered, and then we were out the door.

Belphegor scrunched down in the back as I dove into the driver's seat and Loren hurried into the passenger side. He immediately opened his duffle and pulled out two bulletproof vests.

"This is Raine's," he explained. "You're a bit taller, but it should work."

I ripped off my sweatshirt, pulled the vest on, then replaced my hoodie. It was important to avoid advertising that one was wearing a bulletproof vest. The enemy was more likely to aim for your head if they saw it.

As soon as Loren had his on, I threw the truck in drive and headed toward my brother's apartment on the outskirts of town.

"IF I'M NOT walking out with a guy who looks like me in two minutes, come in." I idled the truck at the curb. I pulled my pistol from my waist holder.

"Wait." Loren opened his duffle and pulled out a stun gun. "Turn it on like this." He demonstrated how it worked. "Works better in close quarters if you can't get a shot off."

I accepted the weapon. "Awesome."

He smirked and grabbed a semi-automatic gun and its corresponding magazine, snapping them together. "Let's do this."

"I can go in alone."

"And make me miss the fun? Please." He opened his

door.

Belphegor climbed out and left the back door open. "I'll stand guard."

I nodded at Loren as I buzzed my brother's apartment. "It's P," I confirmed when he answered. The door unlocked and I held it open. "Going to 5B."

The hallway was slathered in beige and stale smelling, and if I wasn't homicidal, I'd brag about how much better my place was, with the exception of Doris. When we got to 5B, I wailed on Dallas' door. "Open up!"

"What's wrong with you?" He looked up and saw Loren, then attempted to shut the door.

But rage made me stronger, and I pushed my full body against the door then moved in, Loren behind.

Dallas grabbed his weapon from a side table and held it between us. "What's going on?"

Loren closed the door and nodded to me.

"Where is he?" I asked my brother.

"Who?"

I release the safety. "I love you more than myself, but I swear to god I'll shoot you. Where is he?"

"If you shoot me, Mom will be pissed."

"Which is why I'd rather not shoot you."

He looked at me, his eyebrows pulling together in apology. "I can't tell you. You know I can't."

"This guy is former HQ. You don't cooperate, I tell him your entire story."

Dallas turned his gun to Loren. "Jesus, Paris, what the actual fuck? Do you want me dead?"

"Daisy is really sick. Ben is the only one who can save

her. We need information only he can give. Where. Is. He?"

"They'll kill him—then all of us—if they find him," he confessed, his voice low. "And I can't let that happen."

"I love Eliza and I will do anything, and I mean anything for her daughter. So you tell me where Ben is, or I swear on our grandmother's emerald ring that I will shoot you." I swore I felt the ring on my right hand grow warmer.

He didn't move for a long moment, then he lowered his gun. "If we're discovered, bulletproof vests won't help."

The cloudy vision that had taunted me since Thursday brushed across my sight again but didn't offer any new details. "That's a chance I'm willing to take. You in, Loren?"

"I've made a career out of almost dying," Loren explained. "No reason to stop now."

Dallas handed me his gun. I doubled-checked the safety then tucked it into my holster, while I held the other one at crotch height. He looked from the gun to me. "Really?"

"I'm aiming for the part of your body I know you care about the most," I said with a sardonic smile.

We walked out of the building, me in front and Loren in back. Belphegor looked at Dallas as if he were a hair in his food. "Twins are so creepy."

"We have triplet cousins," I offered.

He made a face. "That's just not right."

I turned on the child safety lock and waved Dallas inside the back door. Belphegor followed.

I climbed in the driver's seat and turned around. "Where?"

"Nana's Laundromat and Deli in Holly," he said.

"Loren, can you navigate?"

He nodded. "On it." He checked the screen. "Forty miles northwest. Take 75 North. Traffic is yellow. Looks like a snowstorm is passing through."

"Good thing I have snow tires."

I squealed out of the parking lot, which got a cheer from the demon and a groan from my twin. "Try not to kill us before we get there," Dallas begged.

Loren held on to the handle above the door and glanced over at me. "Fill me in."

"Ben isn't really dead, and he needs to save his daughter."

Chapter Twenty-Seven

Eliza

I SAT ON the hospital bed next to my sedated daughter, her eyes closed and cheeks pink as if she was just taking an afternoon nap while wearing an oxygen mask. I brushed her curls out of her face, soothing myself more than her. I'd sent my parents to get coffee because I couldn't deal with my mom's fretting.

I needed to stay numb. Needed to avoid looking at the tubes and wires. The cartoons playing on the television nearly covered the irregular beeping of the heart monitor. I checked my phone, but my text to Paris was still unread. *Where was she?*

Dr. Marback walked in the room, tablet in hand and a concerned look on her face. "We have calls to our best witches, but they're all several hours away. I've got two on a plane. As long as Daisy's vitals stay stable, and we can keep her sedated, we'll wait. Hopefully a temporary spell will help."

I nodded, all the *what if* questions bottlenecking in my throat. I couldn't let them out, or I'd lose whatever it was keeping me upright.

"Have you thought about a removal?" she asked.

I bit the inside of my cheek, then nodded. "Raine, with the blonde and blue hair, she had a successful removal."

Dr. Marback's eyebrows raised. "Really? I would love to speak with her. Are you considering it for Daisy?"

I tucked my legs under me and scooped up Daisy's tiny hand. "If she was your daughter, what would you do?"

She sat down in the chair next to me and looked at her tablet for a long moment, although she wasn't reading anything. "Sometimes magic is kind of like a tumor. It can be one singular, benign tumor that's in just one area of the body and easily removed. Every procedure would carry risks—damage to surrounding organs and tissues, infection, etc.—but generally in these cases there's a good success rate."

She turned off her tablet and met my gaze. "Daisy's magic is like a metastatic cancer. It's all over her body and creating chaos. There's no guarantee surgery would work, and even if it did, we may not get it all. We could remove her magic, but if we missed some, it could grow back in a more alarming way. We may be able to remove it all but damage her body in the process."

I swallowed hard, trying to get the baseball out of my throat. "I only want to do it if we're out of options. If it's that or…" I didn't finish the sentence. I didn't need to.

She nodded. "Any luck finding out information on her dad's side?"

I shook my head. "I have someone in HQ on it, but there's been nothing yet." I kissed the back of Daisy's hand. "Maybe we'll get a miracle."

Chapter Twenty-Eight

Paris

I HIT THE steering wheel. "We need to get around this traffic jam." We were inching along as the sky threw up snow. It was like heavy fog, and outside of the brake lights on the car in front of us, I couldn't make out anything. I was desperate for an exit sign.

My cell rang and I checked the screen. "Hi, Jake."

"Paris, what the hell? Where are you?"

"Trapped on 75. Semi jack-knifed."

"I could just move the semi," Belphegor grumbled.

"Why the hell are you on 75 and not on your way to the hospital?"

"Can't tell you yet."

"You can't lift a semi," Loren scolded Belphegor. "Not without eating a human soul first."

"What if I make sure they're a really terrible human? There's plenty of those around," Belphegor responded, glancing at Dallas.

"You can't eat my brother," I called back.

"What's happening on your end?" Jake prompted. "Why is Belphegor threatening to eat your brother?

"It's a long story," I explained.

"You keep very interesting company," Loren mused.

"One soul," Belphegor promised. "I can move the whole semi with the strength from one soul."

"Paris," Jake interrupted. "What's your ETA?"

"As soon as I can," I promised. "I'm on the trail of something that could help. I need you to trust me."

There was a beat of silence. "What am I telling Eliza?"

"Tell her I'm trying to save the day."

"Hurry." He hung up and I hit the steering wheel again.

"I've got an idea," Belphegor admitted.

"You're not eating a soul," I returned.

"Don't need one to lift this truck. It's light."

"You're going to what?" I asked.

"Tighten your seatbelts." He stepped out of the truck, straightened his mint green sweater with the black stars, and bent low. Without ceremony, he lifted our entire vehicle over his head, as if we were no more than an egg carton and started walking.

"Oh fuck, the phone calls we're going to get about this," Loren said.

As if on cue, my phone rang. Sienna. I clicked to answer on Bluetooth. "It's Paris." My voice sounded strained as I tried to keep from flopping around.

"Agent Evans, why do I have reports of a large animal carrying your truck through human traffic on I-75 North?"

"Because a demon is helping us out of a traffic jam so I can save Eliza Robinson's daughter's life." Accompanied by several screams and horns, Belphegor made his way up the exit ramp.

"I—" Sienna, who had probably never hesitated before in her life, hesitated. "There are so many violations—"

"It's fine, write me up. If Daisy lives, it'll be worth it."

"I'm scheduling a meeting for Monday," she warned.

"See you Monday!" I said, then hung up.

Belphegor set us down on the shoulder, as gently as if we were a baby bird. I rubbed at the side of my head where it had hit the door twice. The demon opened the back door and climbed in, not bothering to brush the snow off his sweater. "I got grease on my cuff."

I reached around the seat and touched his sleeve. "I can get it out."

Loren turned around to look at Belphegor. "I can't wait to see Paris's report on this."

"Worry about reports later. We gotta fucking hurry. Daisy's my ice cream buddy." Belphegor had found Daisy wandering Applechester one day after she'd snuck out her window to get ice cream, and they've gone together every few weeks since. Between Jake and Belphegor, Daisy had more ice cream in a month than anyone I knew.

I merged into the light traffic. While unplowed, the road was passable and we were finally moving.

I slammed on the brakes, fishtailing, as a large animal, reddish brown and twice the size of a wolf, ran across the road. I wrestled the truck to the shoulder, my heart beating so hard, my head was shaking. "Tell me that wasn't what I think it was?" I breathed in deep then blew it out before merging back on to the road.

"I couldn't tell, but I hope not." He ran a hand down his face. "I need to convince Raine to move somewhere it doesn't snow. I despise snowstorms."

I glanced over at him. "I definitely am going to need this story later."

"I'll tell you on the way back," he promised. "Nana's is coming up, half a mile on your left."

We pulled into the empty parking lot, a sign on the door indicating it was closed Sundays and Mondays. I turned to my brother. "Why a deli/laundromat?"

"Food plus chemicals for clean up," he explained.

Solid reasons. "What are we walking into?"

"Basement utility room with computers, cots, and a small bathroom. Block windows on the west side of the building. A fire exit on south side."

"Firearms? Boobytraps?" Loren prompted.

"I'll go in first to disable them."

I turned around and stared directly into his eyes. "I will shoot you in the crotch if you screw me over."

He held up his hands in surrender. "Paris. I'd never deliberately hurt you. I need you to trust me."

I trusted him. At least, I trusted that he wouldn't shoot me, or let someone else shoot me if he could stop it. I just didn't trust him about Ben. Holding his gaze, I handed him his gun, handle first.

He nodded and tucked it into the back of his jeans. "Ready?"

I glanced at Loren and Belphegor, then nodded. "Let's move."

As we exited the car, a low growl came from our left. We turned to see a giant werewolf, teeth bared.

"Dammit," I grumbled. "It was a hybrid."

"What the hell is this motherfucker?" Belphegor asked.

"Werewolf-vampire hybrid."

"Oh hell no. Not today. Let's go asshole." Belphegor charged the beast. The wolf, who had over twice the mass of the demon, stepped back and lowered its tail. "Go!" he shouted. "I got this."

"Go for the throat," Dallas advised, then moved to the laundromat's glass door. He pulled a set of keys from his pocket and unlocked the door. "Follow me."

We crept through the darkened laundromat, then edged to the fire door and eased down the concrete stairs. Dallas held his arm out three stairs from the bottom, signaling to skip the next one. We eased our way to the ground floor, then moved to the door, where he typed a code into a padlock.

I held my breath as he eased the door open, revealing a basement no bigger than a bedroom. The man I thought I'd killed nearly twenty-nine months ago was sitting in a computer chair, his back to us, facing a table with several computers crammed on the surface.

The years of grief and loss and anger and betrayal and sleepless nights of me blaming myself, memories of me holding my pillow while I cried hit me all at once. I wanted to scream, yell, cry, do anything but stand here silently.

My chest was caving in, rage making my hands shake, and I nearly stormed over to him.

Loren grabbed my shoulder. "Breathe. You can beat the shit out of him later," he whispered. "I'll help."

"Deal."

Dallas moved farther into the room. Then all hell broke loose.

Chapter Twenty-Nine

Paris

THE VISION HIT me immediately, and I tackled Dallas to the ground, kicking Loren's legs out from underneath him. We rolled behind stacks of boxes as bullets whizzed over our heads and hit the back door.

Loren looked over at me. "You're as creepy as Romi. Thank god."

"That reminds me, I need to call her back."

Dallas grabbed the gun he'd dropped and rolled away from me. "Girl talk later. Bullets now."

"I can do both, thanks!" I shot back. "What the fuck is happening?"

"Hey, buddy?" Dallas called. "It's me."

Footsteps shifted over the concrete. "Sorry, Ben's a little…tied up right now," a man announced, then chuckled.

Dallas paled, his eyes going wide. It was that moment, the terror in his gaze as it met mine, that I realized I'd never seen my twin *truly* scared. Even when I threw the smoke bombs, he was more angry than afraid.

"Russell, what are you doing here?" Dallas asked.

"You thought you could keep this a secret?" Russell

asked. "My blood, sweat, and tears went into this, too."

"Fuck," my brother whispered. He turned to me. "Cover me."

"What are you doing?" I whisper-yelled.

"Saving your ass." He stood and raised his hands. "Let's talk about this, buddy. I don't know what you heard but trust me. This isn't something you want to be a part of."

"You just want to escape to your sandy beach with no extradition laws and a foreign bank account while the rest of us suffer? I don't think so. I'm in, or I shoot you both and take the deal myself. I would've already been on the beach if you hadn't fucked me over the first time."

Loren and I crawled to either end of the room and began to advance, staying behind the boxes of cleaning supplies and salad dressing. I felt like these two things should be separated. I leaned around a stack of mayonnaise and eyed the bottom of Ben's chair.

His feet were tied to the base with bungee cords. Russell using impromptu methods of restraint meant two things: he was unprepared and desperate. The first was an advantage but the second made him dangerous.

"Where are your friends, Dallas?" Russell prompted. "I know I saw three on the camera."

"Waiting for my signal to come in," he said. "It's just you and me."

"You're so full of shit."

"How'd you find us?" Dallas prompted.

"Ben is shit at covering his tracks," Russell said on a derisive laugh.

Moving soundlessly, I reached out and unhooked the

cords on the back of Ben's chair. His feet shifted slightly to the left, trying to give me better access. Careful to not let the plastic piece snap and make noise, I eased the elastic away. I started on the cord holding his hands behind his back when the too-warm barrel of a recently fired gun pressed into my temple.

"I don't think so," Russell said.

Ben planted his feet on the ground and slammed his chair into Russell, causing him to stumble backward. He got off two shots as he fell, and white-hot pain barreled through my arm. Another shot rang out as Dallas scooped me up and moved me away from Russell.

My ears rang and my arm throbbed. I swayed when Dallas set me down. "Stay with me sis."

"I'm okay," I promised. "Russell."

"Not a problem anymore."

I looked up to find a hole through the center of Russell's forehead. Dallas was always an excellent marksman.

"He's not, but this is," Loren warned, crouching in front of Ben. Ben was slumped in the chair, blood seeping out of a bullet hole in his chest. "Came through the back of the chair."

"NO!" I screamed. "No, no, he can't die. Not now. We'll lose Daisy." I grabbed Dallas's arm. "Dal, do something!"

"Fuck!" Dallas said, then ran to a safe in the back of the room. He opened it and ran back, two clear capsules with dark pink powder in his hand.

"The vixen is here?"

"Take one for your arm." He dropped one in my hand.

I shoved it into my jeans pocket. "I would never."

"Neither would Ben. I hope he forgives me."

"He will if we save his daughter."

Dallas shoved the pill in Ben's mouth as Loren cut him loose of his bindings.

Loren looked over at me. "I texted Javier and told him to send a helicopter."

Belphegor shoved through the back door and stomped into the room. "Got the wolves secured. Turns out they're not fond of demons."

"Excellent work," I wheezed.

Belphegor looked me up and down as he approached. "One of you call an ambulance for devil's sake. You got this one bleeding everywhere, another one tied to a chair. I fucking stay outside for a few minutes to take care of a problem and it's pandemonium." He grabbed Russell and tossed him over his shoulder. "Need me to take care of this guy? Soul's still fresh. Would take care of that semi-truck."

Dallas shrugged.

"Take it outside, at least," Loren said. "I don't like the sound of souls coming out."

Before walking out, the perpetually grumpy demon wearing a torn sweater with a grease stain on the sleeve reached out and smoothed my hair. "You'll be okay. Only person I know tougher than you is Daisy."

Then he marched out the back door. I hummed loudly as Russell's soul began screaming. A demon taking a soul was a nasty business, at least from what Poppy told me. Thankfully, the sound of the helicopter arriving blocked it out.

Chapter Thirty

Eliza

"BOTH OF THE witches' flights were delayed due to the weather," Dr. Marback explained. "We need to think about attempting to remove the magic. We're losing her kidneys and her heart is weakening. We have an hour or two at most to make the decision."

"I'm not ready to give up," I'd told her, desperately wishing for another solution.

The voices in my head were so loud, my body ached. I laid down next to my daughter, holding her close, when someone crashed into the door.

"You can't go in there!" someone yelled from the hall.

Paris ran into the room, the sleeve of her hoodie cut off, and bloody gauze wrapped around her upper arm. "Sorry I'm late, babe. Had to make a stop." She hurried to me and touched my face. I nearly sagged in relief as my head went quiet. "This is going to be a shock," she warned.

Then Ben walked in, Loren's gun at his back, wearing a scrub top and jeans.

Ben walked in…

Ben walked…

Ben.

Time stopped for a moment, an hour, an entire day. Black dots danced in front of my vision. My entire body began shaking as I burst out in a scream-cry. I was hyperventilating, unable to get enough air in as I tried to make sense of what I was seeing.

Paris wrapped her uninjured arm around my waist. "He's been dosed with vixen, so they probably need to give him a transfusion to reverse it first, but then he'll be able to help Daisy."

My fiancé, who had been dead for over two years, was kneeling at my—our—daughter's bed. He brought her small hand to his lips and kissed it. "I'm here, Daisy," he whispered. "Daddy's gonna make it better."

Dr. Marback ran in, taking in the scene with wide eyes. I tried to explain, but I could only suck in gasps of air between body-wrecking sobs of relief and confusion. Paris wrapped her arm around me tighter then started explaining.

"This is Daisy's biological father. You'll see he's not, in fact, deceased. He was shot through the back at 13:05 and was dosed with vixen about 13:10. Bullet's still in his chest."

Dr. Marback began giving orders to her nurses. "Get another bed in here."

"Not safe to keep us together," Ben warned. "I'm being tracked."

"We're on security," Loren promised. "Do whatever you have to do for Daisy, and we'll cover it."

"We'll remove the bullet, then start a transfusion to reverse the venom. Once his blood is clear, we'll be able to take a sample and create Daisy's treatment." Dr. Marback checked her watch. "We have to move. We only have a few hours at most."

The first nurse ran out and Dallas walked in. "If you could also take the bullet out of my sister's arm, I'd appreciate it."

Another nurse arrived and handed me a small plastic dish and a cup of water. "Alprazolam," she explained.

I shook my head.

"Take it," Paris said. "It'll help."

I held my breath to swallow the pill and water as Paris's hand ran over my back in big circles. "H-how?" I tried, barely able to get words together.

"Later," she promised, then hissed. "After they dig the bullet out of me." She kissed the side of my head. "I love you."

She held me until the medication kicked in, slowing my racing thoughts and my heaving chest. I watched as she left with the nurse, then my eyes moved to Ben, who was studying me. "We have a lot to talk about," I whispered.

He nodded. "Soon."

JAKE TOUCHED MY shoulder. "You asleep?" he asked in a low voice.

"Resting my eyes." I struggled to lift my heavy lids, pushing myself up. Jake sat down on the couch.

"You know this folds out into a bed," he said. He had stayed in the SHAP medical facility with Poppy when she had become human.

"Didn't mean to go back to sleep," I admitted. I checked my phone. I'd been out for nearly an hour. "Dr. Marback?"

"They should be able to get a blood sample from Ben in the next half hour. Daisy's plateaued for now."

I nodded. "Good, okay."

"Drink." He handed me a cup of coffee. "Doc says Paris is out of surgery. She's stable."

I frowned. "Surgery?" My brain was foggy, but I was surprised they hadn't just given her local anesthetic and stitched her up.

"Something about bullet fragments and a torn tendon. It was easier to remove it from Ben since he dosed. They want to make sure Paris heals completely, or she'll be out as a field agent."

"Makes sense." I rested my head on his shoulder, too weary to stay upright. I took a sip of coffee and forced myself to swallow the bitter brew. "We can turn humans into vampires but can't make a decent cup of coffee?"

"Geniuses often fail at the easy things."

"Jake, how did she know? How did she just show up with Ben?"

He sighed and opened his mouth to say something else, but hesitated.

"Just say it."

"She loves you. And Daisy. She could've made a dozen different choices, yes, but I think in her shoes, I would've done the same."

"Jake…"

"Dallas says she found out on Friday morning. Ben was the one who took the trackers from evidence, which is something we need to talk about by the way. The what from where?"

I waved him off. "Later. Continue."

"And he warned her that telling you would put him in danger, and I can imagine after the trauma of last time, that she was scared to say something. When she heard the news today, she showed up at Dallas's apartment and held him at gunpoint to reveal Ben's location."

"Holy shit," I whispered.

"She did what she thought she had to do to keep everyone safe." He studied me. "I'm assuming you hadn't told her about Daisy or the search for Ben's history?"

I shook my head.

"If you had, I don't think she would've waited to say anything. I think she would've had Ben handcuffed to her the moment she saw him on tape, her brother be damned."

"Don't you dare say 'I told you so.'"

He smirked. "I won't. Out loud."

"Is someone sitting with Paris?"

Jake nodded. "Dallas is with his sister. Loren and Mina are doing security for tonight. Neither Dallas nor Ben are sharing any details about this person after them, but we want to be safe."

"Good plan."

"By the way, Belphegor is sitting in the lobby, scaring everyone who passes by. He refuses to leave until Daisy is home."

My eyes stung and pressure increased in my nose, and I covered my face with my hand. "A demon wants to protect my daughter."

"I mean, have you met Daisy? She's literally the best kid in the world."

"And now her dad's back." And there it was. I pulled my knees up and rested my head on them, sucking in deep breaths to try and control the tears.

"And he'll always be her dad," Jake promised. "But it doesn't mean he has to be your anything, unless you want him to be."

I turned my head sideways and looked at my brother. "He was supposed to be mine. We were meant to be. How could I regret any part of my life with him when he gave me Daisy?"

He tugged on one of my curls. "Meant to be doesn't always mean made to last."

"He left." Those two words held twenty-nine months of grief, anguish, desperation, and a host of other emotions I couldn't define.

"He did." Jake's two words held the same myriad emotions. "I don't know the entire story, but I know it was for you and Daisy."

"He hurt people."

Jake nodded again.

"I love him," I mouthed, the words barely even a whisper.

"I know you do. But are you in love with him?"

I lifted a shoulder. If I tried again, maybe I could be. "What do I do?"

He nodded toward Ben. "I think you and Ben need to have a long talk."

"Yeah, we do," Ben said.

I startled and looked over. Ben used his remote to raise the head of his bed, then ran a hand through his messy hair. He looked nearly the same as he did the morning he kissed me for the last time, although his hair was lighter now, and he'd grown a beard.

"I'm going to go find us some better coffee and get the nurse," Jake announced, then grabbed his cane and stood. "Ben, can I bring you anything?"

Ben shook his head. "Thanks, Jake."

We were silent until my brother left, then I moved to Ben's bed. "How're you feeling?"

"Like I was flattened by a steamroller then inflated with helium. Think old Road Runner cartoons."

"That good, huh?"

"Top notch. I recommend this procedure for anyone looking for a fun weekend." He patted the bed and scooted over.

I sat down gingerly, and he reached out, taking my hand. "How are you even here right now?" I asked.

Even after all this time, his hand was familiar, comfortable. But it didn't feel right. *Because it's not Paris's hand.* I shoved the thought aside. My focus was on Ben right now.

"I don't even know how to start," he admitted.

"How could you?" I whispered. "How could you leave? How could you make me *plan your burial* and put our daughter through hell?" My voice had gotten louder with each word, and he shushed me.

"Don't wake Daisy," he warned.

I pursed my lips at him. "She's sedated until they can give her the treatment."

"I'm sorry," Ben admitted. "And I know that's not, nor will it ever be, enough."

"You faked your own death."

He blew out a breath. "I was trying to find a way to safely contact you. I snuck in a few times, but I couldn't figure out a way to leave a note that explained everything but didn't put you in danger..."

"Who am I in danger from?"

He studied my hand, tracing the gold band on my finger. "Someone from my past."

"Am I still in danger?"

"If he ever catches you? Yes. But I've stayed one step ahead of him so far."

"Tell me what the hell happened."

He studied the wall behind me before continuing. "My cover had been blown on a case. Dallas was trying to help and things got...sticky."

"Sticky, how?"

He shook his head. "I can't tell you. At least, not yet."

I narrowed my eyes at him. "You get a reprieve, for now."

"Dallas had texted Paris something stupid, and she lost it—rightfully so. I tried to get her out of there, but we were being followed. I knew if he recognized her, if somehow he connected her, he might find you. I just, I made a spur of the moment decision."

"To fake your own death? So this guy didn't connect me to someone I hadn't met yet?"

He gave me a bashful smile, the one that made me fall in love with him in the first place. "Well, when you say it like that."

"You're a damned idiot."

"I am."

"Why did you stay gone? If you were just trying to lose the tail?"

He hesitated and ran his free hand over his hair. "I decided while I was playing dead, I'd try to take him down from the inside. Make sure that when I came back, it was safe. Permanently safe."

"You could've talked to me. We would've figured it out."

"It was the worst and likely stupidest thing I've ever done, but I did what I thought I had to."

I frowned and sucked in a breath. "The life insurance—"

"Cashed out my retirement fund. There was no insurance fraud."

"Thank god. It's in an account for Daisy."

"God, you're a great mother." He reached up and touched my chin. "And a great woman." He gave me a tight smile. "I missed you so much."

Those five words nearly broke me. A stray tear, then another escaped before I managed to get myself under control again.

Ben, who could never figure out what to do with a crying woman, awkwardly wrapped his arms around me. "Hey, hey, it's okay."

All the grief and anger over losing him and his deception, the shit with Paris, the terror of my daughter being in danger, boiled to the surface. Ben moved one of his arms and then handed me the box of sandpaper tissues from his side table.

"They're going to tear your face off, but at least you won't be snotty?" he tried.

I balled up a tissue and threw it at him, then dabbed at my cheeks. The tissue practically disintegrated in my hand. "When we're alone next, I'm going to scream a lot of obscenities at you."

"Absolutely fair. We'll make sure the place has good acoustics, too."

"You'll have to find a way to get ahold of your parents. They moved to California and didn't leave a forwarding address."

"I'll find them."

"And you need to explain all of this in more detail soon. After she's better and we're out of here."

He squeezed my hand. "God, I've missed you."

I shook my head. "I've missed you," I admitted. "And so has your daughter."

We both looked over at Daisy.

"I missed so much of her life. She's so big now. And the powers!"

"I'll make you a photo album."

He squeezed my hand again. "No. No photos. Nothing to identify her by. At least, not until the threat is neutralized."

"How do we make that happen?"

He shook his head. "I don't know yet. Dallas and I need to talk." He smirked. "Speaking of Dallas's sister…"

I stared at him. "No, I'm not talking about my dating life with my ex-fiancé."

"Ex, huh?"

"Ben...you were *dead.*"

He sighed. "I know. I know about Paris."

I waited for him to continue, but he didn't. "You left."

"I did. And it's fine."

"Paris may be an ex now, too."

He raised his eyebrows. "Does that mean I have a chance?"

I hesitated. "I...don't know. We have a lot to work through."

"Like the fact that I pretended I was dead for two years?"

"Might come up in therapy, yes."

He pinched the bridge of his nose. "Fine. Co-parents only, for now."

"For now?"

"I almost died today. Let me have the 'for now.' You know I get grumpy when things don't go my way."

I laughed quietly. "Monopoly-gate went down in history."

"That game is stupid!"

"Don't worry, Daisy hates it, too."

"Good." He smiled. "What else does she hate?"

"Spelling."

"Naturally."

"Eggplant, all of February, and red skittles."

"Red skittles?!" He pretended to be offended. "Clearly she's not my daughter."

"She hated her dad being gone the most." It wasn't nice to say, but he needed to hear it.

He ran a hand through his hair again. "Yeah. I missed her with every breath." He sighed. "I need to talk to Dallas, he around?"

"He's with Paris. If you're feeling well enough to keep an eye on Daisy, I'll go get him."

"I'm wide awake."

I leaned over and gave him a soft kiss then held his chin in my hand. "I'm glad you're not dead. But when I stop feeling so benevolent and our daughter isn't sleeping a few feet away, you're going to wish you were."

"I have no doubt."

I stood and walked over to Daisy, scanning her face. Her eyes were still closed, her mouth relaxed, lips parted. She looked peaceful. Good.

I moved to the door.

"Wait."

I looked back over my shoulder. "Yeah?"

"How many letters did you write, Eliza?"

I tapped my hand on the doorframe. "Only one," I lied. "And it was returned to sender."

"Good. Because I wasn't worth it."

"No, you weren't." I nodded to Daisy. "But she was."

I'D STOPPED TO give Loren and Mina a quick update, then knocked on Paris's door before entering. Dallas stood and walked over. He had Paris's brown eyes and hair, but his nose was crooked from a few breaks, and his chin was square where Paris's was round. His stride was nearly identical to his sister's, but he held his body differently. Still, if you put them side by side in a lineup, I'd know they were siblings.

"Eliza, it's good to see you."

"You too."

He gestured to one of the two chairs near the bed, and we sat.

"How is she?" I asked, my voice weary.

"Good. She would've been better if they could've given her vixen and then reversed it but..."

"She absolutely wouldn't want that. Not after everything."

"I know."

"She's as stubborn as me sometimes."

He smiled, although it didn't reach his eyes.

"Ben's awake, asked me to send you over to see him. Dr. Marback should be in soon to take a blood sample."

Dallas straightened. "He's awake? And okay?"

"Yes."

His face softened. "Good. I'll go see him right now if that's okay? I don't want her to be alone."

"Of course." I gestured to next door.

He hurried out of the room, leaving me alone with Paris.

I looked at the woman asleep in front of me. She had a drainage tube and bandage around her left arm. The bed nearly swallowed her. She'd risked her life to save Daisy. She'd lied to me about Ben, but she'd do anything to protect my daughter. She didn't run, she didn't leave, she stayed and fought.

"Eliza?" My name on her lips was little more than breath.

"I'm here," I promised, standing, and leaning over the bed. "How are you feeling?"

Her lips turned up at the corner. "Daisy?"

"Should be able to do the treatment in the next hour or so."

She reached up with her uninjured arm and cradled my face in her hand. "Sorry."

I tilted my head and kissed her palm. "We'll talk when you're better, okay?"

"Okay," she mouthed.

"I'm going to wrap up the case. By the time you get out of here, Jim will be off our backs."

She looked sad, then closed her eyes, drifting quickly to sleep.

Chapter Thirty-One

Eliza

AS SOON AS Ben's blood was cleared of vixen, they took a large sample and began work.

"We suspect Ben is descended from a very powerful line of what we call red wizards with some gray witch lineage further back," Dr. Marback explained. "They can play with different types of magic but are best known for their tempers. Hence, red."

I frowned. "Why only suspect?"

"Two reasons." She paused, waiting for a nurse to walk past us in the hall. "The first is, the DNA doesn't match exactly. It's almost as if it were altered."

"Can DNA be altered? How does that affect Daisy?"

"In some cases, yes, especially when magic is involved. I think it's why her magic is overwhelming her. Instead of growing with her, it just dumped all her powers at once." She patted my upper arm. "The ritual will help, especially since we can use source material."

I blew out a breath and nodded. "The second reason?"

"There aren't many red wizards in Michigan. They tend to gravitate toward warm, dry climates. The last one that we knew of has no living relatives."

I laughed without humor. "That tracks, honestly. Two months ago my best friend went from being a grim reaper to a human. Nothing surprises me anymore."

Dr. Marback blinked then nodded. "Understandable. We'll keep looking into it and adjust Daisy's treatment as needed, but I'm confident."

I sagged against the wall in relief. "Thanks, doctor."

"Give me thirty more minutes, and we'll be ready."

THE RITUAL WASN'T what I expected.

"Earrings?" I asked.

Dr. Marback nodded. "We may need to adjust these as she ages, likely to multiple piercings, but at eight I'm hesitant to do more than a single lobe on each side. This should work for the next two or so years."

Ben and I had agreed to not let Daisy get her ear's pierced until she asked, but health came first. I stroked her sleeping face, then her small ear. Mom guilt about doing this without my daughter's permission poked me in the side, but I shoved it away. This wasn't a fashion choice, but a medical decision.

"How do they work?" Ben asked. He was sitting in the chair next to Daisy's bed and was no longer hooked to an IV. He was wearing one of Jake's hoodies that was too short in the sleeves.

The doctor held out the flat silver disks. "They've been charmed to filter and disperse magic. Magic is basically energy that a person can harness and redirect. These earrings will provide a bilateral regulation system, so the energy coming in or exiting doesn't spike, which is what's damaging her body." She moved her hand in a straight line. "They should keep her pretty level."

"His blood did this?" I asked.

"It was the base of the charm, yes," she confirmed. "It allowed us to do a very personalized, Daisy-specific formulation."

"And as she grows, the system grows?" Ben asked. "What happens if..." his gaze moved to mine. "What happens if I'm not around when she needs more help?"

"She may yet grow into her magic and not need additional help, which is what we typically see from young witches over the course of a decade." She looked between us. "We already have additional pieces charmed and stored in her file, along with a blood sample in special serum that will protect it. It's always best to use fresh when possible, but she should be fine no matter what the future brings."

"Good." Ben gave her a lopsided smile. "I always liked to make things difficult. Ask my fiancé."

"Currently ex-fiancé," I corrected him. I thumbed the gold band on my right hand, a reminder of what we'd had. Finally, for the first time in over two years, I was ready to remove it.

Dr. Marback handed me a tablet. "Read through the consent forms together. I need signatures from both of you. Then we'll get started. If all goes well, she should be home by tomorrow night."

Ben sat with his chin on my shoulder as we read, and the

warmth of his body seeped into mine. It was so comforting, yet strange. I wasn't used to his size, his smell anymore. It was like putting on your favorite pair of pants only to find they fit just a little tight.

Did you still try to wear them and hope they stretched back out to the perfect size? Or did you put them in the donate pile? The fact I was comparing a relationship to a pair of old pants was probably a sign itself.

Using my finger, I signed the document, then handed it to Ben.

He signed and then paused before he hit the accept button. "You good?"

I glanced down, eyeing his nearly illegible signature. "You handwriting hasn't improved."

He hit accept and the screen went white. "You know how these electronic signatures are. They never look like the real thing."

"Yeah."

He handed the tablet back to the doctor. "Thanks."

But as he put his hand in mine and squeezed, then turned to study his daughter, I leaned close.

"You didn't sign your real name," I whispered.

"Don't let them connect me with her," he replied. "I'll leave once she's stable."

I wanted to ask him a hundred questions, but they'd have to wait.

"Let's get started." The doctor set down the tablet, then washed her hands at a nearby sink and pulled on gloves. "We'll begin with the right ear, then left."

Ben and I moved to hold Daisy's ankles as a nurse assisted Dr. Marback with piercing each ear, using a needle. Once she'd finished placing the earrings, she handed me an instruction sheet with aftercare.

The earrings seemed to have an immediate effect. Daisy's heart rate steadied. An hour later, her blood oxygen level had returned to normal. Three hours later, her metabolic panel came back within normal range. Her kidneys were saved, with some minor damage.

My family came in, Mom standing right behind me, as Daisy opened her eyes and saw her father. She burst into tears and jumped into his arms. When she'd calmed down and was eating her dinner, while watching her favorite show sitting on her dad's lap, I excused myself.

"I'll stay until she's asleep again," he promised. "Then we need to talk."

"I'll be back in a few minutes. Just need some air," I explained.

Once I left the bustling hospital wing, the rest of SHAP was quiet for the evening. I rode the elevator to my floor and walked into the office I shared with Paris. I sat in my desk chair, covered my face, and cried. The last thirty hours had been too many feelings, too many near disasters. I definitely hadn't slept more than a few hours. And it was over.

The realization made me cry even harder. I didn't want to lose Paris. I loved her being in my life. It was easier to be with her than to live without her. She made me better.

And Ben? Ben would always be my first true love, but learning to live without Ben had been easier than learning to live *with* him. And there was my answer. I didn't know how long he'd be gone when he left this time, but I knew I wasn't going to wait for him to return.

I moved to stand, then paused, eyeing the last orange folder on Paris's desk. I moved to her chair, sat down, and started sifting through it.

Chapter Thirty-Two

Paris

MY EYELIDS WERE weighted sandpaper, dragging painfully across my eyes as I struggled to wake. Gray smoke filled my room, the overhead light flickering on and off as if it were a strobe. The fire alarm rang, a brighter flashing light coinciding with the piercing sound.

The heart monitor warned me my pulse had skyrocketed, and I yanked the sensor off. "Hello? Is anyone there?" I called, my voice scratchy from disuse. A wave of panic forced me to catch my breath. "Daisy!"

I pushed myself out of bed, using the IV stand for support. I ripped open drawers until I found another gown, then dampened it at the sink, before tying it around my face to minimize smoke inhalation. I skated to the door on my socked feet and touched the handle. It was warm but not burning.

I twisted the handle and pushed, but it didn't budge. "Hey! Let me out!" I called, trying to push against the door. I banged on the window and peered out, but all I could see was thick clouds of smoke.

The entire building shook and I held onto the door to

keep from toppling over. Dust from the ceiling tiles rained down and the power went completely out. I tried the door again, frantically pawing at the handle. Sirens grew louder and I pushed myself toward the outside window.

I tripped over a bedpan that had fallen from the table and caught myself on a chair with my injured arm, an explosion of pain stealing any remaining breath from my lungs. I tried to suck in more air but only got a lungful of smoke. I coughed so hard my eyes watered and pulled at my stitches, leaving small pools of blood on my gown.

Gasping and choking, I stumbled toward the window, pressing my face to the cool glass. Even five stories up, I could clearly make out the advancing hoard. Hybrid wolves interspersed between hundreds of people—no—they all moved like dancers. Hundreds of hybrid humans, walking through perfectly white snow.

They were coming for SHAP. Coming for us.

The door behind me flung open and Dallas stood there, blood and tears staining his face. "I'm so sorry," he said. "he took Daisy." Someone grabbed him from behind, and he disappeared into a cloud of smoke.

A nurse holding a syringe and wearing a wicked smile walked into my room. "Time for a little something to calm you down. This will only burn for a moment."

I screamed.

My eyes opened and I sat up, gasping fresh air. *It was a dream.* The same dream I'd been having, but earlier in the story. We weren't done yet.

"What the hell!" my twin cried.

I looked over to find Dallas scrambling from his chair to

the sink to grab a paper towel. He ran back and shoved it under my nose. I looked down and saw crimson stains trickling down my gown and pooling on the top sheet. Well, this was going to be fun to explain.

"Are you okay?!" he asked.

I shifted the towel to a more comfortable position and pinched my nose. "Yeah. This happens after my dreams sometimes."

He moved to a cabinet to grab a new hospital gown, opening the same drawer I had in my dream. My stomach twisted and I forced myself to swallow down the bile trying to escape. Throwing up while dealing with a bloody nose was the worst.

"I didn't know you still got them this bad." He held up a clean gown. "Want me to help you change or should I call the nurse?"

"Don't call. They'll run more tests. Just help me with my left arm. I don't want to tear my stitches." I released my nose, relieved to see the dark blood had turned light pink. Almost done.

Dallas helped remove my left arm from my old gown, then replaced it with the new one. After he turned around, I removed my right arm and yanked the soiled fabric off, pulling on the clean one. "I'm covered. Can you tie me?"

He returned and helped me lean forward as he tied me in the back. "What are we going to do about the sheet?"

"Search the drawers again?" I suggested.

He poked around and found a clean top sheet, then gathered up my blood-stained clothes and shoved them into the biohazard bag. "There."

I gave him a thumbs-up, then closed my eyes, exhausted.

"What was the dream about?"

My eyes shot open as the images crashed back into my mind. "Where's Daisy?!" I demanded.

Dallas grabbed my hand. "She's okay. They did the ritual and now she's eating chicken nuggets with Ben. Mina told me before she went to grab dinner. Loren's watching them."

I sucked in a deep breath, then another. She was okay. She was safe. "God, I'd rather talk to the dead than have these dreams." I dragged the heel of my hand across my watering eyes. "I want to see her."

"You need to stay in bed."

"It's a minor gunshot wound to my bicep, not a cannonball to the chest. I'm fine. I don't even understand why they put me under for surgery." I had fought for local anesthetic. It hurt, but it wasn't unbearable. "When are they letting me out?"

"Probably a few more days."

"Days?! I'm sore, not dead."

"Should've taken vixen."

"I would never." It would've made my recovery instantaneous, with only a small potential side effect of turning into a vampire or dying. But a little pain and a few months recovery were nothing compared to the devastation the venom caused, *will* cause. Plus, knowing my luck, I'd be allergic or something.

"God, you're fucking stubborn."

"Yeah, yeah, I know." Despite having transferred, I'd been pulled back to R&D to help with blood transfusions after the weight loss company Thinner dissolved, leaving thousands of humans at risk for turning into feral vampires. It had been an all-hands-on-deck situation and I'd been happy to help, but I'd seen the damage venom could truly do.

I'd worked with Carma and her best friend Elena, neither of whom could have the procedure reversed. They were vampire hybrids until they died or turned into full vampires. I had sat next to Carma's bed while she'd cried when we told her what was truly going on at her mom's company. I knew venom had practical and life-saving applications, but I didn't want to touch something that poisoned so many lives.

I turned toward the window as a ray of sun came in, and in-between blinks the parking lot changed back to the scene from the dream. I looked over at Dallas and struggled to sit up. "Dal, where's the vixen?"

He raised an eyebrow. "What do you mean?"

"Ben took all the venom and vixen from evidence, then Russell tried to steal it. What happened after Ben and I were loaded into the helicopter?"

"We cleaned up the mess and then drove back here. Why?"

Was he being deliberately obtuse? "What happened to the stash of illicit drugs after we left?"

"What do you mean?"

I searched his face. "Dal, what aren't you telling me?"

"I'm not not telling you anything!"

"Russell didn't take the venom with him when he died. Where is it?"

He shook his head. "Don't ask me that, P. It's safe, I promise."

I fisted the sheet with my good arm, my stomach dropping to the floor. What was my twin mixed up in? "Dallas, why didn't you have to go into hiding? Why only Ben?"

He dropped his legs and leaned forward. "I told you—"

"I know what you told me. Now, I want to know what you didn't say."

"What are *you* trying to say? You need sleep. You're all fuzzy."

I was fuzzy, but not incoherent. Outside of my throbbing arm, I was fine. But Dallas kept touching his eyebrow with his left pointer finger, his tell when he was lying.

"You didn't have to go into hiding…because it's you behind the threats, isn't it?" I whispered, watching his reaction.

He brushed his palms over the thighs of his jeans. The same thing I did when I felt trapped. He swallowed hard then turned on the charm. His eyes softened and he smiled as if he were in a toothpaste commercial.

His attention crept over me like a warm blanket and for a moment, I forgot what I was saying. Then I pushed the feeling away. "No. You can't charm your way out of this." I was one of the only people who could push away his gift. *I was one of the only people who could push away his gift.* "You're manipulating people into doing what you want them to do."

"Are you running a fever? I'm calling a nurse." He reached for the button on my bedrail, but I swatted him away.

"No, tell me the truth. You have the venom."

He shrugged. "What's it matter? It's off the streets."

"What are you going to do with it?"

"What I have to."

I blinked at him. "You're going to sell it."

"I have my orders."

"What are your orders? To make and sell weapons?"

His eyes held mine. "No." His left eyebrow ticked.

My mouth fell open. "SHAP's selling weapons, aren't they? That's why I've been dreaming of a hostile takeover for weeks." My mouth went dry as the tops of his ears turn red. "Because you find out what people want and then use your gift to make it happen."

A wave of dizziness and exhaustion washed over me. "It was *you* testing the venom. Was Thinner an involuntary clinical trial to see if it would work? You just needed someone ruthless enough to carry it out, and Lucinda was the perfect candidate."

"Paris, you're delusional. You got shot yesterday and you just had a bad dream."

I was sweating, my heart monitor's beeps increasing in frequency. I shook my head. "Vixen was supposed to be a modified, safer product, but Fletcher threw a wrench into that with her own plan. No honor among criminals anymore, I suppose."

I gasped. "You put the tracker on my trackers! You knew there was a probability I'd use them for something and catch you. And you were right. That tracker was shitty, by the way, but I guess I'd have made a shitty one, too, if I had to do it with supplies from a chain electronics store."

He frowned at the insult, and I knew I'd landed the blow. My brother the traitor. Panic seized my lungs and I fought to take a breath as the events of the last twenty-nine months shifted into focus.

"Dare I sound like a doctor from the 1950s and say you're hysterical?" He leaned over my bedrail and pressed the nurse call button. "You need a sedative."

"Ben," I whispered. "You needed him. He was a genius at chemicals and—" I covered my face with my hands and shook my head. "Oh my god...you texted me that night to manipulate me. You knew I wouldn't just sit back while you were in danger and that I'd find you and create a distraction."

"Paris, what planet do you live on?"

I gripped the bedrail. "You ordered Ben to make sure I was safe. You're the one who followed him, didn't you? So he'd freak out and play dead, then come work with you without interference?"

I shook my head, trying to make it untrue. "Jim didn't know, did he? At least not until just before Jake resigned. Otherwise, he wouldn't have put his best agents on the Thinner case." I laughed once. "I knew he underestimated Eliza and me. Expected us to just write up a tidy case report and absolve SHAP of any wrongdoing."

"How on earth are you jumping to these conclusions?"

"Because I know you." My eyes widened. "Your favorite movies are *The Departed* and *The Winter Soldier*." I shook my head.

"Do you even hear yourself? You've gone mad."

"You were the boy who beat up my bullies for me and taught me to fight. You spent your life protecting me and now *you're* the bully!"

"I'm still trying to protect you!" he shouted. "Why do you think I pushed you out of R&D? Encouraged you to become an agent? The irony of you being assigned to this case..." He laughed without humor.

He raked his hands through his already disheveled hair, the exact color as mine. "I couldn't let it touch you, I couldn't—" He sucked in a shaky breath. "We didn't know. The orders come through anonymously. When I realized who was behind it...it was too late."

"Dallas—"

"We didn't have an exit plan. So I made myself untouchable to protect you and our family. I *had* to make Ben my lead researcher, no matter what stood in the way. I did what I had to in order to finish the job."

"You hurt so many people." I didn't recognize my own voice.

"I'd do it all again! You're my *twin*. I'll always have your back. But I need you to have mine, okay? After the sale, we just have to get out of the country and we'll be okay. We'll all be okay."

"You can't sell the venom."

He leaned on the bed, hands over his face. "If I don't, we're all dead. The man who ordered it..." He leaned forward and gripped my arm. "The man who ordered it doesn't have limits. We can only hope to distract him long enough to never be on his radar again."

A shiver rolled down my spine. "Ben is with Daisy right now. Is she in danger?"

He didn't answer.

A PA system announcement interrupted us. "Code purple, eight-year-old girl with curly red hair..."

Eliza's guttural scream echoed down the hall.

My spine turned to steel, and I scrambled out of bed. "Oh my god, it's why you convinced them to do surgery on me. So I wouldn't figure out your plan even when I was so close to it. That's why you've been sitting here, to keep me from figuring it out?" My heart rate increased even more, the beeping reminding me of a detonated bomb seconds before it blew. I ripped off the sticky pad and wire.

"To keep anyone from hurting you!" he defended, standing with me. "Ben was supposed to keep Daisy safe!"

The door opened and the nurse I had for the last few hours walked in. She saw the heart monitor and frowned. "We need to get your heart rate down." She turned to Dallas. "You need to leave."

"No." Dallas withdrew his gun and held it on the nurse. "Who are you?"

The nurse was unfazed. She reached into her scrubs and removed a tranquilizer gun and shot my brother in the shoulder. "No guns in the medical suites. Oxygen canisters are very flammable."

Dallas stumbled backward and into a chair. "Paris," he wheezed, "Wingspan Bridge. Run." Then his eyes closed.

"He'll be fine in a few hours. Enough to cool off."

I looked at her, wide-eyed. My blood ran cold. I shook my head, trying to clear it. I needed to get out of here, get to Eliza, help Daisy. "Uh, my brother didn't get much sleep last night," I offered, trying to distract her. She was on the opposite end of the bed, between me and the door. "I'm so sorry."

She put away her own weapon. "Let's get you something to calm you down, too."

She blinked and her eyes went bright yellow for one moment. Everything went eerily quiet. This *wasn't* my nurse. And not-my-nurse was reaching into her pocket to remove a syringe, just like she had in the dream.

As if in slow motion, I scanned the room. My clothes, my phone, and my shoes were gone from the couch. I bet if I looked in the lockbox at the bottom of the dresser where the TV sat, my weapons would be gone, too. I pulled my sheet up over my IV arm and started to peel back the tape that kept the tubing in place.

I studied Dallas, relieved to see his chest rising and falling.

"Don't worry. He's still alive, just resting. He's too valuable to kill, unfortunately. You'll have to serve as the warning." She uncapped her syringe and leapt across the bed, shoving the needle into an injection port on my IV. "This will only burn a little, then you'll just close your eyes."

I thrust my hand upward and hit her nose, causing her to fall on to the bed and release the syringe. I grabbed it, shoved it into her arm, and pressed down, injecting the remaining medication. She screamed, changing into Miriam, my old lab manager, before falling to the floor. So she wasn't a troll, but a shapeshifter.

She cackled. "It's too late for you, too," she wheezed. "It works fast."

I ripped my IV out, ignoring the blood coursing down my arm, but she was right. My energy was already pouring out of me, my breathing labored, my vision nearly double. *Get to Eliza. Find a way to get to Eliza.*

I looked at Dallas. *Vixen. Get vixen.* I stumbled toward

my brother and grabbed the gun out of his hands, then gripped the arm of the chair to keep from tumbling down. If I fell, there'd be no getting up.

Get vixen. Find Eliza.

I clenched my jaw until my teeth were about to break and pushed myself off the chair. I stumbled toward the door, my socked feet slipping a little. I hit the door hard, then yanked it open, crying out as stitches tore.

The wall held me up as I stumbled forward, the gun nearly useless in my bloodied hand. My nurse—the real one—was bent over an unconscious Loren, slumped in the hallway. She gasped when she saw me. "Ms. Evans!"

"I've been poisoned. I need my clothes."

Her mouth opened and closed without sound, then she took a step forward. "Let's get back to your room—"

"Miriam, disguised as you, poisoned me and tranquilized my brother. Get. My. Clothes." I held the gun in my shaking hand.

Eliza bolted out of Daisy's room and stopped dead.

My legs gave out. I tucked my arm between the wall and the railing, my knees useless. My mouth tasted like sweet metal and I could barely hold my head up. "Find my jeans," I ordered, gasping for breath.

Eliza didn't hesitate, pushing past the nurse and running to the nurse's station. She threw open cabinets and drawers, then reached into a trash can and removed a plastic shopping bag.

"You can't be back here!" someone argued, but Eliza was already running toward me, pulling my jeans out.

"Pocket," I breathed.

Eliza reached into the pocket and removed the clear capsule with the pink powder, shaking her head. "You can't," she begged.

I reached out and grabbed her hand, crying out at the pain to do so, and brought her hand to my mouth. *Please don't be one with fentanyl.* I sucked the pill into my mouth and chewed, choking on the powder.

I fell to the ground, unable to hold myself up anymore.

A blistering fire grew inside my mouth, and I feared if I dared to scream, I would burn down the entire building. My heart thundered, the throbbing at my gunshot and IV sites grew so hard, my body shook. Then, the pain eased.

Eliza's heat was wrapped around me and as I shifted, she helped me stand. My strength was returning. Not much, probably not enough to drive, but enough to move. "Let's fucking go rescue our Daisy."

We ran—well, more like stumbled—to the elevator, barely making it before the doors closed. I slammed the lobby button, straightening as the pain gradually faded.

The doors opened, and Sienna stared at us from across the threshold. "Saw an older man carry an unconscious Ben and fighting Daisy out of the building on the security monitors. Shot the guard before he could stop him. I'll drive."

Chapter Thirty-Three

Eliza

"WHERE TO?" SIENNA asked.

"Dallas said Wingspan Bridge," Paris explained, "but it was demolished in 2010."

"And replaced with the Folk River Bridge," I explained. I pulled out a crumpled paper from my pocket. "I hadn't connected the dots yet, but you wrote down the location of every incident report. All were at the bridge."

"Dallas said this guy was a threat to all of us if he didn't get the vixen. But why take Daisy? I'm going to tear that man limb from limb—"

"Get in fucking line," I said, lifting the phone to my ear. My brother answered on the first ring.

"You still at the hospital? Poppy's asleep, but I'm on—"

"Someone kidnapped Daisy and Ben. We think they're headed to the Folk River Bridge for the vixen sale. Bring every weapon you have."

"Roger." He hung up.

"What I want to know," Sienna asked, ignoring a red light in favor of using her horn to weave through the intersection, "is when you're going to figure out Ben's real name."

I stared at Sienna, then looked back at Paris. "Bennett?"

"Bennett as in Bennett Somerville, the missing child of Christian Somerville? The abusive wizard who did oral venom experiments on his own son?" Paris asked. "Was Christian the guy who kidnapped them?"

Sienna made another turn that would've made a regular human's truck flip over. "Where can a wizard go where he won't hurt anyone else?" she prompted. "Because even if you manage to stop him, he'll come after you."

One of Poppy's reaper stories from Saturday evening popped into my head. "Once someone crosses into the afterlife, it's nearly impossible to come back, unless you're a reaper."

"We're going to need reaper help." I dug through my purse and found a pen, then flipped Paris's crumpled note over and began to write.

DEARLY DEPARTED SYLVIA GRIM (GRIM REAPER)

MY DAUGHTER WAS KIDNAPPED AND OUR FAMILIES ARE IN DANGER. RESCUE MISSION. MY DAUGHTER IN EXCHANGE FOR A DANGEROUS WIZARD AND ORAL VAMPIRE VENOM?

MEET US AT FOLK RIVER BRIDGE, 30 MILES NORTHWEST OF APPLECHESTER IN 45 MINUTES.

ELIZA

"Use my blood," Paris said.

"I can't ask you to give up a year of your life. Anyway, you have vampire venom coursing through you. It likely won't work."

"You didn't ask. I offered." She grabbed the paper and rubbed some of the still-wet blood from her hospital gown's sleeve onto the corner of the paper. "There."

Sienna reached into the middle console and handed me a lighter. "Try not to burn yourself or a hole in my leather seats."

I tore off the bloodied corner of the paper, flicked the lighter on, and began scrying. The flame went out twice. "If you can give me like thirty seconds without slamming on the brakes or hitting a pothole, that would help."

"Hmm," Sienna said, then cut across three lanes of traffic and down an off-ramp for the freeway. She cut over the grassy medium and then merged onto the on-ramp to a chorus of honks.

"We're going to die or get pulled over," I warned.

"I've been driving longer than you've been alive," Sienna said. "And no, we won't get pulled over."

"How do you know?"

"Because the police chief is also a werewolf, and I have connections." We entered the freeway and straightened out. "Now hurry up. You have four miles."

Reengaging the lighter, I concentrated on the flame and made a connection. I shoved the words through and then burned the bloodstained paper postage. The receiver pushed back.

This one's on us and closed the line.

I released the lighter and turned to Sienna. "Floor it."

SIENNA SLAMMED ON her breaks, the truck stopping at the edge of the two-lane bridge as the sun faded completely from the sky. The reflectors on the bridge closed signs shone off the banks of snow. Heavy construction tarps flapped overhead. I was out of the truck before it was even in park, Paris at my heels.

"I don't have any weapons," she warned.

Another black SUV pulled up next to Sienna, followed by shouts. I squinted and saw Jake, cane under his arm and gun in hand, move beneath the streetlight. Loren, behind him, paused to hand Paris a revolver and me a stun gun.

"You okay?" I asked him.

"Not the first time I've been knocked out with magic but should've seen it coming. I'm sorry."

"We'll get my girl back," I promised. We would because we had to.

We moved as a group, ducking underneath the tarps and into a dim, dead-quiet work zone. "Hello?" Eliza called. "I'm here for my daughter, you son of a bitch!"

"The toll booth," Loren suggested.

An old-fashioned toll booth sat at the other end of the bridge. Once a working payment station, it was now preserved by the historical society. I wonder if they knew illegal dealings were going down inside.

"Oh, come on," a man said. "You didn't think I'd be so obvious as to use the toll booth, did you?"

We turned as a group to find a man on the opposite banister in a crisp black suit. I knew without question he was Ben's father. The same hair, although more salt and pepper, the same pointy chin, the same charming smile that was meant to disarm and manipulate.

I flipped on my stun gun and ran up toward him, dodging Paris's reach, and stopping nearly nose to nose, the stun gun against his stomach. "Give me my daughter and I leave you alive."

His smile grew as he grabbed my wrist, twisting it so my hand moved away from him, and the weapon fell. It hurt so bad I wanted to shout, but I refused to give him the satisfaction. "I warned you," I said through my clenched jaw.

Christian laughed. "So you're Eliza Robinson of 476 Third Drive?" He released my arm and wrapped his fingers in a vise-like grip around my chin, tilting it left and right. "I see why my son has taken such a liking to you."

"You may know my address, but you don't know the most important thing about me."

He smiled. "I know your parents, Magnolia and Morris live at—"

"Oh, you know all the details you can literally Google in two minutes. Good for you. Did you want a gold star?"

"Hey, Eliza," Jake called. "Can we maybe not taunt the maniac who has Daisy?"

I waved him off. "I'm just getting to know my future father-in-law," I called back. "Well, former future-father-in-law."

His laugh was obnoxious and overly curated, meant to steal something from the listener. "Oh my dear, how I wish I'd gotten to know you before I had to kill you and your friends."

I kept perfectly still but remained aware of Paris on my right side. *Don't look*, I told myself. *Focus on Christian.*

Despite the pain in my jaw, I forced my most dazzling smile, the one that Ben said he fell in love with. As expected, Christian blinked, distracted. Like son, like father. "Here's the one thing your research didn't tell you," I whispered. "Unlike you, I would *literally* move heaven and hell to protect my child."

"NOW!" Paris shouted.

I kneed Christian in the nuts. Hard. He released my chin and I ducked and rolled as everyone with a gun fired.

A green forcefield wrapped around him and the bullets fell to the concrete.

"Probably should've seen that coming," Paris said, then dropped low and kicked his legs out from under him. He hit the ground, then scrambled back upright.

"You have never been sexier to me than right now!" I called.

"Save the dirty talk, babe!" she returned. "I gotta concentrate."

Sienna wolf whistled. "I found Ben and Daisy! He's unconscious but she's okay."

"Jake, get my baby!" I ordered.

Jake took off after Sienna.

"No," Christian said. A blue light flashed, and the air went solid.

We were suspended as if in a photograph. I strained to move my arms and legs, but barely twitched. I tried to shout, but nothing came out.

"Ah, pity. And I was having so much fun," the bastard said. He walked toward me as if he were walking on water, proud and godlike. "This is what happens when you bring a human to a wizard fight."

"You forget, I'm not completely human!" Paris called, pushing through the spell and jumping on his back and holding him in a headlock. He rammed into the concrete wall, trying to loosen Paris, but she didn't let go.

"Leave her alone!" Daisy called. A flash of purple, and the air softened.

I turned and ran headlong at my daughter.

Christian grabbed Paris and hurled her at me. She did a somersault and bounced right back up to her feet. Daisy waved her hand and erected an ice wall between us, as if she were Elsa from one of her favorite movies.

Ben crawled out of the shadows and toward his daughter. "This is what happens when you fuck with magic, Dad," he called, struggling to stand. "You changed my DNA, did you know? Made my daughter as powerful as you at only eight."

I was sick of this. I grabbed Paris's gun and held it directly pointed at Ben's chest. "I know you're not trying to deal with your childhood trauma by using *our* daughter."

"Stay out of this, Eliza," my *very* ex-fiancé warned.

I stepped between him and Daisy. "I'm sorry, what did you say to me?"

"He wants me. Well, revenge on me." He smiled but it looked like a grimace. "I was his biggest failure. Don't make him want revenge on you, too."

"Then you better tell me what the hell is going on and why our daughter is involved."

"SHAP is making custom made-to-order weapons," Paris explained. "Including the venom. Seems Christian gave up on making his own oral venom when his son disappeared and hired Dallas to do it. The irony was, the kid he had experimented on for decades was working in R&D when the order came in."

Ben flinched. "Goddammit, Paris! You just had to stay quiet and stay away from my family and this would've been over. We could've sold the venom to my fucking father, and I could've taken my family and disappeared from him, from Dallas, from all of fucking SHAP."

"No," Paris said. "You couldn't have. He's planning a SHAP takeover. And you all end up dead."

I gasped, looking at Paris. "The nightmare?"

"Almost every night for months."

"Fuuuuuuck, I hate my life." Ben looked resigned. "Being with you and Daisy were the happiest years of my life. Looks like those are the only happy years I'm going to get." He leaned over, kissed my cheek, and then took off running toward his dad.

Daisy looked off to the side and squealed, startling all of us. "Puppies!"

A dozen hybrid wolves stepped out of the shadows. "Oh my god," I breathed. A small black wolf paced in front of them, keeping them in place. *Sienna.*

Daisy took off running toward the wolves, but Paris ran forward and scooped her up into her arms, circling back to me. "These ones aren't super friendly, munchkin."

Daisy's face fell. "Oh, okay."

Belphegor tore through the bridge behind us. "Why did I have to get summoned by the fucking death army to find out about Daisy? None of you could've told me?"

"The reapers are here?" I asked. Humans couldn't see

reapers unless they were about to die.

"You don't have a phone," Paris told Belphegor. "And I didn't have time for smoke signals."

"Don't sass me, woman! And yeah, the reapers are here." He pointed at a spot that looked empty. "This one says she's Poppy's sister." He looked around and spotted his favorite human. "Daisy, you okay?"

"My mom is mad at my dad because my grandpa is trying to hurt us," she explained, gesturing to Christian.

I blinked. What an accurate assessment. I glanced up at the wizard, whose eyes were on Belphegor.

"This grandpa?" the demon asked, pointing.

Daisy nodded. "He hurt Daddy when we arrived and told me he was going to take me somewhere to play with magic, but I don't want to go."

Belphegor carefully peeled off his large sweater and draped it around Daisy's shoulders. "I'll handle this. Keep my sweater safe."

Paris set Daisy down and my daughter ran to me. I scooped her up and pressed her face into my shoulder. Belphegor took another step, his skin turning into molten lava. "Sylvia! This the guy we're taking with us?" he asked.

I covered Daisy's ears as Belphegor wrapped Christian in what appeared to be a hug, cut a hole into the ground, and jumped in.

The black wolf growled and began corralling the hybrids, nipping at their heels until they followed Belphegor into the ground.

"Where's the venom?" Paris yelled.

Ben shook his head. "I can't let you have it! It's my only

way out now. I need to trade it to SHAP for my freedom."

She grabbed him by the throat. "Turning into a hybrid has made me very, very angry and able to tear you apart limb from limb. Where. Is. The. Venom?"

He raised his gun to her shoulder and shot twice, at point-blank range.

My scream echoed through the night.

Paris dropped Ben and stumbled backward two steps before reaching up and pulling the bullets out of her shoulder, then tossing them on the ground between them. "You're going to have to try harder to kill me."

She punched him hard in the jaw. He tried to throw one back, but she evaded and swept his legs out from under him, then kicked him in the ribs for good measure. "Where. Is. It?"

Ben moaned, then gestured to a black duffel bag between two porta potties. She grabbed it and ran toward the hole, then threw it in.

A stack of letters fluttered to the ground as the hole closed.

On top, a letter for Poppy. Beneath, the five missives I'd written to Ben with a note on the top envelope. POSTAGE REFUNDED. UNDELIVERABLE.

Loren ran over and turned Ben on his stomach, then used a zip tie to secure his hands behind him. "Well, I'm glad that's over. Maybe I'll get another six months of relaxing before I have to come out of retirement. *Again.*"

Chapter Thirty-Four

Paris

SIENNA, AFTER CHANGING back into her human form, had literally thrown Ben in her truck and left with orders to take Dallas into custody. Loren, Jake, and Belphegor went with them. Poppy drove Eliza, Daisy, and me back to Applechester, pulling in front of the bed and breakfast, where Eliza had called Dr. Marback and asked her to meet us. There was no way she was returning to the medical center until a thorough investigation was completed.

Daisy's examination went better than expected, with orders for her to rest and eat a lot of calories. While Eliza talked to the doctor, Mina took Daisy into the room with a canopy bed and a giant television, turned on her favorite show, and fed her leftover birthday pie.

Carma directed me to her bathroom to shower and laid out some clothes on the bed. Her shampoo smelled like strawberries, and I was instantly calmer. The scent made me think of berry picking with Eliza and Daisy the summer we were together. I would give anything to be back there.

A knock sounded and I opened the door to find Carma. "Just checking on you."

I stepped back and motioned for her to come in. Her orange and black cat, Cheddar, darted out from under the bed and weaved around her legs. She scooped him up, gave him a kiss on the nose, and set him on her comforter. He stretched and curled into a ball.

She reached out and fussed with the shoulders of the sweatshirt she'd loaned me. "We're about the same height, although your shoulders are bigger. Still, not too shabby." she said. "The tank and pants fit okay?"

"Yeah, thanks."

She perched on the edge of the bed and motioned for me to take the stool at her vanity. "Being a hybrid is surreal, isn't it?"

I laughed once. "Yeah. I can smell everything, and colors are intense."

She nodded. "Everything is heightened. It can be exhausting, even with more energy."

"I was adamant I was going to heal without it. I didn't want to touch it."

"What made you?"

I looked into her bright green eyes. "The people I loved the most in this world were in danger, and I was poisoned. Can't protect them if I'm dead."

She smiled. "I like you, Paris Evans. I think you're the only person in this world good enough for Eliza. And she for you." She nodded toward my arm. "How's the arm?"

I lifted the sweatshirt, showing her the gunshots. She stood and inspected the wounds. The surgical one was completely healed, and the two shots by Ben were smooth and pink. Carma then opened a drawer on her vanity, grabbed her small manicure scissors, and snipped the remaining irrelevant stitches from my surgery. She removed the small threads and ran her thumb over the skin.

"You won't even scar." She looked at me. "You know, you heal faster than I do. It would've taken me at least twenty-four hours to recover from wounds this big." She scrunched her nose. "Physically. I'm sure being shot three times in a week leaves some scars."

"Can't wait to unpack that one in therapy," I admitted. "Why do you think I heal faster?"

She lifted a shoulder. "Maybe you got a higher dose? Or maybe there's some undiscovered magic in you. Poppy still heals fast, despite having reversed the vixen."

"Speaking of Poppy, did she share what was in the letter?"

Carma smiled. "She said it was an update on how Sylvia has taken over the grim reaper council and is campaigning for a bunch of rule changes. I didn't really follow, but she gave two fist pumps before she cried."

"I can't even imagine what it's like, or why the hell they made her a reaper so young."

"I know, right? I mean I logically understand there was a reaper shortage, but it should never have fallen on the shoulders of a sixteen-year-old girl."

"Supernatural life rarely seems to work out fair."

She laughed. "That's the truth. Although it's not all bad." She sat back on the bed. "Have you considered staying a hybrid?"

I shook my head. "No, I haven't. The risk is so high."

"It is. And it's a different type of life. But you wouldn't

have allergies anymore. Is the threat of becoming a vampire really greater than having life-threatening allergic reactions?"

I chewed over her words. I'd dreamed of not having allergies for years. But being able to eat freely wasn't something a hybrid could do, either. Carma couldn't eat human food and instead had a special feeding regimen through SHAP. I was used to a restricted diet, but was I willing to give up part of my humanity for this life?

My gut twinged, knowing the answer before my brain did. Oral venom was an amazing tool, but it wasn't one I wanted to use forever. "I know it must be lonely to be one of the only hybrids," I admitted.

"I have my bestie, Elena. And that's enough." She smiled at me as she straightened my gown. "If you ever want to talk about it, let me know. No matter if you're full human or hybrid, whether you're with Eliza or not. Okay?"

My chest was fuzzy with emotions, as if she'd stuffed cotton inside. "Okay."

She gave me a hug. "I'll leave you to finish getting dressed. And watch out for Lucifer," she warned about the black cat sleeping in the closet. "He loves chewing on toes."

Eliza was waiting for me when I reemerged. I hesitated. We hadn't talked much, except about Daisy. Would she still want me after everything? Would she be able to trust anyone after the way Ben betrayed her?

I cried out when she opened her arms. I dove in, wrapping tightly around her. My forehead pressed against her neck, her hands fisting the back of my sweatshirt.

"I almost lost you," she said, "again."

"You didn't," I promised, wrapping my arms tighter.

"Don't let go."

As if I could. As if I would. "How do we do this? How do we make it work?"

"Together." She leaned back and kissed me softly on the lips. "We figure it out day by day."

"Okay," I whispered.

"Dr. Marback said to call her when you're ready for a transfusion." She brushed a stray piece of hair behind my ear. "Are you going to reverse?"

I nodded. "I am."

She unlocked her phone and pressed the doctor's number from her favorites. "Dr. Marback, Eliza. My girlfriend is ready for a transfusion." She hung up. "She'll be here in an hour."

"Girlfriend?" I asked, the wave of butterflies in my stomach nearly carrying me away.

"It doesn't seem like a big enough word, but it'll do for now."

I dug my hands into her hair and kissed her.

Chapter Thirty-Five

Paris

A SPECIAL COUNCIL was called by Sienna, where the plot with Ben, known as Bennett, and Dallas—confirmed by Carma's convicted mother, Lucinda—was revealed. Bennett had run away at eighteen and was picked up by a SHAP agent who was trailing Christian. That agent—my nosy neighbor Doris Manalin—helped him get a new identity and start over. I nearly passed out in shock when she took the stand.

When the oral venom order came through, Dallas—who knew Bennett's history—blackmailed him to be a part of it. Bennett, who had watched his father try and fail at making the venom, knew what pitfalls to avoid. He hoped by giving his father the venom, his father would focus on something else and leave Eliza and Daisy alone.

With Christian Somerville and the remaining key players dead, the oral venom/vixen case was officially closed by November 30th, just as Jim requested. Next came an investigation of all the weapons SHAP made-to-order, which didn't take long. Sienna had made copies of every order that came in, despite being directed by Jim to take every dark blue envelope directly to Dallas without opening it. As any good assistant would do, she carefully steamed opened the glue, copied the contents, and resealed the envelope. She locked everything in a safe that only she and her sister knew the combination to, waiting for a team she could trust.

Jim was not formally charged, as he never opened or read the files, but he stepped down as the Territory Director, effective immediately. My heart broke for Mina, who had just started rebuilding a relationship with him. She was by his side as security escorted him out, so I had to think there was some hope left.

Sienna was named Interim Territory Director and immediately called me into her office. "Be my right-hand woman. Help me put this place back together."

"You're going to have to pay me a lot of money," I warned.

She wrote down a figure on a piece of paper and I blinked rapidly at the number of zeros. I could retire at forty with that salary. I held out my hand to shake. "I'll start after the holidays."

"Deal."

Eliza and I dealt with our grief over losing people we loved in different, but creative ways. She made enough food to open a bakery. She'd been dropping it off at the bed and breakfast, with neighbors, and LGBTQ+ shelters for the last two weeks. She'd lost her fiancé twice over, and this time when she explained why Ben was no longer around to Daisy, the little girl became completely inconsolable. I knew how she felt.

My twin, my other half, the only person in my family

who gave a shit about me, was gone. We'd never celebrate our birthdays together again, never go to another baseball game, never go to another theater on opening night, and never share another salad. He'd *hurt* people, killed people. He was the reason Carma was in constant risk of turning into a vampire.

Sure, it could be said without the venom, Carma and Mina wouldn't have met, and Poppy wouldn't be back, and Eliza and I may not be together now, but that was the only tarnished silver lining I could find in the aftermath.

"You're dropping stitches," Belphegor said. "Get out of your head and focus."

I blinked at him, then refocused on the scarf I was trying to make Eliza. The neat row of yarn had veered off course. I groaned.

"Do it again."

I glared up at a demon. "I thought Amber was teaching me to crochet."

"She is!" he defended. "You just listen better to me."

I scrunched my nose and turned to Amber. "I'm sorry. I'm just lost in my thoughts."

Amber waved me off. "It's fine. Crocheting is supposed to be fun! No use if it's stressing you out."

I dropped my project to my lap. "I think I'm just hungry. I'll go grab a snack."

"Ah, wait." She opened her large handbag and pulled out a container of cookies. "These are for you! There's one cup peanut butter, one cup sugar, one egg, and a splash of vanilla. You can eat these, right?"

I looked between the container and Amber, my eyes

stinging. I nodded and reached for the cookies. "Thank you," I managed, my throat tight with gratitude. I opened the container and inhaled deeply, my mouth watering at the smell. I broke off a piece of a cookie and popped it into my mouth, my eyes closing at the sweet, creamy texture.

"Glad you like them, dear," Amber chuckled.

"These are incredible," I said through a mouthful.

She smiled at me. "When things are bad and getting worse, keep a cookie in your purse."

"That's the best life advice I've ever heard."

"I'm old. I'm full of good life advice."

The front door opened, and Amber glanced over. "Ah, there she is."

I looked up to find Sienna, my future boss, walking toward us. I sat up straighter and looked between Amber and Belphegor. Amber wore a shit-eating grin and Belphegor's eyes were glued to the newcomer.

"Mina told me Sienna wanted a formal introduction to Belphegor," Amber explained, "so I reached out and invited her to yarn night, if that's okay."

Sienna nodded to me, then reached out her hand to the demon. "Sienna, Interim SHAP Territory Director and werewolf."

Belphegor tried to yank his hand from the yarn he held for Amber, but his claws got tangled. "Fucking hell," he grumbled.

My boss put her hands over his. "Careful, you don't want to hurt the yarn." She eased the fiber away from his claws, then glanced at Amber. "Is this Malabrigo Rios merino wool in Aniversario? One of my favorites."

She smiled. "Yes! Belphegor got this for me for Christmas." She reached over and stroked the back of his head. "He's so thoughtful."

"What a wonderful gift." Sienna sat down next to him. "Let's get this yarn sorted back out."

I didn't know demons could blush, but Belphegor's cheeks turned pink as Sienna wrapped the yarn around his hands again. When she was finished, she opened her own bag and pulled out what appeared to be a shawl.

Belphegor's eyes went from her shawl to me, and he mouthed "What do I do?"

I mouthed "Talk to her" back.

He cleared his throat and opened his mouth than closed it again. I held up my yarn and shook it then tilted my head to her.

"Uh," he started then took a steadying breath. "Sienna, what are you making?"

She smiled and looked up at him. "A shawl, for my sister."

He looked back to me, and I rotated my hand in a small circle, indicating he should keep going. "What kind of…" He widened his eyes.

"Yarn," I mouthed.

"Yarn," he continued, "are you using?"

"Jade Sapphire 4ply Mongolian Cashmere in Earth." Sienna looked over. "Did you understand any of that?"

"Cashmere," he admitted. "Means it's soft."

Sienna leaned back on her chair, her shoulder brushing his. "So soft."

"Tell me more about your sister," he prompted.

I looked over at Amber, who was pulling headphones out of her bag. She winked at me. I took the hint and made a big show of checking my phone.

"Oh wow, look at the time. I've got to make a call." I scooped up the cookies and my hopeless scarf and walked back to my apartment.

The moment I closed the door, the temporary distraction from real life was gone. I dropped to the couch and nabbed a cookie from the container, nibbling the edge. Peanut butter cookies were Dallas's favorite, too.

I unlocked my phone, then locked it again, then unlocked it and dialed SHAP's main number. Following the prompts, I made it to the security desk.

"Prisoner #8394 Dallas Evans," I requested.

I was put on hold, a steady beep marking off time in ten-second increments. One hundred and forty beeps later, my brother answered.

"Hello?" His voice was strong but tired. "Hello, who is this?"

I opened my mouth, but no sound came out. I hadn't seen or talked to him since that day in the hospital.

"P?"

I cleared my throat. "Yeah. It's me."

We both sat there in a minute of silence, a conversation we weren't ready to have filling the space. I took a bite of the cookie to fill my mouth with something other than unending questions.

"What are you eating?" he asked.

I swallowed before answering. "Amber made me Paris-safe peanut butter cookies."

"My favorite."

"Yeah."

He let out a long breath. "I know I'm sorry isn't enough."

"What are you sorry for, exactly? Getting caught? For our parents completely checking out and taking off for Florida?" The day after Dallas was arrested, Mom and Dad were on a plane headed to stay with family. They couldn't miss Dallas at Christmas if they weren't home, they said.

"That too, but mostly for disappointing you. For not being the good man you believed me to be."

"You hurt so many people, Dallas. Including me."

"I know."

"It's going to take time for me to forgive you."

"Can you?"

I took another bite of my cookie, then chewed slowly and swallowed before answering. "I hope so. You're my twin."

"You got all the good genes. Except the allergies."

I laughed, the tension between us lowering a fraction. "Eh, at least my cholesterol is way better than yours since I can't eat much crap."

"Ah, the silver lining." A guard warned Dallas his time was up. "Same time next week?" he asked, his voice cracking with emotion.

I hesitated for a moment. "Yeah."

"I know you may not believe me, but I love you, sis."

I wasn't ready to say it back yet. Of course I loved him, but I was too raw. "Talk next week." The moment the line went dead, I started crying. I shoved the rest of the cookie in my mouth.

Unlocking my phone again, I texted Eliza.

Me: *I called Dallas*

Eliza: *How'd that go?*

Me: *I'm crying while eating cookies Amber made me*

Eliza: *So really well, huh?*

Me: *The best*

Eliza: *I thought you had yarn club tonight? Over already?*

Me: *Amber set Belphegor up on a date. With Sienna*

Eliza: *WHAT?!*

Me: *It was going well, so I left them alone*

Eliza: *Brb*

Out of distractions, I curled up on the sofa, burying my face in my pillow so the nosy ghosts didn't hear me, or worse Belphegor. I was not going to interrupt his date—or whatever it was—with my emotions. I wouldn't be a burden.

Three sharp raps on my door made me sit up so fast, I was dizzy. *Shit.* Someone had heard me. I grabbed two tissues and tried to wipe my face off, then looked out my peephole.

When I opened the door, I just stared. Eliza and Daisy pushed me aside and walked in, arms full. Eliza set down her large plastic container, shed her coat, then wrapped her arms around me. "Come here."

She stroked my hair and rocked me back and forth, soothing me. "I've got you," she whispered.

Daisy gave us a quick hug then dropped her bag. "Mommy said you were sad, so we brought over my pink

Christmas tree. It makes me smile and I told Mommy it would make you smile."

I leaned back and looked at Eliza. "You brought over the pink Christmas tree?" I breathed.

"She was insistent when I told her we were going to surprise you because you were sad," she explained.

"Mommy needs to help because it's sooo tall. Like probably twenty feet or something," Daisy added. "But you can use it until Christmas so you're not sad anymore."

I wanted to fall to my knees and wrap both my girls in my arms. Tell them how much I loved them and how thankful I was for them. Instead, I forced a smile. "Thank you, Daisy. That is so thoughtful."

She beamed at me.

Eliza gave me a soft kiss then tugged the crumpled tissues from my hand to dab my face. "Figured you needed some company."

"Yeah, but I didn't want to burden you."

She smiled and shook her head. "When will you learn *you're not* the burden. Never the burden. You're just *carrying* burdens that we get to share, okay? We're a team."

I searched her ocean eyes. "I thought you wanted to take things slow."

"Forget slow." She brushed a lock of hair away from my face. "We were never good at slow anyway."

"We were awful at it."

Daisy sat on the couch, swinging her feet. "Mommy, does this mean you're a lesbian now?"

"No, baby. I'm still bisexual. That means I like more than one gender, remember?"

"Oh yeah," she said.

"My word doesn't change, no matter who my partner is."

"Oh, okay."

I leaned in and kissed Eliza back. "Thank you."

"Are you two done yet?" Daisy asked. "I want to set up the tree."

Eliza and I broke apart laughing. "For you? Yes," I promised. "Let's set up the tree."

I turned on Christmas music and offered Daisy a cookie, and she danced around while eating it, shooting little sparks of magic in excitement.

"I'm sure it's not SHAP-approved, but she's so cute I don't want to stop her," Eliza whispered. "And she's healthier than she's ever been." She opened the large plastic bin and began sorting the pieces to the tree.

I pretended to zip my mouth closed. "Secret's safe with me." She handed me the base of the tree, and I placed it next to the television.

"How are your parents?"

"Good. It's going to take time to heal, but we'll get there. Mom wants us—including you—to come to Christmas dinner. It'll probably be less dramatic than last dinner, anyway."

I smiled. "I'll be there."

After we'd finished putting the tree together, I plugged it in.

"Whoaaaaaa," Daisy said, the word turning into a laugh.

"She does it every time," Eliza explained.

I gestured toward the tree. "For good reason." Soft lights made the glitter weaved into the pink branches shine. It was impossible not to feel joy when looking at it.

"Let me put the dog up top!" Daisy said, bouncing over.

Eliza held up a dog with a halo over its head. "The Applechester Animal Rescue was giving these away with a donation."

Daisy took the dog from her mom, patted it on the head, then tossed it into the air. With a wave of her hand, it landed perfectly on the top.

"Whoa." I held out my hand. "High five, Daisy. That was badass."

The three of us decorated the tree and sang and shared cookies until Daisy passed out on the couch. I carried her to my room and placed her in my bed, then left the door ajar. Eliza had turned down the music and resealed the cookies. When I returned, she patted the couch.

I gestured toward the parking lot. "Need me to carry her to the car after we pack up?"

"In a few. Come here." She reclined and opened her arms.

I laid down, facing her, her head tucking underneath my chin. We just held each other, calming the storm no doubt swirling in both of us.

"How's she taking Ben being gone?" I whispered.

"The first two days were hard, but she's so used to him being gone that she just kind of accepted it."

I ran my hand over her back in a slow circle. "What about you?"

She lifted a shoulder. "When he died—or I thought he'd died—I grieved the man I loved and planned to spend my life with. Now, I'm grieving the partner I *thought* I had, the person I thought he was, and all the time wasted."

"That makes sense." I was grieving the brother I thought I had and every day away from Eliza. "You going to keep in contact with him? For Daisy?"

She hesitated. "I'm not sure. He's still her dad, but he did unspeakable things. He tried to kill you and endangered her. I don't think I can ever forgive him." She gave me a soft kiss then sighed. "But he's still Daisy's father, so I'm going to talk to my therapist, and Daisy's. And probably my lawyer."

"Very wise plan."

"Why thank you." She pressed her lips to my neck. "What about Dallas?"

"He's my twin. We have that twin-thing, you know? But I'm not sure. I'll take it week by week."

"And your parents?"

"They're with my aunt for the holidays, which I think is perfect. They needed a getaway. My mom asked if I could come over and teach her to cook something for me when she gets home."

"I'll come with you," she promised. "I'm pretty good at it."

"You are." I kissed the top of her head. My stomach filled with butterflies at the thought of how easy this was, how comfortable. "Are you sure we're ready for this? Again?" The words were like razor blades, slicing everything open as they came out. "I don't want to be your rebound or escape."

She pulled back and looked up at me. "Paris, I've been in love with you since the moment you made me a daisy crown while I sat on the sidewalk and cried. I just needed to get out of my own way. I'm all in, okay?"

"Even when you hated me?"

"I'm really good at burying my feelings."

I smiled and kissed her nose. "I know."

"This can't go bad," she breathed. "I can't lose another person."

I wrapped myself around her. "I've always been all in. You're the love of my life. So is Daisy. I don't need to be psychic to know that."

"Then it's settled."

"What is?"

"You'll have to move in. Daisy loves the backyard and makes far too much mischief to have close neighbors."

I laughed softly. "Yes. Let's get through the trial first though. Too many changes, even good ones, will make you stress, and you've already fed the entire neighborhood."

Her breath came out in a puff against my skin. "And then some. Okay, deal."

I looked up at the pink tree and for the first time in so long, felt joy. "That tree really does make me smile. I'll bring it back tomorrow."

"I think it's Daisy's excuse to make sure we see you every day. We can move it back to my place on Christmas Eve, and you'll just have to spend the holiday with us."

"This is in no way a hardship."

"Better stay through New Year's, just in case."

"Deal."

She lifted her head and kissed me tenderly, her lips brushing mine over and over again. I kissed her back, softly, gently, and each kiss pieced my broken heart back together. A vision flashed in front of my eyes, of Eliza and I walking down an aisle holding hands with Daisy, of me slipping a ring onto Eliza's finger and a bracelet around Daisy's wrist, of us being pronounced an official family. My breath hitched, hope flickering to life.

"What?" Eliza asked.

"Just really, really happy." I'd suffer through it all again if it ended with this moment.

"Finally."

Epilogue

Mina

September, the next year

I REALLY NEEDED to get this crying thing under control. It was absolutely Carma's fault. I never cried before I met her, and now I was literally crying in front of an entire room of people. Thankfully, my tux had pockets for tissues.

I could blame it on the pollen from the gorgeous hot house pink peonies which covered the arch, the glare of the thousands of twinkle lights that lit the room, or from the anxiety of wedding planning, but it would be a lie. And if we learned nothing else in the last year, it was there could be no more lies. Not after what we went through as a group.

"Mi Minita, you've got to stop crying!" Reggie whispered to me from the front row.

Sebastian nodded. "You don't want to look like a nocturnal animal."

"My dudes, it's waterproof mascara and eyeliner," I shot back.

Eliza turned to them. "We can fix it before photos."

Paris held up her clutch. "I've got back-up everything."

I shook my head. "I should've known better than to put

you all in the front."

"I'll keep them in line," Evie promised, glaring at Sebastian and Reggie.

"Get it the fuck together," Belphegor called. "It's not a funeral."

"I can cry because I'm happy, too!" I shot back.

He grumbled, but ran a hand over his new sweater that read "Mina & Carma" across the chest with a rainbow heart beneath. Sienna smoothed the sweater down, and I knew without a doubt she'd made it for him. Who knew a demon and a werewolf could find love, through yarn of all things? Amber and George sat on Belphegor's other side, beaming.

When Raine started playing our favorite Sorry Charlie song, I looked up to find Carma standing at the end of the aisle, with Jake beside her. My hand flew to my mouth as my vision blurred. We had agreed to not have anyone stand up with us, but if I did have someone, it would've been Jake. This surprise meant the world to me.

"Breathe, Mina," Magnolia whispered from her place beside me as the officiant.

I blinked rapidly so I didn't miss a single moment of Carma walking toward me. Her dark hair was down with soft curls, her pink peony bouquet with a black sequin spider on top, and her dress…

What were words? What was breathing?

I couldn't take my eyes off her.

Her vintage-style black ballgown was hand-painted with pink flowers and black embroidered embracing skeletons that only appeared in certain light. I nearly dropped to my knees. She was the most beautiful person (or supernatural creature)

I'd ever seen, and she was about to be mine.

I was living inside a fairy tale. Well, a fairy tale if Tim Burton directed it.

I don't think I managed a single breath until Carma reached me and immediately pulled me in for a searing kiss. The room erupted in hoots and laughter. I chased her lips when she leaned back.

Jake touched my arm. "Hurry up and get married and you can keep doing that," he teased.

We pulled him into a quick group hug before he went to sit next to Poppy, who was next to Hanelore and Elena, Carma's best friends. Elena didn't look like she wanted to murder me where I stood, so at least that was a slight improvement.

"You ready for this?" Carma whispered.

"From the moment I met you."

I didn't remember the ceremony, but to hear Jake tell the story, I was bouncing up and down in excitement the entire time. I cried again when I slipped the vintage pink sapphire band on her finger, and one more time when she slipped a ring she'd designed onto mine. It was a decorative gold band with a single teardrop-shaped ruby in the center, reminiscent of a drop of blood.

I started happy crying. "I love you so damn much," I said, not caring that I was interrupting.

The entire world stopped when Carma kissed me as if I were the most precious thing in the universe. Her strawberry scent wrapped around us, and I fell in love with her even more. It could have been an hour, a week, a year, but I didn't care. It was the best kiss of my entire life, and I was happy to live in this moment forever.

Eventually, Carma pulled away, wiped her lipstick off my mouth, and whispered, "We're married!"

I scooped her up into my arms and carried her down the aisle to thunderous applause. "Let's celebrate my awesome wife!" I called.

In the ten months since the venom case closed, the bed and breakfast launched and was now booked out six months in advance. Sebastian retired from SHAP and had moved from Jake and Poppy's place to join us, so he could be with Evie. With Reggie and Clint visiting as often as possible, we had four in-house ghosts most nights. When things became too busy for Carma, Poppy, and me to handle, I reached out to Maggie, my old manager when I was undercover at Thinner, who was our new assistant. She may not be able to see ghosts, but she could *sense* shenanigans, and things had been smooth sailing ever since she came on board.

Jake and Poppy had eloped in April and showed up to family dinner with rings on their fingers. "Life's short. We didn't want to wait any longer," Poppy explained. They did throw a big reception at the bed and breakfast, which appeased both Poppy's love of planning weddings and Magnolia (who'd cried for an unprecedented hour after she found out they'd eloped).

As a wedding gift, Jake had given a year of his life so Poppy could write a letter to her sister to tell her the news. Poppy tried to argue, but in the end, it was the most generous gift he could give her. With Reggie translating, Sylvia and Poppy spent the entire day together catching up. She was even able to take Poppy's journals back to share with the rest of their family.

Lucinda's, Dallas's, and Ben's trials had finished in July, each of them landing significant time behind bars for their crimes, but everyone involved with weapons development had been incarcerated and finally, our group was safe. The sentencing hit Carma, Eliza, Daisy, and Paris hard. We went on a girls' trip to Hayvenwood soon after. Daisy had the time of her life and still talked about how her new aunts were also witches, or in Raine's case, a former witch. Life was complicated, but our found family was more than we could have ever asked for, and we were all in this together.

Paris had moved in with Eliza right before Daisy went back to school in August. They had decided to allow Daisy to write supervised letters to her father but wouldn't open other lines of communication until she was older. Daisy had been through significant trauma this year and safeguarding her was the number one priority. Daisy, Paris, and Eliza had become a beautiful family so easily, it was hard to remember a time they weren't together. Eliza promised to let Carma and me help pick out Paris's engagement ring after we returned from our honeymoon. Little did Eliza know, we'd promised Paris the same thing.

Sienna moved from interim to official Territory Director of SHAP in February and started major restructuring. Paris, acting as her assistant, had uncovered the Dead Letter Department was using the blood of unwilling prisoners to send SHAP sanctioned letters. They immediately stopped the practice. SHAP was on a mission to find alternatives. For now, only the most essential contact, or personal appointments, were carried out.

The research and development department was completely revamped, with Paris overseeing all projects. The security system was also upgraded, to prevent anyone else from discovering backdoor access points. The international office had been so impressed, Sienna's and Paris's project was implemented at all locations and hefty bonuses were given.

My dad turned into a different person after he left SHAP. He retired, his savings and investments enough to keep him comfortable. He bought a van, converted it into a camper, and took off to visit anywhere he could drive. He was making up for decades of skipped vacations.

While we were still working on our relationship, he did send me a postcard from every new place he visited, and I'd pinned them all up in my office. I hadn't fully forgiven him for the role he played by turning the other way as Dallas and Ben tried to destroy SHAP, but I was working on it. We decided it was best if he skipped the wedding but promised to get dinner after Carma and I returned from our honeymoon.

Carma wrapped her arm around my waist and held a plate in front of me with a grilled fruit kabob. "Fenton did an amazing job with the food." She leaned in and whispered, "Describe it to me."

Keeping my eyes locked on hers, I popped a pineapple chunk in my mouth. I chewed slowly, then licked my lips, building anticipation. "Sweet and tangy, heaven on my lips. Like you after your third orgasm," I whispered back.

"We better do a comparison test really quick," she teased.

I grabbed her hand and pulled her down the hall to our bedroom and did just that. We were a half an hour late for dinner and had to get Eliza and Paris to help us fix our hair and makeup, but it was totally worth it.

After our first dance, the floor opened for everyone. Sebastian turned to Evie and held out his hand. "My lady, I am a century and a half overdue for this, but may I have this dance?"

"You may," Evie said, beaming.

They danced around in a waltz, completely lost in each other.

"Did you ever think we'd see the day Sebastian was in love?" my wife asked.

"Nope," I replied, "and I will tease him about this for the rest of my life."

She kissed the back of my hand. "That's why I love you."

"My pettiness?"

"And your perseverance."

Jake walked over and held out his hand to Carma. "Can I take my new sis-in-law around the floor?"

She put her hand in his. "Only if you tell me more embarrassing stories about Mina."

"Hope you're ready to dance for the next hour, then." He smiled at me, then handed me his cane. "I'll be okay for a dance," he promised.

As I watched Carma dance with Jake, laughing at whatever story he was sharing, Sebastian appeared at my side.

He crossed his arms and smiled. "I was correct."

"About what?"

"Everything."

I rolled my eyes but smiled. "Just so."

He laughed then disappeared as my wife walked up to me, a silly smile on her face. "I've heard a story about shaving cream and an alpaca that I'm going to need details about."

I groaned. "Just you wait, Jacob Robinson!" I called. "Payback's a bitch!"

Magnolia and my mom yelled "Language!" at the same time.

"That's why I eloped!" Jake returned.

Magnolia turned to Eliza and Paris. "If you elope, I will make your lives a living hell."

Paris held up her hands in surrender. "Promise we won't."

Eliza nodded swiftly. "Yeah, Mom. We will make sure to have an actual ceremony."

I lowered my voice. "Welcome to the family, officially," I told Carma. "We're all mad here. You should've run while you had the chance."

Carma kissed my nose. "No way. You're stuck with me."

"Yeah?"

"Yeah. Forever."

I pretended to think it over for a moment, then kissed her softly. "I was yours the moment you smiled at me."

"I didn't know you were such a hopeless romantic."

"No. I'm a hopeful romantic. After all, I get to keep you."

"Yeah. You do." She sealed her promise with a kiss.

The End

Want more? Check out Mina and Carma's story in *Blood Thinners*!

Join Tule Publishing's newsletter for more great reads and weekly deals!

Acknowledgements

I don't even know how to start these acknowledgements except to say thank you! Yes, to *you*, dear reader. The messages of love and support I've received since starting this series, especially stories of how my books have helped people come out to loved ones, speak up about their own disabilities, made them feel seen, or comforted them in their grief have humbled me. It's more than I could have wished for.

Next, I'd be nowhere without my Tule team! Thank you to my editor Sinclair, and to Nikki, Meghan, Cyndi, Jane, Lee, Voule, and everyone who had a hand in creating this series: Thanks for all you do. This is truly a dream come true.

Shout out to Mr. Heather, who believes in me more than I believe in myself somedays.

I would be nowhere without my support staff: My alpha readers Janna Bonikowski, Elyssa Mann, and Sarah Estep, translator Andrea Véliz García, assistant Joanne Machin, sensitivity readers Jenna Walsh and Amber Young, my sister Kate who can spot a typo from fifty paces, and my Tule sisters who provide so many strong shoulders to lean on. Special nod to Dana Nussio, Thien-Kim Lam, Liz Zerkel, Elaine Reed, and Eric Aech for rallying behind this series—and me!

Love always to the wind beneath my wings: my Tacos, Intellectual Hotties, Sister Wives, Dolls (especially Mel and Cheryl), my hypopara sisters, and my Fantoms. Shout out to the people who keep *me* running (my family, my besties, my medical team, my cleaners).

As always, Katie V, Eliza, Ci, Jen T, Erika C, Jen M, and Keara. And of course, my guys from Nicotine Dolls, for all the inspiration.

If I haven't mentioned you by name, know it is just a side effect of my brain fog and not because I don't treasure you—you're forever in my heart. Can't wait for my next adventure with you all!

Wishing You Laughter & Good Books,
-H

If you enjoyed *Dearly Departed*,
you'll love the other books in the…

Love Me Dead series

Book 1: *Blood Thinners*

Book 2: *Grim and Bear It*

Book 3: *Dearly Departed*

About the Author

Bold, Breathtaking, Badass Romance.

When she's not pretending to be a rock star with purple hair, award-winning author Heather Novak is crafting sex positive romance novels to make you swoon! After her rare disease tried to kill her, Heather mutated into a superhero whose greatest power is writing stories that you can't put down.

Heather tries to save the world (like her late mama taught her) from her home near Detroit, Michigan, where she lives with Mr. Heather and a collection of musical instruments. She is part of the LGBTQ+ community and believes Black Lives Matter.

Thank you for reading

Dearly Departed

If you enjoyed this book, you can find more from all our great authors at TulePublishing.com, or from your favorite online retailer.

www.ingramcontent.com/pod-product-compliance
Lightning Source LLC
LaVergne TN
LVHW041108080826
845145LV00007B/1737